How could she have fallen for him?

"Laura," Anatol called quietly, "why don't you come to bed?" When she didn't respond, he rose and padded across the room to stand behind her, resting his hands gently on her shoulders.

"I never planned to get so involved with you, Anatol," she said sadly.

"No, and I didn't choose to fall in love with you, either. But I have. I love you deeply, Laura."

A rumble of thunder echoed through the room as the threatening storm drew closer. Laura shivered and stepped away from the window, shrugging off his touch. She hadn't expected Anatol to declare his love, and it frightened her that he had.

She'd known all along that she'd have to leave Russia eventually. But she had imagined she'd be able to control her feelings. How foolish she'd been.

ABOUT THE AUTHOR

"I wrote *Russian Nights* because I believe that people are the same everywhere," says Kelly Walsh. "Strong, idealistic and wildly romantic, my hero, Anatol Vronsky, could easily be an American. But he happens to be Russian." Kelly Walsh lives in Florida, and keeps an aviary full of exotic birds.

Books by Kelly Walsh

HARLEQUIN SUPERROMANCE
248—CHERISHED HARBOR
286—OF TIME AND TENDERNESS
336—A PLACE FOR US
360—A PRIVATE AFFAIR
415—STARLIGHT, STAR BRIGHT

Don't miss any of our special offers. Write to us at the following address for information on our newest releases.

Harlequin Reader Service
P.O. Box 1397, Buffalo, NY 14240
Canadian address: P.O. Box 603,
Fort Erie, Ont. L2A 5X3

Russian Nights

KELLY WALSH

Harlequin Books

TORONTO • NEW YORK • LONDON
AMSTERDAM • PARIS • SYDNEY • HAMBURG
STOCKHOLM • ATHENS • TOKYO • MILAN

Published March 1991

ISBN 0-373-70445-3

RUSSIAN NIGHTS

CHAPTER ONE

WAITING IN THE LONG LINE at customs at Leningrad's Pulkova Airport, Laura was startled when someone grasped her arm. She swung around and looked up at a tall, unsmiling man in a trench coat.

"You are Laura Walters?" he asked in Russian.

"Da," she answered.

He inspected her from head to toe, giving Laura the uncomfortable feeling he was with airport security and was about to accuse her of having done something illegal. When he pulled her out of the line, she was sure of it.

"Is something wrong?" Laura asked with false bravado, freeing her arm from his grip.

Noting the confusion in her expression, he said, "I'm Anatol Vronsky. Didn't you know I'd be meeting you?"

"No, I didn't," she admitted, taking note of his alert hazel eyes and the light brown wavy hair that framed a ruggedly attractive face. "I thought the plan was that I would meet you at your office after I checked into my hotel."

Vronsky shrugged off the mix-up and put out his hand. Laura smiled and offered her hand in return, but drew it back quickly when she saw his palm turn upward.

"Your travel documents, please."

"Oh, yes," she said, digging into her purse to retrieve the leather organizer where she kept her papers.

He took them without explanation, strode behind the customs counter and spoke to one of the clerks, who immediately stamped her travel papers.

Some welcoming committee, Laura thought, deciding Anatol Vronsky's manner was overly formal if not downright abrupt.

"All processed," he announced briskly, returning from the customs desk and handing back her documents. "Your luggage is being taken to my car. Yuri Chernov is waiting at my office. Do you mind if we go directly there?"

"Not at all," Laura replied pleasantly, but she was less than thrilled with the reception Anatol Vronsky was giving her. Knowing she had just traveled almost five thousand miles, a more considerate man would have given her time to get settled in her hotel or at least given her the opportunity to freshen up before meeting Yuri Chernov, the man she was going to be working with. *So much for Russian hospitality,* she thought, following him to his car.

As they drove through the outskirts of Leningrad, past block after block of tall apartment buildings, Vronsky remained silent, and Laura wondered if perhaps she wasn't what he had expected.

Laura's company, Biomed, had just entered into a joint venture with a Soviet medical supply firm under the supervision of the Ministry of Health. As a management analyst, her assignment was to work with Yuri Chernov, the director of the firm. A squad of American managers would arrive in December, and she and

Chernov were supposed to decide how Soviet and American managers could work together harmoniously.

At the moment Laura sensed anything but harmony. As they passed over a canal, she decided she couldn't take the silence any longer. "I can see why Leningrad is called the Venice of the North," she remarked. "It seems to be a city of islands."

"Have you been to Venice, Laura?" he asked, surprising her by switching to a first-name basis.

Thinking she might have misjudged him, she relaxed somewhat and brightened her voice. "I vacationed there two summers ago and fell in love with it."

Vronsky glanced her way and smiled. "Leningrad has canals and palaces, too. I hope it will affect you the same way."

"That would be great," she agreed, thinking that he should smile more often; even in profile his smile was effective, to say the least. To keep the conversation going, she asked, "Are you familiar with New York?"

"I make two trips there a year as an adviser to Amtorg Trading Corporation, a private firm that's been coordinating trade between our two countries since the twenties. Whenever I'm in New York, my first stop is always at the Kentucky Fried Chicken on Broadway."

"Ah, a devotee of American cuisine."

"Among other things," he said, a playful lilt in his voice. "You're to be complimented," he went on. "Your Russian is fluent."

"Thanks to Irina, my roommate in college. She was born in Moscow."

"An exchange student?"

"No. Her family immigrated to the States fifteen years ago. They opened a Russian restaurant near Columbia University in New York. That's where I met Irina. I helped her with English, and she helped me with Russian. Her parents just about adopted me as a second daughter. Irina's still a close friend."

Soon they crossed the Neva River and turned onto the eight-lane Nevsky Prospekt, joining the crush of compact cars that wove their way around lines of crammed buses. On the sidewalks pedestrians bustled past churches, cinemas, shops and cafés. The scene reminded Laura of rush hour on Madison Avenue in Manhattan, where she lived and worked.

Some of the women she saw were stylishly dressed. Others wore colorful babushkas, print dresses and dark jackets. Soviet soldiers and sailors were also mixed in the crowd, as were younger people who, in their jeans and sweaters, looked like teenagers everywhere.

"How was your flight?" Vronsky asked.

"Fine. After dinner I nodded off during the movie, so I slept halfway through the trip." She checked her watch and reset it. "My body thinks it's only 6:00 a.m."

"I apologize for not taking you directly to your hotel."

"No problem. I'm looking forward to meeting Mr. Chernov."

Vronsky let several moments pass, then said, "You'll find that not everyone is in favor of this joint venture with an American company."

"Mr. Chernov, for one?" Laura asked uneasily, sensing that Anatol Vronsky felt the need to prepare her for her meeting with the director of the Pavlovsk plant.

"He's not exactly sold on the idea, but he'll come around when he observes your managerial skills. I'm told that's where you excel."

Laura accepted the compliment silently, but his remark about Yuri Chernov disturbed her. "The ultimate success of this venture is going to depend on his willingness to work with me."

"He will. Our law now states that businesses that go bankrupt are to be closed down."

"Bankrupt?" Laura repeated, the word sending a shiver of suspicion rushing down her spine. Her eyes riveted on Vronsky, she said, "The production reports he sent us indicated a healthy growth at the plant."

"It's in good shape right now, but every tenth enterprise in this country is operating at a loss. Chernov knows that some changes have to be made at his plant if he's to keep it healthy."

Laura's eyes narrowed. "The production reports we received were totally accurate, weren't they?"

"Over there," he said, nodding toward his right. "The Alexander Nevsky Monastery. Tchaikovsky, Rimsky-Korsakov and Rachmaninoff are buried there. Do you like classical music?"

"If it's soothing and has a melody," she replied warily, realizing he had effectively changed the subject.

"We agree on something already. Shostakovich and much of Stravinsky make me nervous. You might say I'm a romantic at heart." His eyes slid toward hers. "As far as music goes, I mean."

"Yes, I understood you," she said, noting the glow of amusement in his eyes. Romance was the farthest thing from her mind at the moment. The job that lay ahead of her was going to be difficult. Nothing in her work experience had prepared her for working jointly with the Russians. But she was determined not to fail at the assignment she had fought hard to get.

"Here we are," Vronsky announced, pulling up in front of an ornate stone structure that looked to Laura as if it could have been some nobleman's palace.

Inside the building she followed him up the wide marble stairway to a reception room on the second floor, where he spoke briefly with his secretary before leading Laura into his private office. A tall, slender man stood quickly when they entered.

"Welcome to the Soviet Union, Miss Walters. I'm Yuri Chernov."

Laura smiled and offered her hand to the middle-aged man whose plastered-on grin did little to soften the angular lines of his face. "It's a pleasure to meet you. I'm looking forward to our working together." She imagined there would be more life in a dead fish than in his handshake.

"An American who speaks our language. How nice," Chernov commented, and Laura wondered if she'd heard a note of sarcasm in his compliment.

"Please," Vronsky said, gesturing Laura toward one of the two vinyl-covered chairs in front of his desk. "To say that your job here will be an easy one would be overly optimistic," Vronsky began. "Both the supporters of *perestroika,* of the restructuring of our economy, and—" his eyes shifted to Chernov "—those who oppose it will be watching closely to see if the joint venture at the Pavlovsk plant becomes operational by the first of January."

"There's no reason why it shouldn't," Laura said confidently, "if we cooperate."

Chernov eyed her sideways. "According to legislation, we retain a fifty-one percent share of the company."

Laura matched his robotic smile with one of her own. "I realize that, but Biomed is entering this venture with the written agreement that management of the plant will be on an equal basis between your people and ours. In the day-to-day functioning, my company must have an equal voice if profits are to be increased."

Chernov's voice darkened. "But we cannot increase profits at the expense of the workers."

"Enlightened managers realize that satisfied and motivated employees are more productive."

Adjusting his chair to face her head-on, Chernov asked, "Just how are you planning to make our Soviet workers satisfied and motivated? By giving more money to productive employees?"

"Managers should have that option."

Chernov leaned back in his chair and began rubbing the point of his chin with a middle finger. "What will you do about jealousy on the part of those workers who are not as productive? Will you suggest we chain them to their work stations until they meet their quotas?"

"Mr. Chernov," Laura replied calmly, "what I suggest is that your knowledge of working conditions in America is lacking if you think our employees are chained." She could feel the warmth creeping up her neck. "For the past year Biomed has gone through endless negotiations to lay the groundwork for this venture. I was told that a spirit of cooperation existed and that everyone here realized that the Soviet economy is only going to improve if the workers become more productive."

Vronsky glanced at Chernov, lifted his eyebrows, then sat down behind his desk to observe.

Grinning, Chernov asked, "Miss Walters, are you planning to improve our economy single-handedly?"

"Hardly, but just as I hope that I can learn from your managerial techniques, I believe that you might learn from ours. Of course that would require an open mind on your part."

"And you've judged that my mind is closed. Tell me, are you this blunt with American colleagues or just with backward Soviet citizens?"

Laura turned toward Vronsky, expecting some support from him. None came, and it further annoyed her that he seemed to be enjoying this verbal duel. Well, she didn't need anyone's help in holding her own. Bracing herself, she returned her attention to the plant director.

"'Backward' is for you to decide, Mr. Chernov. On the plane I read that ten more Soviet children have been infected with the AIDS virus, apparently by doctors using syringes that hadn't been sterilized after being used on other infected children."

Vronsky eyed Chernov and said quietly, "An example of the backwardness of our health care." He shook his head, then faced Laura. "Our lack of disposable syringes and our outdated methods of sterilization are a national scandal."

"And that's why I'm here," Laura said, softening her tone. "Biomed makes the best medical supplies in the world."

"Back to incentives for productive employees," Chernov said. "Working for profit is new to our people. Most of us believe that making a profit is a form of criminal activity."

Suddenly Vronsky leaned forward, and his voice turned razor-sharp. "We're not here to weigh the advantages and disadvantages of our two systems of government, Comrade Chernov. On Monday morning Miss Walters will be at your plant to meet your department managers. I know you'll do everything possible to make her visit to our country productive and enjoyable."

Chernov rose, gave Anatol a perfunctory nod and offered Laura a flimsy smile. "One word of advice, Miss Walters. If you oversell capitalism, we will not buy it at all."

A sinking feeling settled in Laura's stomach as Chernov exited, closing the door behind him. Turning to Vronsky, she asked, "You are his superior, aren't you?"

"These days I'm more of an adviser, and Chernov's plant is just one of twelve joint ventures I oversee around the country. But it is an important one. The project is a pilot program, the first under the aegis of the Ministry of Health. Some of their top people were against it from the first when I suggested it."

"From what I've read of shortages of medical supplies here, I find it hard to believe that anyone at your Ministry of Health would be anything but supportive."

"Our ministries are very powerful, and often they use that power to inhibit change, as do most bureaucrats."

Laura lifted her chin, holding back from reminding Vronsky that he, too, was a bureaucrat. Instead she asked, "Why did you leave me dangling there for a while with Mr. Chernov?"

"I wanted to see how you would handle him. He can be rather abrasive." Vronsky paused, then said, "A word of warning, Laura. Don't push him too hard. If you expect him to compromise with you, you must learn to compromise with him."

A feeling of annoyance tensed the muscles around her lips. An ambitious woman, she didn't particularly care to have anyone sabotaging her career plans. She had worked long and hard to rise in the ranks at Biomed, and she knew that if she were successful in her present assignment, she would be able to write her own ticket with her company. But after meeting Comrade Director Chernov, she realized she might be going up against a brick wall. Considering Anatol Vronsky's warning, she wondered if he would add to her difficulties.

Rising, she tugged at the hem of her jacket and looked him square in the eye. "Compromise, of course, is a two-way street, but if Chernov and I are to meet the January first deadline, he must understand that identifying problems is what my job is all about."

"In this case, though, you can only suggest changes at the plant," Vronsky pointed out.

"I understand that perfectly. But tell me, and please be honest, will he even consider any suggestions I might make?"

"He will, but don't expect changes overnight. It won't work. Not here."

Anatol studied her concerned features, wondering if she would heed his warning. He still wasn't sure what to make of this American from New York. From the moment he had laid eyes on her at the airport, she had surprised him. Not because she was a woman, but because he hadn't expected her to be so attractive.

Not that he wasn't used to meeting beautiful women, but for some reason, he'd found it difficult to make even polite conversation with her. She made him feel almost like an adolescent again—bashful, tongue-tied and ready to fall in love at the drop of a hat.

He had taken it for granted that she would be knowledgeable and intelligent. But so strong-minded? That surprised him also. And it pleased him. He had been afraid that Chernov would be too much for her to cope with. But by standing up to him the way she had, she'd put that fear to rest.

Smiling at his ruminations, Vronsky said, "I hope you won't take Comrade Chernov's welcome as indicative of our hospitality. We Russians are basically a warm and friendly people."

At the moment Laura questioned that seriously. Her dubious eyes followed Anatol's graceful strides as he went to the credenza along the side wall and picked up a gift-wrapped box.

Offering it to her, he said, "It would please me if you would accept this as a gesture of welcome."

Smiling quizzically, Laura opened the package and withdrew a lovely sable hat. "It's beautiful," she exclaimed, running her fingers over the soft fur.

When she looked up at him, she met his eyes, and in their shining warmth, she saw something that made her feel truly comfortable for the first time since arriving in this country.

"I was sincere when I said I wanted your visit to be enjoyable as well as productive," he told her.

Laura's sincere smile broadened. "I'm sure it will be."

"If you like," he suggested, "I'll drive you to your hotel. Then we can continue our business discussion over dinner."

"Yes," she said, her spirits lifting even more, "that would be fine."

But she was confused by Anatol Vronsky. One minute he was warning her, lecturing her on how to do her job; the next, he was charming her socks off. Lowering her eyes to the sable hat, Laura decided that the next three months might not be a total disaster, after all.

AT THAT MOMENT, in a park across town, a man named Dmitri Karnakov was sitting on a wooden bench, his cashmere-jacketed arm resting casually on the bench's upright back. His gaze rose to the gold dome atop Saint Isaac's Cathedral, and he felt the sun warm his Hollywood-handsome face. "I love Leningrad this time of the year," he told his companion. "It's not hot and it's not freezing."

Dmitri's attention drifted to the children who were frolicking in pools of shade under nearby trees. Large brightly colored bows bobbed in the girls' hair. "Sweet, aren't they?" he remarked, then his expression turned cold as he faced his companion. "If Misha again mentions quitting the organization, you know what to do."

"It's Laura Walters I'm worried about. She could be a real problem at the plant. It will be difficult keeping things from her. Apparently she speaks and reads Russian like a native."

"You worry too much," Dmitri told him. "Even our American guest can have an unfortunate accident."

CHAPTER TWO

SOFT STRAINS OF MUSIC floated through the restaurant as Laura finished the last of the flaky pastry loaf with salmon filling that Vronsky had ordered for them.

"That was delicious," Laura complimented their waiter when he removed her plate and replaced it with a small bowl of chilled vegetable soup. Looking over at her dinner companion, she said, "I'm not sure where I'm going to put the main course, Mr. Vronsky."

"Anatol, please," he requested.

"Anatol," she repeated softly, then sipped from her wineglass. Setting it down, she said, "You've been so considerate that I'm beginning to feel I'm on holiday rather than on business. First the beautiful welcome gift, and now this charming restaurant. Again I find myself thanking you."

"I'll try to make that a habit," he said, an easy smile forming on his sensual lips.

The man has eyes to die for, Laura decided, lowering her own and reflecting that only yesterday she had been in New York, and now she was in a charming restaurant in Leningrad, listening to balalaika music and dining with an attractive man. And loving every minute of it! What a difference a day makes.

Raising her eyes, she found herself smiling back at Anatol, but when their eyes held, she thought she saw something in his that she could only describe as being too intimate for comfort. She had already noticed that he wore no wedding ring. Of course, that didn't mean he wasn't emotionally involved with someone, she told herself. "Other than the Pavlovsk plant, what kinds of joint ventures do you oversee?" she asked, steering their conversation back to business.

Captivated by the way the candlelight reflected in her lovely blue-gray eyes, his response came rather absently. "One is a chemical plant located at Tengiz on the Caspian Sea. We work jointly with an American, an Italian and a Japanese company."

"That must keep you fairly busy."

"Yes," he said, wondering if her silky golden blond hair would feel as soft as it looked in the candlelight. Realizing a vacant silence was hovering between them, he forced his concentration back to the topic at hand. "Another factory I oversee—at Tbilisi—used to make aircraft for the military. Now they're manufacturing civilian business planes with an American company. We build the frame, landing gear and the engine, ship the planes to California, and your people fit them with electronic devices, install cockpit equipment and take care of the interior design."

"Mr. Chernov," she said, an edge to her voice, "doesn't seem to share your enthusiasm for working with foreigners. I have the uncomfortable feeling that he may not be the easiest man to work with."

"Yuri's afraid you might want to undercut his authority."

"With his attitude, I probably will."

Anatol leaned back in his chair and offered her a mock frown. "Haven't we talked enough business for one day?"

"I suppose so," she said hesitantly, "but you said that's what you wanted to do."

"Learning more about who you're dealing with is talking business." After their waiter served the chicken Kiev, Anatol asked, "What do you do in New York when you're not working?"

"The usual things . . . entertain, attend the theater. I enjoy movies, but we usually watched them at home on our VCR."

"We?" Anatol asked, glancing at the single pearl on her left hand.

"Roger, a friend," she said, cutting her chicken with vigor as she recalled the final words he had flung at her the day she'd moved out of the apartment they'd shared for a year, *"You'll fail in the Soviet Union and you'll come rushing back to me."*

Not in a million years, Laura now answered mentally.

Seeing that her features had tensed, Anatol asked, "Have I been too personal? If so, I apologize. You see, I'm as straightforward as you seem to be. Does that bother you?"

"No, not at all," she lied. Then, to change the subject, she added, "I hope I'm not taking you away from your family this evening?"

"I live alone. I'm divorced."

"Oh."

When she had first laid eyes on Anatol, Laura had decided that he would stand out in a crowd of men. There was an aura of strength about him—strength of character, not just physical ability. It was obvious in the way he walked, the way he held his head high. It was also apparent in the way he could speak with authority without offending, as he had with the clerk at the hotel when he'd directed the clerk to change her room to a larger one that overlooked the Neva River.

Anatol was indeed a man she would like to know better, she mused, but what would be the point? The job that lay ahead of her wasn't going to be easy. Why ask for complications?

After dinner Laura and Anatol went for a walk. When they came to the Neva River, they stood silently, resting against the waist-high stone wall that edged the shore. A cool breeze swept over the rippled water, and Laura raised the collar of her maroon coat. Although the sun had set, a blue-silvery haze hung over the city, muting the tall gold spire and dome of a cathedral across the narrow waterway. Hearing quiet laughter, she glanced over her shoulder toward the park behind them. A young man and a woman, lovers, she thought, meandered down a pathway toward a small stone bridge.

"It's lovely here," Laura said, facing the river again.

"Yes, it is," Anatol agreed, his gaze steady on her face, which was softly lit in the fading light. After a moment he said, "I'm curious about why you agreed to take on a job so far from home."

Having mulled that over many times before leaving the States, Laura didn't hesitate before responding. "The joint venture is a first for my company, and I saw the job as a challenge."

"And you like challenges."

"I like succeeding at my work." She paused, then added, "Also, relations between our countries are warming, and I find it exciting. I want to be part of it."

He glanced at her ring finger again. "Have you ever been married, Laura?"

She shook her head, then began walking slowly alongside the wall. Anatol met her stride and slipped his hands into the pockets of his trench coat.

"I've been busy establishing my career," she said, surprised that she felt comfortable discussing her personal life with him. "Perhaps I'm also a little leery, considering that back home half our marriages don't work out."

"Our peoples have more in common than we think. In our cities the divorce rate is about the same."

Smiling, she said, "I suspect that the divorce rate indicates women are no longer as docile as men would like. At home men have a way of saying their wives are equal partners—" she thought of Roger momentarily "—but when it comes to daily decision-making, some men seem to forget that." Since Anatol was being so direct, Laura decided she would be. "Did you?" she asked lightly.

Anatol chuckled softly. "Yelena, my ex-wife, is anything but docile. Maybe it's her being a doctor that makes her used to giving orders. We divorced two years ago. She and our son live here in Leningrad."

"How old is he?"

"Valentin is seventeen. He's bright, but..." As Anatol's words trailed off, Laura noticed a shadow of concern shade his features. "But he's confused right now." After a pensive moment, Anatol asked rhetorically, "Why should he be different? It seems everyone here is confused nowadays. We're going through a period of problems ... changes in the government, the economy, fragmented families, alienated young people."

"Seventeen is a confusing time for any teenager," Laura commented, thinking of her own seventeenth year when her parents had divorced.

She'd adored her father, who had managed a government plant in Merrick on Long Island. After the divorce, he'd packed up and relocated to Chicago. His letters to her had dwindled, then stopped. Soon after the divorce her mother had remarried, but Laura and her stepfather hadn't gotten along. Feeling she was in the way at home, she'd decided to live on-campus while attending college.

"Do you like rock music?"

Anatol's question drew her back to the present. "Not if it hurts my ears."

"The same with me, but Valentin is a fanatic about it. He even wears a gold earring." Shaking his head, Anatol said, "I don't understand it. He was raised a member of the Komsomol—sort of a Communist version of your Boy Scouts, but co-ed. Now he belongs to a protest group. All he thinks about is rock music and groups with bizarre names like the Grateful Dead, the Scorpions, the Motley Crue. When he's not ruining his hearing, he's demonstrating against pollution."

"What's so terrible about that? When I was his age, I marched with antinuclear groups on Long Island."

"All the same, I worry about him. Next year he goes into the military. Then what? He should be planning for his future now, deciding what he wants to do with his life."

Stopping, Laura leaned back against the railing and studied Anatol. "When you were seventeen, did you have your future all planned?"

"Times were different," he said, resting his hands on the stone ledge and gazing out over the river. "My life was mapped out for me. At seventeen I entered the army. Four years later I was assigned to work on a collective farm for two years before going to Leningrad University to prepare myself for state service. I didn't have a choice. But Valentin does. Now he says he's not sure what he wants to do with his life."

"Well," Laura suggested, "I guess when you're young it's simpler when you're told what to do rather than to have to make decisions. Times certainly have changed since you were your son's age, but from what you say he doesn't seem so different from young people I know back home."

Facing her, Anatol said, "It's late and you must be tired."

"Yes, the trip is catching up with me," she said, making a mental note that whenever Anatol became uncomfortable with a topic, he abruptly switched to another.

"If you like, I'll arrange for a driver to show you Leningrad this weekend. I'd like to do it myself, but I have a meeting in Moscow."

"I appreciate the offer, but I'd prefer wandering around on my own."

He nodded. "As you like. Monday morning I'll drive you to Pavlovsk. I've arranged for you to have an apartment near the plant."

"Oh?" she remarked, having thought she'd live in Leningrad. "Pavlovsk is only a short drive from here. I thought I'd rent a car and commute."

"Winter comes early in this part of the country, Laura. I'm quite sure you'd be more comfortable living near the plant."

So much for joint decisions, she thought.

OVER THE WEEKEND Laura went on a walking tour of the Venice of the North. By Sunday evening she felt as if she had traversed each of the city's 376 bridges and passed every one of its historical palaces. After sampling the Swedish buffet in one of the hotel restaurants, she returned to her room to finish writing notes on the postcards she had purchased.

As she completed the one to her secretary in New York, Laura's eyes drifted to the sable hat that lay on the dresser, and she remembered the way Anatol had smiled as he'd offered her the gift-wrapped box.

Yes, she thought, moving to the window and gazing down at the streetlights reflecting in the dark water of the Neva River, her life had changed dramatically in recent days. She wondered what part Anatol might play in her future. Not much, she decided, since she would be in Pavlovsk, he in Leningrad when his work didn't take him to far parts of the vast country. Smiling softly, she realized she was looking forward to seeing him in the morning.

A LITTLE AFTER NINE on Monday morning, Laura and Anatol began the twenty-minute drive to Pavlovsk. Just outside Leningrad, they passed a satellite town, and Laura looked in vain for the shopping malls that were so prevalent in the States. Farther into the countryside, they whizzed by low wooden houses. Behind swaying white-washed fences, women in heavy sweaters and boots hung the laundry, while others cared for tethered goats. Glancing down one dirt road, she saw two teenage girls on bicycles, herding cows.

"Would you like to go to your apartment first," Anatol asked, "or should we go directly to the plant?"

"Let's go right to the plant. I'm anxious to see where I'll be working."

"The people there, all six hundred of them, are just as anxious to meet you."

Smiling, Laura asked, "Is that another warning?"

"Most of them have never met an American. They probably aren't sure what to expect."

"Don't let word get around, but I'm not sure, either, not after meeting Comrade Chernov."

"You'll like Olga Batyunin, the assistant director. She's sharp and has a degree in economics. Sergei Angizitov, who manages inventory control, is a good friend of mine. We were in the army together, but he stayed in long enough to get wounded in Afghanistan. When you meet him, don't feel awkward about the scar on his face. He's not overly sensitive about it, and he's got a great sense of humor."

"After meeting Yuri Chernov, that will be refreshing. On Friday I got the distinct impression he'd eaten something bad for lunch."

Anatol grinned, then said, "Sergei and Olga share an apartment not too far from yours." His eyes flicked toward Laura to catch her reaction, but he saw none.

She was scanning a field of sunflowers, her expression noncommittal, but she wondered if Anatol had been thinking of her having lived with Roger. Not that it really mattered. Her relationship with Anatol Vronsky was purely a business one. He'd take her to the plant, then drop her off at her apartment, and after that she would see him rarely, if ever.

"There's the plant," Anatol announced, nodding toward the right.

In the distance, beyond a field covered with blue and yellow wildflowers, she saw a gray U-shaped, two-story building just on the other side of a narrow river. Numerous wind turbine vents stuck up from the roofs, and a line of semitrailers was parked outside at a long wooden loading dock.

"It's not air-conditioned," Anatol said as he parked in front of the building, "but with our climate very few places are."

"That's understandable," Laura commented, the morning temperature being a brisk forty-seven degrees.

"You'll find that it's well heated, though," Anatol assured her.

As they went through the double glass doors at the entrance, the first things that caught Laura's attention were the two huge photographs on the wall behind the receptionist's desk: one of Karl Marx, the other of Lenin. Between them was the slogan Glory to Labor.

"Comrade Vronsky," the smiling young receptionist said.

"Good morning, Lydia," he returned before introducing Laura.

Lydia's green eyes inspected Laura with interest. "The director is waiting for you and Miss Walters. Please go right in."

Inside, Chernov was standing by his desk, and a woman was seated in a chair by the window. She wore a lavender silk dress and a green smock. The morning sun rayed over her shiny black hair, which fell to her shoulders and framed her attractive face. There was an alluring hint of Asia in her almond-shaped dark eyes and an enigmatic smile.

Chernov introduced the woman as Olga Batyunin, his assistant director, and Laura remembered Anatol having mentioned her in the car. Introductions made, Chernov gestured Laura to the wooden chair next to Olga's and waited until Anatol moved another one closer to the grouping.

"I understand that this is your first visit to the Soviet Union," Olga said to Laura with a cautious smile.

"Yes, but I hope it won't be my last."

"I took the liberty of stocking the pantry in your apartment. Just staples, of course. I had no idea of your preferences in food."

"That was thoughtful of you...may I call you Olga?"

"A first-name basis would be fine," Chernov interrupted, answering for his assistant. "Except in front of the workers. I've scheduled a tour of the plant for you, Miss Walters. Olga will take you while I speak with Anatol."

Laura set her purse on the floor beside her chair, rose and smiled at the assistant director.

"Olga," Anatol said, "Laura hasn't been to her apartment yet. Perhaps a very *brief* tour would do for this morning."

"I understand," she said, opening the office door for Laura.

As Olga led the way down a narrow corridor lined with Worker of the Month photographs, she remarked, "We've seen pictures of Biomed's plants in America. I hope you won't be too disappointed with ours. It's not as modern."

"But your production figures are quite impressive."

"Not everyone thinks so. Each month the government increases our quotas." Offering Laura a friendly smile, she said, "With your help, maybe we can meet those quotas." Stopping at the first door on the right, Olga took a moment to study Laura's outfit. "Your suit is beautifully made, and I really love your blouse." She smiled as she opened the door. "But then I love nice clothes."

Anatol was right, Laura thought, she was going to like the assistant director. Inside the long room, Laura was introduced to a department manager, an older tight-lipped woman, who followed and scrutinized Laura closely as she walked behind the seated green-uniformed employees who were assembling kidney dialysis machines. Laura's questions about quality control were answered curtly, making her realize that not everyone at the plant was going to be as friendly as Olga. Laura was surprised to learn that there were actually three managers in charge of the department. One was on holiday, the other at a party meeting at the local Soviet headquarters.

As the tour continued, Laura received cool welcomes from several department heads. Then Olga led Laura to Misha Vinokurov's office, the manager in charge of quality control. He jumped up from behind his desk when they entered, obviously feeling nervous or anxious.

He was much younger than the other managers she'd been introduced to—in his late twenties, she estimated. Unruly black hair draped over his high forehead. Wire-rimmed glasses framed his pale blue eyes. His face was somewhat elongated, his complexion rather pallid.

After being introduced, Laura smiled at him, trying to put him at ease. "I don't envy you your job, Misha. Assuring the quality of everyday products is important, but assuring the quality of medical supplies is imperative."

"Yes, I agree," he said, speaking quietly, hesitantly.

"Have you been at the plant very long?"

He glanced at Olga, then replied, "Almost two years now."

"Misha's our youngest department manager," Olga remarked, placing a hand on his arm. "We're fortunate to have him."

Laura noted Olga's gesture and wondered if she'd done it to calm the young man. "I'm looking forward to working with you, Misha," Laura said. "A firm's reputation depends on the quality of its products."

"I take the responsibility very seriously," he said, seemingly forcing the words out.

Seeing how uncomfortable he was, Laura signaled an early departure by shaking hands. His was cool and clammy.

The next stop Laura and Olga made was at Sergei Angizitov's office, the manager in charge of inventory control.

Sergei was Anatol's friend, Laura recalled as the brown-haired man smiled broadly and pumped her hand. As Anatol had told her, the left side of Sergei's face bore a swath of scar tissue from his temple to the edge of his full mustache. It was apparent that minus the scar he would have been quite a handsome man. She was, however, impressed by the sincerity and warmth of his welcome. The other managers, with the exception of Misha Vinokurov, seemed to have gathered behind an impenetrable wall of suspicion and animosity.

"Would you like some tea?" Sergei asked as Laura settled herself in a chair.

"Please."

"Fruit jelly or lemon?" Sergei asked.

"Lemon, please." When he automatically added a spoonful of fruit jelly to Olga's tall glass, Laura remembered that the two of them lived together.

"Have you ever been to the top of the Empire State Building?" he asked enthusiastically, handing Laura her tea.

Laura smiled at the unexpected question. "Like many New Yorkers, I'm afraid I haven't."

"Sergei has had a fixation about the Empire State Building ever since he saw the movie *King Kong*," Olga explained. "He actually cries when the beast falls from the top of the building."

"So I'm sensitive," Sergei said, shrugging. He faced Laura. "I love what the man says at the end of the movie: 'It was beauty who killed the beast.' Someday," he added, thumping his chest ape-style, "I'll visit New York and go to the top."

Chuckling, Olga remarked, "By way of the elevator, I hope."

"That's your trouble. You're too practical." Turning back to Laura, he smiled broadly and crossed his arms. "So, what do you think of our plant?"

During the brief tour, Laura had taken note of the primitive computers, the advanced age of the majority of the managers and the general lack of employee enthusiasm—none of which she wanted to discuss right now. "It's difficult to form an opinion based on such a quick tour," she answered diplomatically. "But I feel certain the joint venture will be mutually beneficial to Biomed and to your plant."

Sergei beamed. "With the high-tech computers your company is shipping, we should outproduce every other medical supply plant in the country."

Olga placed a hand on Sergei's arm. "All he talks about now is computer-controlled inventory."

"The system we have here," he complained, "is little better than using an abacus. I can't be sure where half our products go."

"Don't say things like that," Olga said half joking, half as a reprimand.

"Why not? It's not as if I'm the only one who can't keep track of things in this country." To Laura he said, "Last night on TV they reported that twenty thousand railroad cars are missing. They just can't find them."

"Stop it, Sergei," Olga said. "Laura may turn around and go back to New York."

Smiling, he shook his head. "I don't think so. I've read that American businesspeople love a challenge."

Not this much of a challenge, Laura thought realizing that during the next three months she was really going to earn her salary.

"Once you're settled," Olga said, "please have dinner with Sergei and me. We live only a few streets from your apartment."

"I'd like that," Laura answered sincerely, then checked her watch. "I didn't realize the time. I don't want to delay Anatol longer than necessary." She extended a hand to Sergei, who kissed it and shook it warmly.

"Again, welcome to the Soviet Union," he said, his smile effervescent. "I know we will be good friends."

"We will," Laura agreed, then she and Olga returned to Chernov's office.

"WELL, LAURA," Anatol asked, standing by the window, "what do you think of Yuri's managerial staff?"

No sense beating around the bush, she decided. Bolstered by Olga's friendly smile, Laura looked squarely at the director, who was crouched over his desk, hands folded, eyes glued on hers. "I've had only a cursory look at your setup here, Mr. Chernov—"

His hands flew upward and he smiled. "There are no workers present. Yuri, please."

"Yuri," she repeated, almost feeling the hostility behind his pleasant facade. "I prefer to think of people as employees, not workers. As for the brief look I've had at the way your managers operate, I can see quite a difference from the way we do things at Biomed."

"How?" Anatol asked quickly.

Happy for a reason to turn from Chernov, Laura said, "Our managers at Biomed are primarily organizers. They work at a fast pace and have only brief encounters with personnel."

"You make them sound like machines," Chernov said dryly.

"Hardly. At Biomed we stress the ability to get along with employees. Our managers are trained to understand employees as individuals and to help them. But they don't do it by constantly hovering about. We believe that too much managerial hands-on attention to what each employee is doing is not only undesirable but counterproductive."

Anatol asked, "And that's what you saw this morning?"

"Yes, but perhaps the managers were doing what they thought I'd want to see. I don't know."

Olga switched her attention from Laura to Anatol. "I think Laura's assessment is quite perceptive."

"Do you?" Chernov asked, lifting his eyebrows.

"Yes, Yuri, I do. If we're going to meet the new government quotas, we'd better get all the help we can."

Realizing she needed to build good relations and not tear down existing ones, Laura said to Chernov, "I'm not being critical of your managerial staff. I am saying that when their American counterparts arrive, they'll have difficulty functioning under the present mode of operation."

"Then we'll adjust our present mode of operation," Anatol announced.

Flushed, Chernov sprang up from his chair. "Comrade Vronsky, I don't—!"

"Comrade Director," Anatol said calmly, "we'll have to make changes if we're to work with the Americans."

Olga turned to Laura. "Yes, we'll work together. We'll take the best advice you have to offer, Laura, and in turn, you'll respect our advice. It's a cooperative venture, no? Now, go and get settled in your apartment."

Rising, Laura returned Olga's friendly smile. "We *will* find a way of working together." She glanced over at Chernov. "Olga showed me my office. I'll be here at eight in the morning. Goodbye...Yuri."

"Goodbye...Laura," he said, emphasizing her name.

As soon as she and Anatol left the office, Laura heard Chernov start in on his assistant.

CHAPTER THREE

LAURA GRIMACED as she fastened her seat buckle in Anatol's car. "Chernov's aim in life is to make my life miserable."

"You'll handle him. I feel sure of that."

"I wish I felt as certain. All of a sudden the first of January seems like it's right around the corner."

Checking the rearview mirror, Anatol backed up and pulled out of the parking area. "Are there that many problems in the plant?"

"From what I saw there are more managers than employees, and there wasn't a smile on anyone's face."

"Don't go by that alone. They were probably primed for a week about your showing up today. That could make anyone nervous."

"It's Chernov I'm really worried about. He's going to resist any new ideas I present. When George arrives in December—that's George Hardcastle, who will be Chernov's codirector," she explained, "I'll probably be sent home in a slow-moving, leaky freighter."

Laura bit down on her lower lip, then added "What I don't understand is why Chernov is so hostile. If he doesn't want to be involved in a joint venture, why doesn't he transfer elsewhere?"

"Unlike you Americans, we Russians are used to staying put. And we need government permission to work in a different city. That's Pavlovsk Park we're passing," Anatol remarked, changing the subject. "It's within walking distance from your apartment."

He turned onto one of the tree-lined lanes and drove into the lushly landscaped park. Statuary was set on spacious lawns surrounded by oaks, silver birches and elm trees. Laura scanned the stately green-domed yellow palace with Corinthian and Doric columns that was situated high on a hill in the distance. Continuing down the lane, Anatol pointed out a lovely circular Greek-style structure that he called the Temple of Friendship. It appeared to Laura to be a smaller version of the Jefferson Memorial in Washington, D.C.

As they exited the park, Laura noticed the contrast between the well-kept palace grounds and the town itself. The streets were paved, but the wooden buildings were in need of repair and a fresh coat of paint. The lawns and vacant lots were overgrown. She missed seeing bustling downtown department stores and shops. Remembering her bout with Yuri Chernov, she decided the only thing she didn't miss about Manhattan was the subway.

Moments later Anatol pulled up in front of a two-story concrete-block building. "Your apartment is on the second floor," he said, hopping out of the car.

From the sign over the front door, Laura saw that she would be living over the local Soviet headquarters. She wondered if Anatol had arranged that purposely. And if so, why?

Inside the apartment she felt more relaxed. It was small but cozy: a living room, bedroom, kitchenette and bathroom. Not quite the luxury apartment she and

Roger had shared in New York, but Laura felt comfortable in it.

In the living room a colorful embroidered afghan was draped over a blue sofa that rested on a faded Oriental rug. The blue-and-white wallpaper appeared fairly new. She took note of the radiator and the fireplace, then went to the French doors, opened them and stepped onto the small balcony that overlooked a neatly kept garden below.

"It's charming," she said, turning toward Anatol, who was carting her garment bag to the bedroom.

She crossed to the doorway and watched him hang the bag in a carved armoire, aware that having dropped her off, he would leave and return to Leningrad. An unexpected feeling of emptiness took hold of her, increasing her awareness of being in a strange country, so very far from home. Anatol was the only person in Russia she could call a friend.

"Thank you for all your help," she said softly. "I hope I'll be seeing you again."

"I'm not going anywhere yet," he said, closing the armoire door. "I've decided to stay here for a day or two, just to make sure Chernov is agreeable. I have a dacha—a country cottage—on a lake here in Pavlovsk."

"Oh." Laura turned quickly to hide her relief that he wasn't running off. Beginning to unpack a suitcase, she asked, "Won't that interfere with your work in Leningrad?"

"The success of this joint venture is part of my job," he reminded her, "a big part right now. If everything goes smoothly here, it will open the doors to ventures at medical supply plants across the country."

"Make sure Biomed is included in some of them," Laura remarked as she transferred clothing from a suitcase to a dresser drawer.

Anatol braced a shoulder against the doorjamb, studying Laura's graceful movements. Ever since he had first laid eyes on her at the airport, he had felt a surprising inner stirring that had nothing to do with business. So many things about her captivated him: the warmth of her smile, her soothing voice, the pleasant aroma of the fragrance she wore. He was intrigued by the way light would play in the depths of her exquisite eyes, and the softness of her lips fascinated him.

When Laura turned, the quizzical look in her eyes made him realize he was staring at her. "While you finish unpacking, I'll see what kind of a job Olga did in stocking your pantry," he offered, retreating toward the door.

"Anatol," Laura said quietly, "again I find myself thanking you."

Her smile jarred his insides, but he merely nodded before going to the kitchen.

As she organized her lingerie in a dresser drawer, Laura decided that her assignment in the Soviet Union might not be as trying as she'd feared. Anatol, Olga and Sergei had made her feel sincerely welcome. The only fly in the ointment so far was Comrade Chernov. But during her ten years with Biomed, she had come up against strong-minded managers who had opposed change. Using reason and determination, she had met the challenges successfully. She would succeed with Chernov also, she decided. Suddenly her assignment seemed to have a lot of good points.

"Olga made sure you wouldn't starve for the time being," Anatol announced, reappearing in the bedroom doorway.

"She seems very thoughtful," Laura said, closing the suitcase and placing it on the floor next to the armoire. "I'm sure I'm going to like her."

"I could tell she already likes you." *But who wouldn't?* he added silently, knowing he shouldn't have decided to remain in Pavlovsk. His desk in Leningrad was piled high with work to be done. But, he rationalized, it was important that Laura's adjustment to his country be made as smoothly as possible.

Moving to the foot of the bed, he asked, "Would you like to see my country cottage?"

Laura's eyes lingered on his, and she realized there was a great deal she wanted to know about Anatol Vronsky. "Yes, I would," she said quietly. And shortly they were off again in his Lada.

"IT'S BEAUTIFUL!" Laura exclaimed, standing by Anatol's parked car and gazing out over the lake.

Wrapped in the arms of birch and willow trees, the expanse of calm blue water mirrored puffs of sunlit clouds and wild geese flying high overhead. Graceful white swans glided nearby. Birds twittered, harmonizing with the rustle of leaves in the surrounding woods.

Laura inhaled the cool fresh air, then turned toward the dacha, which was unlike any cottage she had ever seen. Of natural wood, its wide windows were sided with ornately carved shutters, painted blue as were the fretted eaves. The wooden door was a miracle of intricately carved flowers, animals and birds, all seeming to be fairy-tale creatures.

Stepping up to the narrow veranda, Laura ran her fingertips over the carved rosettes on one of the square columns. She turned toward him. "Someone put in a lot of time doing all this."

"Wood carving is a hobby of mine," he explained. "Come inside."

Laura followed him, seeing that one inner wall was of rough stone with a recessed fireplace. She noticed a pair of ice skates hanging on a peg and a set of skis leaning in the corner. Another wall held a built-in bookcase. One shelf was filled with works by Russian novelists; the others held wood carvings: decorative mugs, boxes and small animals. On a narrow table by the bookcase she saw several framed photographs. She guessed the handsome teenager was his son and that the others were relatives.

Picking up a wooden flute, Anatol said, "My grandfather taught my father wood carving, and he taught me." His eyes roamed over the rustic but cozy room. "This is where I'm the happiest. I like the peacefulness here and the change of the seasons." He turned, his face brightened by a sudden thought. "Do you enjoy ice skating?"

Laura smiled and rested her hands on the back of the upholstered chair by the fireplace. "My experience is limited to a few precarious circles on the rink in Rockefeller Plaza."

"The lake will freeze over next month. Come skating with me then. I won't let you fall."

For a few silent moments Laura stood immobile. Anatol was silhouetted by the sun that shone through the window behind him. In a flight of fancy she imagined herself skating with him, his arms holding her securely.

He placed the flute on the little table next to the sofa and took hold of her shoulders. "Will you come skating with me?" he asked again.

As the warmth of his hands penetrated her jacket, Laura shivered—but not from cold. It was quite comfortable in the sun-splashed dacha. "I didn't think to bring my ice skates with me."

"I'm sure I can find a pair in Leningrad that will fit you."

"In that case, yes, I'd love to. But don't say I didn't warn you. I'm not very good at it."

"I have the feeling that you'd be good at anything you set your mind on."

When Anatol's fingers tightened on her shoulders, she felt a surprising wave of excitement surge through her. Suddenly feeling heavy, her eyelids closed slowly. But then he released his hold on her, and her eyes snapped open as he moved away from her.

An awkward silence lingered between them for a moment. "If I'm going to be here a day or two," Anatol finally managed, his voice husky, "I'll have to stock up on some groceries."

"Yes," she said quickly, wondering if she had misread his intention. She'd been certain he was going to kiss her, and she wondered why he hadn't. What surprised her greatly, though, was that she had wanted him to. Confused by the rush of emotions she felt, she started toward the door.

"Laura," Anatol called, and she turned. "If you'd like, I'll drop you off at your apartment to give you time to settle in, then I'll do my shopping. I could pick you up later and we could have dinner here. I remember how lost I felt my first evening alone in New York."

His kind invitation caused her confusion to dissipate, and to be sure, she wasn't looking forward to spending the evening alone. "There's nothing I would like more."

A light glistening in the depth of his hazel eyes, he went to the bookcase and picked up an intricately carved four-inch-high sitting squirrel and offered it to her. "Please, take this for your apartment."

Accepting it, she ran a finger over its smooth head. "It's charming," she said, then smiled at him before exiting the dacha.

DURING THE NEXT TWO DAYS, under Anatol's watchful eyes, Chernov's attitude toward Laura changed for the better. At times he even appeared enthusiastic. She herself was less than enthusiastic when Anatol announced he would be returning to Leningrad.

Ever since she'd arrived in the Soviet Union, except for the weekend he'd spent in Moscow, Anatol had been her constant companion. Monday evening he'd fixed dinner for them at his dacha; Tuesday she'd reciprocated in her apartment. As they had talked late into the night, there was much that she found to admire in him: his unassuming sense of right and wrong, his vision of a brighter future for his country and his willingness to work hard toward that goal. She also liked his tendency to laugh openly and to touch casually, innocently. In the strange new world she'd entered, Anatol had become a generous source of support and comfort.

Now, standing by the window in her office that overlooked the narrow river that snaked between two hills, she turned toward him. "Of course I understand you have to leave. It was more than considerate of you to spend as much time here as you already have."

"I can't promise that Yuri's attitude will remain as cooperative after I'm gone," he told her candidly. "Just remember what I said about not pushing him too fast or attempting to make changes overnight."

"Anatol," she reminded him, more upset by his leaving than his warning, "I know what my job here is. It's not to make changes, only to suggest them when I can back them up with solid business reasons. Remember, January is only three months away."

"Yes, I know," he said quietly. "If you have any problems, or if you . . . if I can be of any help, don't hesitate to phone me immediately. Will you promise me you'll do that?"

She nodded, seeing his features register the same intensity she had noticed in his dacha when she'd thought he was going to kiss her, the same quizzical look he had given her several times during the past two days when he would glance her way.

"I'll miss you, Anatol," she said, fidgeting with the gold chain at her throat. Forcing the semblance of a smile, she added, "I guess that's natural. You're the first friend I've made here."

Taking hold of her hands, he ran his thumbs over her smooth skin. "You'll make many other friends."

The warmth and pressure of his strong hands sent a shock wave of intimacy rushing through her, causing her heart to flutter wildly. Her eyes holding his, she said, "A first friend is always special."

She noticed Anatol's Adam's apple move as he swallowed and wondered if their parting could possibly be as difficult for him as it was for her. Of course not, she decided immediately. He had colleagues in Leningrad, as well as friends and family, while she was quite alone in a foreign country.

"A first friend," he repeated, his words soft-spoken. Then he reached for a pen and a small pad on her desk. "This is the number of a private line to my office. And this is the number for my apartment phone. Call me anytime, even if you just feel like talking...to a first friend."

"Yes," she said softly, filling her eyes with him as he started toward the office door. "Anatol," she called, and he glanced back. "After I get the feel of things here, I'd like to see more of Leningrad. Perhaps we could have dinner—my treat the next time."

Her suggestion brought an easy smile to his ruggedly handsome face. "I'd like that very much."

Laura's smile matched his but waned when he quietly closed the door behind him.

Going to the window, she gazed out and caught sight of the automobile parked next to his, the silver Lada Anatol had arranged for her to use. Once again she was reminded of his thoughtfulness. She straightened when he came into view. Following his sturdy strides to his car, she noted how the afternoon sun glistened on his hair. After opening the car door, he looked back toward the window and waved.

Laura's hand rose automatically. "Goodbye, Anatol," she whispered, and rested her fingertips against the cool windowpane.

"WELL," Olga remarked in her office the following week as she and Laura finished their luncheon salads, "you seemed to have charmed Yuri. At this morning's department head meeting he ordered everyone to give you their utmost cooperation."

"Charmed may not be the right word. Besides, I'm suspicious of people who change like chameleons. So far so good, but I'm waiting for your boss to show his fangs again."

"He's not all that bad."

"How long has he been plant director?"

"About ten years now. Yuri started here as an apprentice when he was fifteen. He worked hard and advanced quickly. A few years ago he was awarded the title of Hero of Socialist Labor."

"Impressive," Laura commented, trying to hide her amusement as she thought of her own boss receiving such an accolade. Of course it would have to read Hero of Capitalist Labor. That thought did bring a smile to her lips. Changing the subject, she said, "I spoke with the home office last night and they confirmed that the computers were shipped by air."

"That will thrill Sergei. I'll phone the routing clerk at the Ministry of Health. She can find out when they should arrive here. It'll be a job getting our paper records computerized, but Sergei will work his staff day and night until it's done. Then we'll finally have some inventory figures we can rely on."

Laura scanned the notes she had made on a yellow pad. "Something as basic as syringes...how could there be a shortage? Surely other plants are producing them, too."

Olga groaned. "Only the Ministry of Health knows who's producing what. First we are told to manufacture disposable dishes, needles and paper products, then orders were changed to produce autoclaves, but we had to wait to get parts for our machinery. As you've noticed, some of our equipment is outdated."

"But the production statistics we received at Biomed were great."

"Yes, they did look nice," Olga agreed quietly. Then she said, "Everyone's talking about reforms and changes, but we haven't seen much evidence of that here." She smiled, leaned forward and patted Laura's hand. "You're going to change all that, aren't you?"

"I didn't think to pack my magic wand," Laura confessed, and frowned. Biomed was depending on her to pave the way for a lucrative profit-making endeavor. But Olga's remarks about the Ministry of Health's erratic instructions made Laura wonder if her company had thoroughly checked things out before signing on with the venture.

"Magic wand or no magic wand," Olga said, "you've already pumped some new blood into the plant."

"And made a lot of your managers nervous," Laura added, reaching for her tea glass.

"Sergei says it's good to see some of them shake. It's the only indication he has that they're alive."

"That Misha sure is an anxious young man. I said hello to him in the cafeteria this morning and he looked as though he was going to faint," Laura remarked.

"Managing quality control around here would make anyone nervous."

Laura eyed her suspiciously. "Are you about to give me some more good news?"

"Well, it's not all that bad. It's just that Misha's job is one that none of the more experienced managers wants. Supposedly he's in charge, but his reports have to be double-checked by a quality-control official from the Ministry of Health in Leningrad and another from Moscow."

"What on earth for?"

"It's the system."

"Olga, the more I learn about the system, the more I feel that you people give new meaning to the word bureaucracy." Laura shook her head and forked up the last piece of cucumber on her paper plate. "No wonder Misha's a bundle of nerves."

"He has good reason to be upset."

Something in Olga's tone made Laura glance up at her. "What reason?"

"Nothing, really," Olga said, her voice a bit too bright. "It's just that he lives alone and hardly socializes anymore."

"That's sad. I like Misha, but as pleasant as I try to be, I can't get a smile out of him."

"Sergei's about the only one who can."

"He could make anyone smile. How long have the two of you been together?"

"Almost three years. I'd been here just eleven months when we decided to live together. Apartments being as scarce as they are, we were lucky to find ours. By the way, we'd like you to come to dinner tonight."

"Not tonight. I'm taking some work home with me."

"Again?" Leaning against the side of her desk, Olga folded her arms. "I'm beginning to believe that Sergei's right. He says you're probably afraid of his cooking."

Laura laughed. "It's my own that worries me now. Back home I ate out a lot. Give me a rain check, will you?"

"You, my friend, are a workaholic. But even workaholics have to eat. Sergei will be disappointed if you don't come tonight."

"He's a thoughtful man. I can see why you like him."

"Sergei's all right, but I think he's developing an ulcer."

"Is inventory control giving him problems?"

"Let's just say he's anxiously awaiting the arrival of the new computers." Olga gave one last try. "You've got to come to dinner tonight. Sergei said I wasn't to take no for an answer."

Laura smiled in defeat. "What time do you want me to show up?"

"Sevenish?"

"Fine." She glanced at the clock on the wall and pushed herself up from the chair. "I've got a meeting with Yuri at one o'clock." She hesitated, then said, "Olga, yesterday I was going over last month's production reports. I saw that ten X-ray machines were listed as ready for shipment, but the department manager told me they hadn't even started making them yet."

Olga dropped the paper napkin she'd been wiping her hands with into the wastebasket by her desk. "That's one of the problems Sergei's having with inventory control. What we actually produce and what we say we've produced don't always match up."

"But that's false reporting!"

"Laura," Olga said matter-of-factly, "playing the statistics game is a national pastime. Everyone plays it, every bureaucrat knows it and expects it."

"Is that what Yuri will tell me when I ask him about the nonexistent X-ray machines?"

"He'll say that he'll check on it and get back to you, but don't hold your breath."

"Thanks for being candid, but that's a hell of a way to run a business," Laura said, dismayed as she headed for her office.

THE JOINT VENTURE was headed down the drain. She'd asked Chernov about the invented production figures, and he'd promised to get right back to her. Two hours later she'd learned he'd gone out to a meeting of the local soviet.

She considered calling Anatol. But if *all* bureaucrats played games with statistics, did that mean he did, too? If it was his job to oversee the plant, Anatol would have to be aware of what was going on, wouldn't he?

Laura reached for the phone, then pulled her hand back. "Damn," she muttered.

It would be simple to report the situation to her boss in New York. But then what? Return home in defeat, as Roger had gleefully told her she would?

No way! She was staying right here. And if she had to make waves to make this venture work, she damn well would. She'd make a tidal wave!

Glancing at her watch, Laura saw that it was four-fifteen and no "Comrade" Chernov yet. She calmed herself, buzzed his office once more and learned he hadn't returned from his meeting at the local soviet.

"So much for my causing a tidal wave," she mumbled looking up when Olga rushed in, Sergei close behind.

"Biomed's computers," Olga said, her face flushed. "They've been rerouted to a plant in Siberia."

"Siberia!" Laura shouted, springing up from behind her desk.

"That's what the routing clerk told me when I phoned her."

"We'll get them back," Sergei said hopefully. But he didn't sound as though he believed it.

Laura's wide eyes darted from him back to Olga. "Who ordered Biomed's equipment rerouted to a plant in Siberia? That's stealing!"

"The clerk wasn't sure, but she guessed it was ordered by the State Planning Committee."

"Anatol's committee?" Laura asked in disbelief.

Sergei planted his knuckles on Laura's desk. "Or it could have been rerouted by someone at the Ministry of Health." His head jerked toward Olga and his tone turned sarcastic. "By your friend Dmitri Karnakov, maybe."

"Dmitri isn't responsible for everything the ministry does."

Exasperated, Laura slumped onto her chair. "Just how many ministries and committees plan to divvy up Biomed's computers, and what makes them think they have the right to?"

"The State Planning Committee decides who gets what," Olga told her. "That's the committee's purpose."

Laura stared up at her. "You're not really suggesting that Anatol knows they were rerouted, are you?"

"Not necessarily."

Sergei chimed in again. "With the SPC, usually the right hand doesn't want to know what the left hand is doing. I doubt if Anatol's even aware of the rerouting."

"And maybe he is," Olga interjected. "Most bureaucrats protect one another in spite of what they say."

"I'm learning that fast," Laura said. "Yuri still hasn't gotten back to me about the funny production figures."

"I told you not to hold your breath," Olga reminded her.

Laura jumped up again. "Well, I'm not going to hold my breath while he explains to me how he's going to reimburse Biomed for half a million dollars worth of computers." She started to the door. "If he's not back yet, I'll sit in his office until he does show up."

Quickly Olga said, "He's not coming back today."

Whirling around, Laura asked, "Where's our wandering director now?"

"He went right from the meeting at the local soviet to one in Leningrad."

Storming back to her desk, Laura flipped through an address book, then dialed a number vigorously, rocking the phone as she did. "I'm going to get some answers from someone, and right now."

She waited for what seemed like an eternity, then, after a brief conversation, she replaced the receiver and looked at Olga and Sergei, a pained expression on her face. "Anatol has gone to Siberia."

CHAPTER FOUR

AFTER SIPPING the bourbon and water Sergei had given her, Laura scanned the elaborate hors d'oeuvres that Olga was placing on the lace-clothed table in the living room: various canapés of smoked salmon, egg, anchovies and capers; blinis with black caviar; creamy mushroom croustades and herring in sour cream dill sauce.

Sergei looked casual in his blue denims and a yellow knit sweater, but Olga appeared quite fashionable in a lovely paisley-print jumpsuit, a sculpted gold chain draping over the low-cut neckline.

Resting back against the cream-colored velour sofa, Laura decided that the shortage of consumer goods hadn't affected her friends' life-style in the least. But, she reminded herself, just as she and Roger had pooled their incomes, Olga and Sergei were probably doing the same.

"This is lovely," Olga remarked, holding up the long-sleeved silk blouse that was in the package Laura had given her. Checking the label, her eyes widened even more. "It's a Chanel!"

"From Saks in New York," Laura said, smiling at Olga's obvious delight. "I had my secretary ship it by air. It just arrived today."

Laura looked over at Sergei, who had finished unwrapping the gift she'd given him, a stainless-steel letter opener, the gold-plated handle a likeness of the Empire State Building, seemingly his favorite edifice in the world.

"This," he said enthusiastically, "is the next best thing to being there. Thank you, Laura. I'll keep it on my desk at the plant."

His mentioning the plant caused her thoughts to return to Biomed's computers that had been rerouted.

Seeing that she had become pensive, Sergei asked, "Are you still thinking about your company's equipment?"

"I haven't thought of much else since we found out."

"Just because Anatol is in Siberia," Olga said, "that doesn't mean he had anything to do with it."

"That's true," Sergei agreed. "He does work with other joint ventures there."

"Well," Laura said quietly, "we'll know one way or the other pretty soon."

"Let's not think about it anymore tonight," Olga suggested, heading to the kitchen. "Start in on the snacks. I'll be right back."

"Your apartment is lovely," Laura remarked, glancing around the well-furnished living room that was twice the size of hers.

"Olga likes nice things, but—" he shrugged and arched his well-shaped eyebrows "—they cost money."

"You should see the prices of quality items in New York," Laura quipped, then her voice became serious. "Speaking of quality, I understand that Misha's having a hard time with quality control."

"Why do you say that?"

"He seems to be wrestling with quite a complicated procedure. From what I understand he has two other people outside the plant breathing down his neck while he's trying to do his job."

"Misha shouldn't have complained to you."

"I didn't hear about his problems from him," Laura said, surprised by Sergei's judgmental tone.

"I'm glad to know that. Since I've been at the plant, I've seen three quality-control managers come and go. Misha's the best of the lot of them. He loves his job and he's got everything under control."

"Then I must have misunderstood," Laura said, wondering why Olga had told her just the opposite.

Pouring himself more vodka, Sergei said, "Anatol's the man who has too many people breathing down his neck, particularly some in the State Planning Committee. When he suggested setting up zones of free enterprise in this country, he said the whole building began to shake."

"Free enterprise," Olga repeated, coming out of the kitchen. "That will be the day. Fix me a drink, please, Sergei." She picked up the canapé tray and held it toward Laura. "You haven't touched a thing. Try the caviar."

Laura took one, commenting, "That's a lovely outfit. Silk, isn't it?"

"Uh-huh," she said, beaming as she turned around to afford Laura a complete view.

Sergei handed Olga her glass of bourbon, then sat down beside Laura again. "That bourbon and the outfit she's wearing were gifts from a friend of hers at the Ministry of Health in Leningrad. Have you noticed how often she has to attend meetings there?"

"It's my job," Olga announced curtly.

"Dmitri doesn't take Yuri to lunch when he goes into the city." Sergei glanced at Laura. "Dmitri Karnakov is the bright star nowadays at the ministry." Switching his eyes back to Olga, they turned darker. "Why doesn't he take Yuri for lunch?"

"Probably because Yuri wouldn't know which fork to use for what." She eased onto the chair across from Laura and leaned back. "Are American men as jealous as Sergei is?"

Laura smiled. "I imagine men in love are the same everywhere."

Sergei's eyes shifted to Olga. "Here, it used to be that when a man loved a woman and she supposedly loved him, they got married."

"I'm not ready to get married," Olga said flatly.

"You just don't want to settle down."

"Marriage isn't for everyone." Still looking at Sergei, she gestured toward their guest. "Is Laura married? No."

"If she were," Sergei said, "her husband probably wouldn't let her travel around the world the way she does."

"Tell him, Laura," Olga said. "Tell him that men in America are more modern in their thinking than Soviet men."

Attempting a neutral position, Laura remarked, "I really don't know that many men here to make a valid comparison. I can tell you, though, that Roger, the man I was seeing in New York, wasn't at all happy with my coming here."

"You see!" Sergei said triumphantly to Olga. "You're the one that's odd. You should want to settle down and have children, my children."

"To grow old and fat before my time? Ha! That will be the day." Olga faced Laura and smiled impishly. "He makes me sound like an ogre, but he knew from the beginning that I have plans for my life, and they don't include being stuck here in Pavlovsk forever."

Sergei snickered. "She has grandiose plans, like living in Moscow and rubbing elbows with important people."

"And what's so wrong with that?" Olga asked.

"Not a thing, especially for a little country girl who once thought Samarkand was the biggest city in the world." He looked back at Laura. "Olga grew up in a village with fewer than a dozen families in it."

"And I've come a long way since then," Olga added haughtily. "I was the youngest of nine children," she said to Laura, her expression taut. "Until I was sixteen I never had a new dress. The ones I wore were hand-me-downs from my older sisters." Olga lowered her eyes and her voice. "I swore then that my life wouldn't be like theirs or my mother's." Her lashes flicked up and her eyes sparked. "So I worked hard in school and was accepted into Tashkent University."

"She wanted to work in Moscow even then," Sergei said, getting up from the sofa and sitting on the upholstered arm of Olga's chair. "But she was sent here. That's when we first met."

Placing a hand on Sergei's thigh, Olga shook her head. "Four very long years ago. My first day at the plant he managed to spill a glass of tea all over a dress that had cost me two weeks' salary."

"You turned too quickly in the cafeteria line. Besides, I got your attention, didn't I?"

Standing, Olga said, "I doubt if Laura finds this walk down memory lane very interesting."

But Laura did, for having learned a little about Olga's background, she could now understand why the woman was so intent on carving out a secure place for herself in life. Yet, as the evening progressed, Laura became disturbed. Whenever Olga would talk about the glitter and glamor of Moscow or Leningrad, Sergei would pounce jealously on her relationship with Dmitri Karnakov.

At one point Laura's thoughts turned to Anatol, and she decided he probably wasn't a jealous man. Thinking of him, however, brought a resurgence of her suspicion that he might have had a hand in rerouting Biomed's computers to Siberia. It was something she didn't want to believe, but if the State Planning Committee had ordered the rerouting, how could he not have known? And what was he really doing in Siberia?

IN HER APARTMENT that evening, Laura paced in her robe, too upset to sleep. Her head ached, and she had taken another antacid after reviewing the phone call she had made to her boss in New York earlier in the day, informing him that the company's shipment had been "mistakenly" rerouted to another medical plant. She had been less than thrilled when he had told her it was her responsibility to get it back.

"What am I supposed to do?" she muttered to herself, collapsing on the sofa. "Hitch up a team of huskies and head east over the Urals?"

She drew her legs up, propped an elbow on the arm of the sofa and rested her chin on her palm. *I don't need this,* she complained silently. *Coming here was a big mistake. Right now I could be vacationing in the Bahamas. This is a crazy country, and it's making me crazy.*

Roger had been right, she decided grimly. She wouldn't last three whole months, not in a country where people had no qualms about stealing medical supplies.

Her head jerked toward the door when she heard a sudden knocking. Cautiously opening it a crack, her jaw dropped.

"I know it's late," Anatol apologized, "and I should have phoned first, but I wanted to talk to you in person."

She opened the door wide, and he entered, looking so troubled that Laura's first impulse was to place her hand against his face to try to soothe away his worries.

His eyes drifted over her peach-colored robe. Concerned, he asked, "Did I wake you?"

"No, no," she said, closing the door.

When he removed his car coat, the blue sweater he wore made his shoulders appear even broader than she remembered. And she noticed how his thick, wavy hair shone in the light from the lamp.

"I just got back from Siberia."

"Yes. I know you were there," she said quietly, averting her eyes. "I tried to reach you at your office."

"And you also know about the rerouting of Biomed's computers," he guessed from her downcast expression.

Laura nodded, then crossed to the chair near the archway to the kitchen. Hugging her arms, she focused her eyes directly on his. "Were they rerouted by the State Planning Committee?" she asked, her words a crisp accusation.

"Under orders from the Ministry of Health," he explained.

"You did know about it," she said brusquely.

"Not until after the equipment had been rerouted. I caught the first plane I could and went to the plant. Biomed's equipment, all of it, is now en route to Pavlovsk."

Laura's grasp on her arms relaxed, and she emitted a relieved sigh. "Thank you," she said softly, massaging the side of her neck. "Please, sit down. You must be exhausted. Can I fix you some tea or coffee?"

"Coffee would be appreciated."

"Take off your sweater if you like," she suggested on the way to the kitchen. "I keep it rather warm in here."

Anatol slipped his sweater off, laid it over his car coat and turned back the cuffs of his white shirt. Sitting on the sofa, he glanced around the room, taking note of the personal odds and ends Laura had placed about: a photograph of a woman he guessed was her mother, copies of *The New Yorker* magazine and the little wooden squirrel he'd given her. A pretty vine wreath hung over one of the French doors to the balcony.

He smiled at Laura when she returned and handed him a cup of coffee and a napkin. "Thanks," he said. "Aren't you having any?"

"I had some a little while ago." Sitting in the chair across from him, she adjusted the robe over her matching nightgown. "To be honest," she admitted, "I had some anxious moments when I learned of the rerouting."

After a swallow of coffee, Anatol put his cup down on the end table. "I thought you would. That's why I wanted to see you personally to explain."

"There's no need to explain," she interrupted, not wanting him to feel any worse than he apparently already did. "Biomed's shipment is secure, and that's all that matters."

"Not quite, Laura," he said, leaning forward.

She examined his tense features. "What's that supposed to mean?"

"I learned who ordered the rerouting...Dmitri Karnakov."

There was that name again, Laura thought, then said, "Sergei believed he might be involved. Just what gave him the right to do that?"

"Karnakov's one of the top men at the Ministry of Health. He thinks he has a right to do whatever he wants. He wields great power and his orders aren't questioned."

"So it seems, but why was he so interested in my computers?"

Anatol stood and walked slowly to the French doors. Turning, he slipped his hands into his pockets. "He claimed they were rerouted by mistake, but I believe he wants you to fail to meet the January first deadline at the plant."

Laura rose quickly and moved closer to Anatol. "Are you saying he's trying to sabotage the joint venture?"

"Yes, I think he is."

"But why? Our success at the plant could only be good for the general health of his people. It doesn't make any sense!"

"Change of any kind doesn't make any sense to many members of the Communist Party, particularly the older, more conservative ones."

With one hand on her hip, the fingers of the other at her forehead, Laura chuckled dryly. "I think I could handle Yuri's antagonism, but I'm certainly not going to take on the entire Communist Party."

"I'm a party member," he reminded her. "A progressive one, however. You're to be commended for the work you're doing at the plant, and please believe that I'm one of your biggest fans."

The warmth of his voice and his compelling eyes sent a shiver of excitement rippling over her skin, but it was more than just a physical reaction. There was something in the way Anatol was looking at her, something in the unguarded trust of his words that drew her to him emotionally.

For the past few days she had felt so isolated in the vast country, so strange, so much like an interloper. She needed to feel welcome and respected for the hard work she was doing. More important, she needed to feel needed and appreciated. Anatol had just succeeded in making her feel that way.

Without thought she went to him, her fingertips barely grazing his shoulders as she kissed him lightly on the cheek. "Thank you for your vote of confidence," she murmured. Struck by his intense reaction to her casual gesture, Laura backed away, then turned from him, trying to calm the confusing emotions that assailed her.

Suddenly Anatol was behind her, his hands cupping her shoulders. His mere touch, his closeness, was like an aphrodisiac, awakening her entire body. "Laura," he whispered, his warm breath teasing her ear, "You've been on my mind . . . a lot."

His voice was so soft and so caressing that Laura's eyelids slipped shut. She wasn't certain if she had leaned back against him, or if Anatol had drawn her closer, but now his arms were cradling her, his warmth penetrating her back.

"I thought about you, too," she admitted in a thready voice.

"You did?" he asked tentatively.

She placed her hands over his forearms, her fingers tingling from the sensation of their soft hair and their warmth. Her heart began pounding a rhythm so erratic that she could hardly think. "Yes," she whispered.

"I was afraid you wouldn't even miss me."

"I did," she confessed, her silk robe rustling as she turned in his arms. Her hands slid up the front of his shirt, and his body heat under her fingers further loosened her restraint. "I missed you even more than I thought I would."

He smiled. Then gently and softly, as though testing the feel of her lips, he kissed her. In the next instant he pulled her up against him, and the gentle exchange gave way to a deepened kiss that sent her emotions spinning.

Her arms streamed over his shoulders, and she guided her fingers through the soft hairs at his nape. Their lips locked until she felt as if he had inhaled all the breath from her lungs.

Unsteady, she tilted her head back and murmured his name. Everything seemed to have happened so fast that Laura wasn't sure how it did, but her sensitized lips and her body pressed against his assured her it had.

When he drew his head up, she gazed at him, seeing his face flushed with desire, his eyes burning with raw need. They frightened her, because of what she saw in them, because they mirrored her own need. Instinctively she pressed her palms against his chest and took several steps backward, raised her hands and ran nervous fingers through her hair, not able to tear her eyes from his.

"Do you want me to leave?" he asked, his voice deep, throaty.

"No," she managed with difficulty, shaking her head. "Just give me a minute to organize my thoughts."

Half turning, she gathered the lapels of her robe over her wildly beating heart. *What are you thinking!* she chastised herself. *Don't you have problems enough? Problems? That kiss wasn't exactly a problem for me or Anatol, but it could certainly lead to problems.*

"Laura, I—"

She faced him, thinking that her expression must be as tense as his. Like a released spring that had been too tightly wound, her words came tumbling out. "First of all, neither of us should read more into what just happened than what actually did."

"You kissed me and I kissed you," he said, trying to understand her reaction.

"That's what I'm talking about. I was merely excited about getting the equipment back."

"Oh?" he remarked dubiously.

As though not hearing him, she continued. "And it was just natural that . . . that . . ."

"That you wanted to thank me."

Her eyelids flickered nervously. "Yes, that I appreciated you're having done what you did."

"I don't believe you. That was no thank-you kiss."

Laura clasped her hands so tightly that her knuckles whitened. Pacing, she rambled on. "I fought hard to get this assignment, and I don't want to get sidetracked."

"You believe I'd sidetrack you?"

Her eyes darted to his, but only for a second. "My work here is going to be more difficult than I realized."

"I'm trying to make it less difficult."

"I need to be able to concentrate, Anatol. I have to channel all my energies into my job."

Lowering himself to the sofa, he spread his arms out over the back of it and continued to study her aimless movements—and to listen to her excuses.

Trying to sound reasonable, she continued. "As I said, my work's important to me. If I'm successful here, I'll be able to write my own ticket with Biomed."

"You're going to wear yourself out," he advised, taking hold of her wrist when she wandered near the sofa. Gently he pulled her down beside him, her tense expression causing him to smile softly.

"I'm serious," she said firmly, "and I take my career plans just as seriously."

"I admire you for that, but you can't work twenty-four hours a day. You have to eat, sleep and rest part of the time."

"I know that," she retorted, moving back a little when he leaned closer.

"There's a saying that all work and no play isn't good."

"I'm not here to play."

"But you'll admit that you do have to eat, sleep and rest. Maybe we could eat . . . and rest together at times, and discuss business along the way."

"At times we could," she agreed cautiously, her eyes following the movement of his arm as he rested it behind her on the back of the sofa.

"Come into Leningrad this weekend," he said, his features softening into a smile that made her want to kiss him again.

Laura sensed her resolve failing and felt as if she had returned to square one as far as convincing him she didn't want an intimate involvement. Or did she?

"I think I'll fix some tea," she said when she felt his fingertips glide down over her neck. Quickly she stood and looked down at him. "Would you like some?"

"I haven't finished my coffee."

"Oh . . . yes." Like a freed caged bird, Laura took flight from the room.

Anatol followed, leaning against the archway, watching silently as she readied the teakettle. He still wasn't sure what to make of her. In business she seemed strong-minded, totally in charge, ready to do battle if necessary. But what was she like as a lover?

She'd kissed him first. He wasn't used to that. But he liked it. He liked it a lot. It was a hell of a turn-on, one he still hadn't recovered from. The thumping in his chest lingered, as did the insistent heaviness between his thighs.

He sat down on one of the two chairs at the small kitchen table and rested his shoulders back against the wall. Sensing her vulnerability excited him, but at the same time it filled him with a strong desire to protect her, another new emotion for him. Something warned him to be wary of Laura Walters. Something else told him that that warning had come too late.

Seeing that Anatol was sitting, Laura joined him, waiting for the kettle to boil. Without thought she took a napkin from the holder on the table and spread it over her lap. Then she reached for another and started to drape it over the first. She caught what she was doing, refolded it quickly and laid it on the table.

Cocking his head, Anatol asked, "Am I making you nervous?"

She shook her head. "No, it's just that I don't want you to make any snap judgments about me."

"Such as?"

She cradled her teacup with her hands, then realized it was empty and lowered it back onto the saucer. "I don't want you believing I go around kissing every man I do business with."

"I don't," he said sincerely, "but I'm happy you did. You're a beautiful woman, and not just physically." He paused, searching for the right words, then admitted, "I'm not very good at saying what I feel when it comes to things like this."

He rested his elbows on the edge of the table and rubbed his palms together, his smiling eyes holding hers. "At the movies I hear men on the screen saying clever things to women, and it makes me realize how inadequate I am when it comes to talking about how I feel sometimes. What I'm trying to tell you is that I care about you, not just because you're lovely, but—" Raising a hand, he rubbed the back of his neck. "I guess it's the way you think, your straightforward approach to life, the way you do things, your sense of fair play." After a moment's silence, he asked, "Does any of what I'm saying make sense to you?"

Laura sat quite still, feeling she could easily drown in his beautiful eyes. Fighting a strong desire to reach over and touch him, to tell him he made a great deal of sense, she jumped up, poured the boiling water from the kettle into the teapot and placed it on the table.

Anatol watched her uncomfortably. Why didn't she say something? he wondered, feeling hurt and foolish for having exposed his feelings. Maybe he shouldn't have. Maybe she took it as a sign of weakness.

That thought sent a stinging heat surging up his neck. "Well," he mumbled, "I probably don't match up to the sophisticated men you know in New York, men like...what's his name...Roger." Before she could utter a word, Anatol asked, "He is sophisticated, isn't he?"

"Too much so," she said, sitting back down.

"I suppose he can't wait for you to come back to him."

"He's not waiting. I moved out of our apartment before I left New York."

"Trouble in paradise?" Anatol asked, unable to restrain the hint of a smile that curved his lips.

"There wasn't at first, but then I found myself living according to his rules. He wanted the luxury apartment and the vacation at the ski resort. He thought children were cute, but he didn't want any, nor did he want me to take this assignment. In fact, he accused me of being too gung ho about my work."

"So you moved out, and now you're footloose and fancy-free. Good. There's no reason why you can't come to Leningrad this weekend. You can use my apartment, and I'll sleep at a friend's."

"Your apartment?" Laura stared at him. "You have it all planned out, don't you?"

"I'm just trying to make your stay here more enjoyable."

"For whom?"

"For you, of course."

"Of course," she repeated, the corners of her lips lifting slightly as she poured her tea. "I'll have to add noble to your list of admirable qualities."

"I'll have to add suspicious to yours."

"Shouldn't I be?"

He leaned back in his chair and tilted his head. "How can you be suspicious of something you should already know?"

Having regained her composure, she said confidently, "Don't talk in riddles, Anatol. What is it I'm supposed to know?"

"That I want us to be good friends, close friends. I feel strongly about you, Laura, and my feelings increase every time we're together. But just because I feel that way, I'm not taking it for granted that you do. Or do you?''

Her composure was short-lived, and her words came out uneasily. "As I said, I'm here to work."

"Then I apologize for being so blunt. I thought perhaps you cared for me . . . a little."

"I do," she insisted, "but our getting involved emotionally just doesn't make any sense. I'll only be here for a little more than two months."

"People have been known to fall in love in less time than that."

"Love?" Again he caught her off guard. "Anatol," she said firmly, "I have no intention of falling into anything while I'm here. And I'm just not good at getting involved in brief affairs that have no chance of leading anywhere. I mean . . . look at the situation clearly. We live such totally different lives. Our backgrounds are so different. And who knows? Next week something could happen to change the warming relations between our countries. I'd probably have to leave right away."

His eyes sharp and assessing, he said, "I doubt if Biomed would have entered the joint venture if they were as concerned about future relations as you seem to be."

He let that sink in, then said, "I wasn't thinking about world politics when I was talking about us. I was thinking of a man and a woman. And you're not just any woman. You're special, Laura. I knew that the moment I saw you. Something happened to me when I first saw you at the airport. I can't explain what, but I've never been affected like that by a woman before."

His expression and his warm and tender words seemed so honest and compelling that she felt herself being drawn into a losing battle, one she wasn't certain she wanted to win.

But neither could she surrender totally.

"Do you understand what I'm saying?" he asked.

"Oh, yes," she whispered, then sipped her tea while garnering all her emotional strength.

"I'm saying that I want us to get to know each other well, very well. Come into Leningrad this weekend ... please."

Putting her cup down, Laura focused her eyes on it. "I need time, Anatol, time to think things through carefully."

"We don't have a great deal of time," he reminded her. "But I won't rush you. It has to be your decision. You have to want what I want, or it will be no good for either of us."

Her eyes drifted up to meet his imploring gaze.

"Will you spend this weekend with me?" he asked softly, disarming her with an alluring smile. "As I remember, you said dinner would be your treat the next time."

Her pulses racing, she said, "Yes, I remember that."

"And, yes, you'll come?"

After a moment she nodded.

"Good," he said, reaching across and covering her hand with his. "I'll arrange to be at the plant Friday afternoon. Then we can drive into the city together." He glanced at his watch. "It's late. I'd better leave so you can get to bed."

In the living room he slipped on his sweater and car coat before taking hold of her hands and gently kissing her forehead. Grazing her cheek with the back of his fingers, he said quietly, "I'll see you Friday."

Slowly Laura closed the door behind him, wondering if she had done the sensible thing in accepting his invitation. Or was she just asking for trouble?

Whatever the answer, she had to acknowledge the warm glow that flowed through her and the tingling sensation she felt on her forehead where he'd kissed her.

CHAPTER FIVE

"REALLY, LAURA," Chernov said, staring at her from behind his desk, "you don't actually expect me to dismiss half my managers."

"That's not at all what I expect you to do. What I'm saying is that there's an unbalanced age structure in the existing staff. Two-thirds of them are about to retire."

His eyes narrowed. "Socialism gives them that right. They've earned it."

"I've no quarrel with that," she insisted, "but when they retire en masse, the American managers will find themselves working with inexperienced Soviet counterparts."

Crossing his arms and resting them on the desk, a smirk of satisfaction settled on his face. "And your Americans won't be able to handle it? I thought there was no end to your business capabilities."

"Yuri," she said calmly, "whatever your problem is, don't make it mine. I haven't time for your sarcasm, and I resent it. It's my job to give you an honest assessment of management conditions here and to make recommendations, solely recommendations. I'm not only willing. I'm anxious to hear yours also. We both have the same goal—to increase this plant's productivity and profits."

"Why start by suggesting I fire older workers?"

"I'm *not* suggesting that." The man was thick! she decided. Or else he just didn't want to understand her.

Rising from her chair, she poised her fingertips on top of his desk. "Listen carefully. One, you have too many managers assigned to most of your departments. Two, the majority of them have retired on-the-job. Three, I am suggesting that some could be reassigned, with no loss in pay, pending their retirement. Four, you're not using your younger, more capable supervisors. You could consider giving them responsible managerial slots."

"I take it you plan to let me stay on here," he said with the hint of a smile.

Laura returned his relaxed expression and stood erect. "Let's just get this show on the road, and in two months you won't have to lay eyes on me again."

"Hmm," he mumbled, stroking his chin. "I can see what you mean by giving workers incentives to produce." He pushed a lever on his intercom and instructed his secretary to tell Olga to come to his office.

While they waited, Laura decided that he looked like many other men she had worked with who felt they were being cornered into making a decision they didn't want to deal with. But in Chernov's case, she thought he was overly troubled by doing so.

"Olga," he said when she closed the door behind her, "Laura has some *recommendations* about reorganizing the managerial staff. I want you to work with her on coming up with a reasonable alternative. But, and it's to be understood by both of you, not a word of possible changes is to reach the workers. Is that clear?"

"Certainly, Yuri," Olga said, then glanced at Laura. Thinking she was about to protest, she took hold of Laura's arm and hustled her out of the office.

As the two women headed down the corridor, Olga grinned. "You're going to make an avowed capitalist out of him."

"I'd settle for an efficient socialist," Laura countered.

"I've got the list of retirement dates you asked for in my office. Should I get them?"

"No, there's something else I need your help with first."

After they reached Laura's office, she went around her desk and opened a side drawer. Removing a folder, she spread out some papers on the desk. Still standing, she said, "I was going over September's inventory-control reports, and something's not right."

"What isn't?" Olga asked, examining the papers.

"Here, for instance...the surgical instruments. Twice as many sets were produced as were shipped, yet our inventory is depleted, according to Sergei's monthly report."

Olga flipped through several other pages, then said, "What you don't have here is Misha's quality-control report. It would indicate the number of defective sets that were rejected."

Laura stared at her. "Fifty percent were rejected?"

"In this case, apparently. I admit it's unusually high."

"High? It's astronomical! Who has the final say on defective products?"

"On paper I do. Naturally I don't check out every item personally. I take the word of our quality-control manager."

"Misha," Laura said uneasily.

"I told you about the problems he has in his department."

"Those other two inspectors," Laura said, recalling what Olga had told her about the cumbersome quality-control procedure.

"Either one of them or Misha can determine that a batch might not be suitable for sale. Of course they each file a report. Misha submits his and theirs to me, and I pass them on to Sergei's department."

"No wonder Sergei's drowning in paperwork." After a moment's thought, Laura asked, "What happens to the defective items?"

"Sometimes they can be reworked here, sometimes they're shipped to whatever factory produced the raw material, and sometimes the items are discarded."

"How are they discarded?"

"They're taken to a dump site."

"A dump site?" Again Laura looked at her in disbelief. Sitting down behind her desk, she concluded, "So the disposition of the defective surgical instruments would be listed on the quality-control report I don't have."

"Yes," Olga said. "Do you want me to try and find it?"

"No. Let's get started on the reorganization project. I'll check with Misha later."

NEAR CLOSING TIME Laura went to Misha's office and found Sergei with him. "Excuse me," she said cheerfully. "I didn't mean to interrupt you. Misha, when you have a minute, I'd like to talk with you."

"Come on in," Sergei told her. "I was just leaving." He turned to Misha and lowered his voice. "Remember what I said."

As Sergei left, Laura couldn't decide if his parting words were offered as friendly advice or as a warning. Pleasantly she asked Misha, "Could I see your copy of the September quality-control reports?" She was taken aback when his expression changed from dismal to near panic.

He turned quickly, went to his file cabinet, partially opened the top drawer, then closed it slowly. His back to her, he said, "Uh...the September reports. I remember now. I forgot to make copies of them before I passed them on to Olga."

"Oh," Laura remarked, thinking it more than odd that the reports she wanted weren't available. And why did he just about go into shock every time she talked to him? Attempting to reduce his anxiety, she said, "I've forgotten to do things like that when the work piles up. Was last month unusually hectic for you?"

"Yes," he said, turning slowly, his eyes moving nervously. "There was a lot going on. We knew Biomed was shipping computers, so all departments began boxing records that Sergei's staff would be computerizing."

"The transition period is a mess, but once everything is in the computer, obtaining copies of records will be a snap."

"That's what Sergei was just telling me...about the new system, I mean."

Wanting to leave Misha in a more pleasant mood, Laura smiled. "Do you have any great plans for the weekend?"

"No. I'll be spending time here at the plant to try to catch up on some paperwork."

Laura knew he had an adequate staff and wondered why he thought it necessary to put in overtime. "Are your people behind in their work, Misha?"

"No, no, it's not that. There are some things I feel I should take care of personally."

"If you find that work is piling up, you might want to talk with Olga about getting temporary assistance. She's very reasonable."

"Yes, she is," he said oddly. "She and Sergei are my best friends here."

"They think highly of you and praise your work." When he didn't respond, Laura said, "If you should come across the September reports, give me a buzz, okay?"

"Yes, I will."

Thanking him, Laura exited his office, wondering why it was that Misha went around in a continual state of anxiety. And he was too good a department manager to forget to make copies of reports before sending the originals on. She glanced at her watch and decided to wait until everyone left before checking the file room herself.

From the side window in her office, she saw the employees file out of the plant. Some streamed across the field. Others boarded buses in the parking lot. After Olga and Sergei left in their car, Laura went directly to the file room.

It was an awful room, a file clerk's nightmare. Someone could easily get lost in the maze of file cabinets. The air was musty due to lack of ventilation, and with half the bulbs burned out, the overhead lighting did little to relieve the dour atmosphere.

Pushing up the sleeves of her blue sweater jacket, she started in on the cabinet marked Quality-Control Reports. The September folder was exactly where it should have been, but there was no report on surgical instruments in it.

She checked several adjacent folders, thinking it might have been misfiled, but still she couldn't locate it. Glancing over the tops of the more than twenty rows of cabinets, she realized they probably held records dating back to the opening of the plant. The reports she wanted could be in any one of them, she decided; papers did get stuck together.

But, she reminded herself as she shut the drawer, if they weren't misfiled, a lot of surgical instruments were unaccounted for. That possibility didn't set well; missing inventory meant missing profits.

She opened the folder she had brought with her, ran a finger down the list she had made, then checked the file cabinet for disposition of EKG machines. As with the surgical instruments, their figures hadn't tallied, either. Searching, she quickly discovered that there was no September report on defective EKG machines. She had a sinking feeling that if she checked the other medical supplies she couldn't account for, the quality-control reports on them would be missing, as well.

Hearing a noise on the other side of the file room, she turned toward the door—just in time to see it being closed. Her heart skipped a beat, and she listened attentively for the sound of footsteps, not certain if someone had entered or left.

She heard nothing. For that she was grateful. Quickly she closed the file drawer, picked up her folder and cautiously made her way to the row of cabinets by the door. She could see over the top of them, but just to be sure she peered around the side. Breathing a sigh of relief, she hurried from the room.

As she reached for the knob on her office door, a hand touched her shoulder. She gasped and jumped at the same time, whirling around to see Chernov smirking at her.

"Working late?" he asked. "Such dedication."

Laura wanted to suggest he wear a bell around his neck. Instead, she said, "You startled me. I thought everyone had left."

"The workers have, but as the director, I have to make sure that nothing goes amiss in my plant. Sometimes that requires keeping a sharp eye on what's going on."

She wondered just how sharp his eyes really were. "Yuri," she said casually, "I was just in the file room looking through last month's quality-control reports. It seems some of them are missing." His only response was a narrowing of his eyes. "Do you have any idea where they could be?"

"If you've been in the file room, you know how disorganized it is at the moment. I'm sure the reports will turn up during the computerization process."

"I see. Well, do you recall that fifty percent of the surgical instruments manufactured last month were defective?"

"Is that what the records show?"

"As best as I can figure out from the ones I can find."

"We'll discuss this further when the quality-control reports turn up." Laura opened her mouth to challenge him, but he cut her off. "You'd better leave soon. There seems to be a bad storm brewing. You wouldn't want to get caught in it, would you?"

"Thanks for the warning," she said, wondering if he were giving her more than advice about the weather. "I'll be leaving in a few minutes."

Laura entered her office, closed the door and went to the window. There were dark clouds on the horizon. In more ways than one, she thought.

The nonsensical scenario that Olga had outlined for rejected products at the plant was scary enough, but if someone was helping himself to inventory, the responsibility for knowing it would ultimately fall on Sergei. It was his job to be aware of what happened to plant products. But what if he did know they were missing? she wondered, not at all liking that possibility. Not only had she become fond of him, but he was a good friend of Anatol's. Two reasons, Laura thought, for her to be cautious before blaming him. Still, she had an obligation to Biomed.

A rumble of thunder drew her attention to the darkening sky once more. Sullenly she gazed up at the heavens and mumbled, "Give me a break, will you?"

"PLEASE," CHERNOV PLEADED the moment Anatol stepped into his office Friday afternoon, "will you try to talk some sense into this woman?"

"The man is inflexible," Laura stated stiffly.

"Well," Anatol said, "at least you two have agreed to disagree. That's a start, I suppose. What seems to be the problem this time?"

Laura thrust her managerial recommendations at him. "At Yuri's request I spent two days and nights coming up with this suggested reorganization plan. Now he'll have none of it."

"Replacing older workers," Yuri said, "is callous and capitalistic."

Anatol scanned Laura's recommendations, then asked Chernov, "Have you discussed this with the head of the labor and wages section?"

"I did, and she agreed that changes of this magnitude would make it impossible to reach our end-of-the-year quotas."

As calmly as she could, Laura said, "Effective managing means long-range planning as well as meeting short-range goals."

Anatol's eyes swept to the stone-faced Chernov, then back to Laura. "I agree," he said, "but I told you that you can't expect change to take place here as rapidly as you're used to in America. What you should be able to expect is a spirit of compromise. This is, after all, a *joint* venture."

"But—" Laura started to object.

"That's not all," Chernov interrupted smugly. "She also wants to initiate a job-evaluation program."

Through clenched teeth, Laura said, "A five-point scale to assess employee performance isn't unrealistic."

Chernov leaned back in his chair and smiled sarcastically. "Workers are to be treated like children in school. Those who get A's are to receive bonuses. The

E's—'' he waved a thumb through the air ''—out the door.''

Laura wanted to rip Yuri's thumb from his hand. Instead, she squared her shoulders and faced Anatol. ''Department managers would do the assessing. Employees dropped from the payroll would include an extremely small minority who aren't pulling their weight. Those who receive a D would be asked to improve their performance before the next evaluation period.''

''I can appreciate Yuri's concern,'' Anatol said firmly. ''Some people here would quit if they learn they're expected to work harder.''

''Those who did would be doing the plant a favor. We could actually increase salaries for those who stayed and were productive. It's my estimation that competent people would compete for jobs here at decent salaries.''

''Laura,'' Chernov reminded her, ''you're here *only* to offer recommendations. You've done so. Thank you.''

Anatol heard Laura suck in a long breath. Before she could respond, he assumed his role as peacemaker and intervened. ''My guess is that the two of you have thrashed these recommendations around enough for one day.'' He slipped Laura's papers into the inside pocket of his suit jacket. ''Give me a chance to study the reorganization plans. After I do, Yuri, you and I will sit down and go over your objections again.'' He took a gentle hold of Laura's arm. ''Let's get your things.''

''Have a nice weekend,'' Chernov said, smiling broadly at the glare Laura sent his way.

As Anatol hung her garment bag in his car, Laura blurted out, "I didn't expect you to side with him."

"I didn't side with anyone," he protested, walking around to the driver's side.

Plopping onto her seat, she slammed the car door. "You gave a good impression of doing so."

"That's funny," he said, fastening his seat belt. "I thought I used the word compromise."

"Which means Yuri will do whatever he damn well pleases—as usual."

"Not necessarily." After backing up, he glanced over at her. "I warned you that you can't expect him to react immediately to changes you have in mind."

"Ha! It would take a firecracker in his shorts to make him move on anything I suggested."

Anatol grinned. "My, but you have a vivid imagination."

"Right now I'm imagining myself trying to explain to my boss why I couldn't make Chernov see reason. I'm supposed to be an expert in managerial communication."

"I was impressed with your reorganization plan."

"Wonderful! Why don't you switch jobs with Chernov?"

"You are upset, aren't you?"

"And you're particularly perceptive today. I don't understand this hesitancy of his to move forward. It's as obvious to him as it is to me that the plant's not producing up to potential."

"Laura," Anatol explained calmly as he pulled onto the highway, "workers in the Soviet Union have a saying. 'We pretend to work, and they pretend to pay us.'"

"It's the pretense I'm trying to eliminate, at least from one plant. Can't you and Chernov see that?"

"I do, but he doesn't want you undercutting his authority."

"Someone has to if I'm going to be able to do my job here."

"Does your job mean so much to you that you'll let it spoil our weekend?"

"Are you able to turn off thinking about your job at five o'clock?" she asked curtly.

"When it's a weekend with you I am."

Still angry and frustrated, Laura faced the side window and muttered, "You sound just like Roger." He'd always accused her of being too gung ho about work.

"Unlike him," Anatol said, looking straight ahead, "I haven't asked you to live with me... yet."

Her head spun toward him again. "What?"

"They're doing some construction work down the highway. Better fasten your seat belt," he suggested. "There's a bumpy road ahead."

CHAPTER SIX

ENTERING ANATOL'S APARTMENT on Tchaikovsky Street, Laura glanced around, struck by the difference between it and his dacha by the lake. The dacha was unmistakably warm, its coziness heightened by Anatol's many personal items. But his apartment hardly looked lived-in.

Modern Danish furniture was placed on pearl-gray carpeting. The draperies were white. The prints on the wall were uninteresting landscapes. Everything was exactly in its place, giving the room a rather cold appearance. Vainly she searched for an indication of the warmth she knew Anatol possessed. Shown the dacha and the apartment, she would have supposed that two different men lived in them.

Returning to the living room, Anatol said, "I put your coat and garment bag in the closet and your suitcase on the rack at the bottom of the bed."

Laura scanned the room again, wanting to say something positive about it, but all that came out was, "This is nice."

"It's convenient to my office." He saw her attention go to the wilting philodendron hanging in a basket by the window. "I don't have much luck with plants in here," he said, and went to the kitchen to get a glass of water for the drooping plant.

As he tried to revive it, he commented, "This poor thing needs more attention than I've been giving it." His gaze slid toward Laura. "I guess we'd all do better with a little more tender loving care. I imagine the plants in your apartment in New York are in great shape."

"I don't have any in my new apartment, not yet."

"That's right," he said, a mischievous smile curving his lips. "You no longer have a roommate to water them while you're gone."

Laura still hadn't forgotten the comment he had made in the car. Of course he hadn't been serious about planning to ask her to live with him, she told herself again. You don't kiss someone once, then start picking out furniture. No, he had just been teasing her, trying to get her thoughts off Comrade Chernov.

Carrying the empty glass back to the kitchen, Anatol remarked, "Having a roommate does have its advantages." He stopped at the doorway and glanced back at her over his shoulder. "If I had one, my plants would be a lot happier."

"Yes," she agreed, smiling snidely. "But would your roommate be?"

"I'd see to it."

"That's another thing I like about you, Anatol . . . your humility."

Tilting her chin up in satisfaction, she went into the bedroom to change for dinner.

As they dined in the upstairs room at the Baku restaurant, Anatol said, "I looked over your managerial reorganization plans. I'm impressed with what you're trying to do at the plant."

"There's just one big problem—the director. But I'd rather not talk about him while I'm eating." After wiping her lips with a napkin, she said, "Just one question. Are the other plant directors you work with like him?"

"Bureaucrats are bureaucrats everywhere, I suppose." He chuckled wryly. "But here we have eighteen million of them giving orders to only half a million plant and factory directors. Trying to get anything done is like umpiring a soccer match where half the team runs toward one goal and half heads toward the other."

"You have my sympathy," Laura said sincerely.

"I'd rather have your friendship," he said, his hazel eyes reflecting the soft candlelight.

"You have that already," she said, wondering how good a friendship they'd have once she told him about Sergei's problem with inventory control at the plant. Not wanting to ruin the evening, she decided to put it off until morning.

After their waiter served them coffee, the small orchestra began playing a slow ballad. Anatol said, "I'm no Baryshnikov, but would you like to dance?"

"I'm no Ginger Rogers, but I'd love to." She saw that the name didn't register. "One of America's great dancers," she explained.

"My curiosity about things American has soared lately. I'm hoping to get an education from you. I promise to be an attentive student."

Feeling quite relaxed and content from the wine and spicy Caucasian food, Laura smiled softly. "I do a lot of teaching in my job."

"That's what I'm counting on," he said as he reached for her hand.

Guiding her between other candlelit tables to the dance floor, he embraced her fox-trot style. The white crepe dress that Laura wore was cut into a low V in the back, and she could feel the tantalizing warmth of Anatol's hand on her skin. His easy pressure sent a ripple of intimacy spiraling through her body. His other hand, holding hers, created an equally disturbing sensation. No, not disturbing, she had to admit; it was delightful. Gently he eased her closer, and she felt the side of his face caressing her temple.

"Umm," he whispered, "you smell good."

"It's the perfume," she said, snuggling against him.

"Uh-uh, it's you," he insisted, his voice low and soothing. "You make me think of early spring at the lake when it's cool and crisp and there are sweet-smelling wildflowers everywhere."

Nestled comfortably in his arms, Laura decided that for a man who claimed to have trouble expressing his inner feelings, he was doing a bang-up job.

Further relaxed, she moved her hand across his shoulder and eased the tip of her thumb over his warm neck. "You're a good dancer," she said softly. "Easy to follow."

"You're easy to hold like this, very easy."

Her eyelids closed when she felt his lips brush her temple, the gesture sending a sensual warmth coursing from her head to her toes. Suddenly she was keenly aware of the pressure of his broad chest on her breasts, the rhythmic movements of his thighs against hers, the throbbing pulse at the side of his neck. Her senses heightened, she felt as if she were floating, held securely by his strong arms. It was such a pleasurable feeling that she never wanted it to end.

But it did. Laura opened her eyes and realized the music had stopped.

"That was nice," he said, still holding her.

"Uh...yes," she agreed, then preceded him back to their table.

Lifting his little glass of brandy, Anatol looked deeply into Laura's eyes. "Just the aroma of brandy from Azerbaijan is intoxicating," he said quietly.

Sampling from her glass, she felt its warmth lingering in her throat. "It is heady, isn't it?"

After sipping from his glass, Anatol said, "Tomorrow, I thought we might take the hydrofoil excursion to Petrodvorets and tour the palace of Peter the Great. How does that sound?"

In Anatol's expression Laura thought she saw questions other than of excursions and palaces, questions that she wasn't ready to answer. She had to admit that she was strongly attracted to him. She missed him terribly when he was out of sight; she basked in his closeness when he was near, just as she had while they were dancing. But the force of her wanting him seemed so much more dangerous suddenly, for now she was positive he wanted her just as much.

"Would you like that?" he asked, wondering why she was hesitant to respond.

"Yes," she said quickly.

Reaching across the small table, he took hold of her fingers and stroked them with his thumb. "You look particularly lovely this evening. Are you enjoying yourself?"

Laura smiled and nodded, wondering what she was rushing headlong into. It was clear to her that with just one word from her Anatol would sleep in his own bed tonight. And that one word would be so easy to say. But was that what she really wanted? she asked herself. The response followed instantly: *yes!*

So what? she argued silently. *You'd like a full-length mink coat, an adoring husband and two healthy, intelligent children, too. Wanting something isn't enough. You've got to be sensible. You're a mature businesswoman who's on a difficult assignment. You can't party it up for the remainder of your stay and hope for the best as far as your job is concerned.*

"It's been years," Anatol said, "since I've taken time to go dancing."

Pulled from her mental battle, she admitted, "It's been a while for me, too."

"We can dance the night away or go back to the apartment whenever you want."

"The apartment?" she repeated inanely, still unable to come to a decision. "I do feel bad about putting you out of your own bed."

"Don't. I'll only be two floors down." Withdrawing his hand, he said, "Unfortunately my friend's place is a little crowded. His brother-in-law visited unexpectedly."

One word, Laura reminded herself, but she couldn't get it out.

Sensing that his friend's being deluged suddenly with company wasn't impressing her, Anatol asked, "How long would you like to sleep in the morning?"

"I'm used to waking up early."

"So am I. I hope the mattress isn't too hard for you."

"I prefer a firm one," she said, still debating about the sleeping accommodations.

"Well...I guess we should call it a night."

"Yes," she murmured, reaching for her evening bag.

THE MOMENT Anatol closed the apartment door behind them, Laura froze. She felt she was standing at the edge of a precipice. One step—or one word—and there would be no turning back. But what would happen in the morning? The days would pass, the weeks—and then it would be time to go home. Would she leave part of herself with him and return home incomplete?

"Do you feel like having a nightcap or some coffee?"

Anatol's question plucked her from her unsolved problem. Turning, she managed a tentative smile. "No...thanks."

Placing her evening bag on the chair by the stereo, she began to slip off her coat, but Anatol was right there to assist her.

"Thank you again," she said. Then she added, "It seems I'm always thanking you for something."

"I told you I wanted to make that a habit for you."

Her eyes searched his, and in them she saw the same longing and the questions she was struggling with herself. What would be fair to him? What would be fair to herself? But what did fairness have to do with the way she felt about him?

Time, he had offered, and time was what she desperately needed, she decided.

"I did have a lovely evening, Anatol," she said, retrieving her coat, which he was clutching with both hands.

"Uh...I did, too, but I guess I should say good night and let you get some sleep." After several thundering heartbeats, he nodded to the left. "The bedroom's in there."

"Yes...I know," she said, her response barely audible.

Oh, how she wanted him to take her in his arms, sweep her off her feet and carry her into the bedroom. She wanted him to make all the decisions right now, to take charge, to think for her.

When he moved closer, Laura caught another whiff of the pleasant after-shave he wore. She'd noticed it first while they'd been dancing, and now the aroma brought back the intense arousal she'd experienced in his arms then. Suddenly she felt her resolve shatter. She smiled and closed her eyes, promising herself she'd have no regrets in the morning. This night with Anatol was meant to be. Destiny had brought them together, and who was she to argue with destiny?

Feeling his lips kiss her forehead gently, her eyes flicked open.

"Good night, Laura. Sleep well."

Seconds later he closed the door behind him, leaving her alone with her feelings of utter frustration. She might get some rest, she told herself, slipping the chain on the door, but sleep? Maybe she'd manage ten or fifteen minutes—at best.

As THE SLEEK HYDROFOIL skimmed over the sunlit water of the Gulf of Finland, Laura quietly told Anatol of her suspicion that someone at the plant was helping himself to medical supplies.

"Damn," he muttered, shaking his head. He glanced at the nearby passengers, then lowered his voice. "I thought the Pavlovsk plant was safe."

"Safe? Safe from what?"

"Organized crime." Seeing her blank stare, he explained. "Organized crime is a big problem throughout the Soviet Union. Stealing state-owned property is a lucrative business for them."

"So much for a crime-free country," she mumbled, imagining Biomed's profits being hauled off in the dead of night. "Can't the KGB put a stop to it?" she asked, impulsively raising her voice.

Hearing the name of that organization, the woman in the seat in front of them glanced over her shoulder and examined Laura with cool blue eyes. Then she rose and moved across the aisle.

Anatol cupped Laura's shoulder and squeezed it, his action instructing her to lower her voice. He let a few moments pass, then said, "The KGB has its hands full. My country is experiencing a lot of trouble lately."

"I don't mean to sound insensitive to your country's problems, Anatol, but I'm interested in what's going on at the plant . . . or going out the back door. What makes you think organized crime has anything to do with the missing medical supplies?"

"They're the kind of things that would bring big money on the black market."

"If this black market business is so rampant, why didn't someone mention it to Biomed before we signed on to the venture?" she asked, glaring at him.

"Look at it this way. The black marketeers are operating in the only true free market in this country. They cater to supply and demand and charge what the market will pay."

"What kind of logic is that?"

"I'm not trying to be logical. I'm just explaining how things are."

"Well, explain how we're going to protect the plant from them."

"The best I can do right now is to request an audit."

"What good will an audit do?"

"It will tell us for certain whether supplies are missing. But it'll take time to get one scheduled. My request will have to get through a maze of bureaucratic red tape."

Laura groaned. "Everything takes so much time in this country. I don't see how you can put up with it."

"You can get used to almost anything in life if you have to. That's not an original idea of mine. It's something Sergei kept telling me after he was wounded."

"Maybe Sergei should tell you where the supplies went. He *is* in charge of inventory control."

"I hope you're not suggesting he has anything to do with the equipment you think is missing."

"Look, I like Sergei, and I'm not accusing him of carting anything away personally, but it's his job to keep track of inventory. Why isn't he?"

"It's not that simple."

"It's not that complicated, either. Only basic arithmetic is involved."

Anatol shook his head. "You don't understand, Laura. So many bureaucrats are involved in factories here that it's all but impossible to track down who's paying who to look the other way when products or supplies are being taken. As for the plant, if supplies are being stolen, I'd blame Chernov, *not* Sergei. I know Sergei," he explained. "He wouldn't be involved in anything illegal. When I met him in the army, he never had a bad word to say about anyone. I wish he had gotten out the same time I did, but—''

Anatol paused. Then when he began speaking again, his voice was full of compassionate concern. "When I visited Sergei in the hospital, his face all banged up, he was bitter and confused, trying to figure out what he'd been doing in Afghanistan in the first place. He went through three plastic surgery operations, and after he was discharged from the hospital, he started to drink heavily, something he never did before he was wounded. Finally I talked him into a retraining program and got him the job at the Pavlovsk plant. Little by little the good-natured young man I'd known returned. Now he has Olga, and he's happy. No, Laura, I just can't imagine him doing anything illegal.''

"I hope you're right," Laura said quietly, adding *faithful friend* to her growing list of Anatol's admirable qualities.

WHEN THE HYDROFOIL docked at Petrodvorets, Laura and Anatol joined their fellow passengers for the walk along the tree-lined canal to the gold-and-white Great Palace situated at the top of a hill.

Standing on the sun-splashed marble terrace that overlooked a cascading waterfall, tiered fountains and graceful statues in the park below, Laura rested her hands on the stone wall. "It's lovely," she remarked.

Anatol leaned down beside her. "Yes, life in the days of the czars was beautiful...for the select few. The revolution was supposed to change all that, but today our bureaucrats are a privileged class."

Laura tilted her head toward him, a smile teasing her lips. "You're a bureaucrat."

"But one who's true to the ideals of our revolution. The people are supposed to own everything and reap the benefits, not the leaders, the members of the Party—the privileged few."

Hearing the seriousness in his voice, Laura asked him something that had been bothering her. "If you're so against the privileges that go with being a member of the Communist Party, Anatol, why did you join?"

"Because I wanted to do more than complain about how difficult daily life is here for most Soviet citizens, and I knew I couldn't do much serving in the army or working on the collective farm. To do anything meaningful, I realized I'd have to have some power. Here, that means political power, and I got that by completing my studies in economics at Leningrad University and becoming a Party member."

"You're certainly making a difference now," Laura remarked, her estimation of Anatol increasing as she realized he had laid out his life's plan in order to better the lives of his countrymen.

A smile settled on his face and brightened his eyes. "Wasn't it your President Kennedy who said not to ask what your country can do for you, but to ask what you can do for your country? Isn't that what you're doing in a way?"

Laura's eyebrows arched briefly. "If I'm helping to better foreign relations, I guess so, but to be honest I've never connected patriotism to being a successful businesswoman...nor have most of my colleagues at Biomed, as far as I know. But I do want the Pavlovsk venture to be a success, Anatol, and not just for the profits Biomed can reap."

"So do I. I put my career on the line by insisting the plant could be a model for other medical plants here. Some people in the State Planning Committee don't seem to understand that it doesn't do any good to raise people's standard of living if they don't have access to good medical care."

Concerned for him, Laura asked, "Could the failure of the venture at the plant really jeopardize your entire career?"

"There are people at the Planning Committee and the Ministry of Health who would make sure it did."

IT WAS LATE AFTERNOON when Anatol left Laura in his apartment to go to his office. Although it was Saturday, he was scheduled to be in Kiev on Monday and didn't want to wait until he returned to Leningrad to fill out the staggering amount of paperwork necessary to request an audit at the plant.

While Anatol was gone, Laura showered to get ready for the evening out he had planned for them. Wearing only her terry robe, she was towel-drying her hair when she heard a knock on the apartment door. Not removing the chain, she opened it a crack and saw two teenagers peering back at her, a boy and a girl. "Yes?" she asked hesitantly.

The young man's jaw dropped, and he glanced at his companion before asking Laura, "Is my father here?"

She froze for an instant, then opened the door. "No," she said, "but he should be back shortly."

"We could wait," the girl suggested, smiling as she nudged Anatol's son inside.

After closing the door, Laura brushed back a damp tendril from her brow. "You must be Valentin," she said with a nonchalance she certainly didn't feel.

His eyes drifted over her robe, down to her bare feet, then shot up to her face. "Yes," he said tightly.

"I'm Katya Kashinkova," the young woman announced brightly, offering Laura her hand.

Laura returned the gesture, thinking that the attractive girl's dark hair and the Tartar slant to her eyes reminded her of Olga. Valentin, however, looked like a transplant from an American TV soap opera.

Medium-cut sun-streaked brown hair fell casually around his well-shaped face that was partially hidden by dark sunglasses. A small gold loop hung from his left ear. He wore a bulky fisherman sweater and tight jeans. Not exactly radical dress, Laura decided. It was easy to see that he was his father's son. He had Anatol's straight nose and sensual lips. He was also tall like his father and had his broad shoulders and proud stance.

"Please, make yourselves comfortable," she suggested. "Would you like a soda or some fruit juice?"

"No, thank you," Valentin answered curtly, removing his sunglasses, his judgmental brown eyes riveted on her.

After an uncomfortable silence, she explained, "I'm Laura Walters, a business associate of your father's." She saw Valentin glance down at her bare feet again. "Uh...would you excuse me for a moment?" she asked, smiling awkwardly. Within seconds she was in the bedroom, dressing.

When she returned to the living room, Katya had removed her coat and was sitting on the sofa, smiling pleasantly, her legs crossed. Valentin stood stiffly, gazing out the window.

Hearing Laura close the bedroom door, he turned. "I'm happy to see that my father is finally taking time to...relax on the weekends. It's something he hasn't done for years."

Anatol, Laura ordered silently, *get back here!*

"Valentin," Katya said brusquely, "what your father does with his weekends is his business, not yours."

"Actually," Laura explained, "he's working at his office, but he said he wouldn't be long." To initiate conversation, she said to Valentin, "Your father told me you were interested in ecology."

"Valentin is interested in stirring up trouble," Katya cut in.

"When the ozone layer's gone," he informed her, "you'll wish people like me had stirred up more trouble."

Disregarding his comment, Katya looked back at Laura and asked cheerfully, "You're an American, aren't you, Miss Walters?"

"Yes, I live in New York."

Katya's dark eyes glistened. "Is it difficult for a woman to get an assistant designer job in New York?"

Laura eased herself onto the sofa next to her. "I don't know much about the business side of the fashion industry, but I imagine there's fierce competition for designer jobs everywhere." She took note of the oversize yellow cardigan and the tan suede miniskirt and matching calf-high boots that Katya wore.

Moving behind the sofa, Valentin placed his hands on the girl's shoulders. "Katya's studying design. She wants to work for Dom Modeli, the fashion house in Moscow."

"When I finish school, I'm going to," she told Laura. "Or I may work for Dom Moda. I modeled sportswear for them this summer."

Laura smiled at Katya's enthusiasm. "Knowing people in the industry should make getting a designer job with them easier."

"If Valentin stays out of trouble. He thinks he can cure all the country's problems just by raising a ruckus in the streets."

"A peaceful demonstration isn't a ruckus," he corrected her. "It's my way of protecting our future."

"*If* we have a future together. The man I marry will have to offer me a secure and stable life."

"No one is going to be able to offer you a secure and stable life if the air we breathe is contaminated and the water is polluted."

"Things are changing."

"Not fast enough."

Returning her attention to Laura, Katya said, "We wouldn't have to worry about our future if he wasn't so obstinate. His father's an important man in the government." She glanced back at Valentin. "He could help you, just like other government people help their children. Look at Nikolai and his wife."

To Laura, she said, "Nikolai's father also works for the State Planning Committee. When Nikolai married Tatyana this summer, his father gave them a trip to Paris, and when they came home he arranged for them to move into a new apartment building."

"I'm not Nikolai," Valentin protested, "and I don't plan on living a privileged life because my father's a bureaucrat. I want to earn the money we'll live on."

"If we wait until you can earn enough," Katya said, "we won't be married until the turn of the century." Her eyes slid back to Laura. "My parents teach at the Academy of Art and can't help us much financially. Valentin and I would need our own apartment and furniture, and raising children costs a lot of money."

When Katya sighed, Laura said, "Back home most young people I know face the same problems when they're starting out as a family."

"But are they fired from their jobs if they're arrested for demonstrating?" Katya asked.

"Peaceful demonstrators are no longer arrested," Valentin cut in.

"So far!" Katya said.

Laura listened as the two young people continued to go at it as though she weren't present. Katya was lovely and obviously career-oriented, and Laura felt she wasn't at all sympathetic to Valentin's intense beliefs.

As for Valentin, Laura could see many of the father's traits in the son. Both were committed to what they believed in and both were willful. At one point, though, when Valentin took one of Katya's hands in his and softened his voice, Laura realized that like Anatol, Valentin could be tender also.

"Laura," Katya asked, "do young businesswomen in America feel compelled to have children?"

"Of course they do," Valentin declared. "It's women's nature all over the world."

"You're still thinking with a Stone Age mentality, Valentin. Not every woman—" Katya began, stopping abruptly when the apartment door opened and Anatol entered. He closed the door behind him. His eyes darted from the two guests to Laura, who smiled weakly. "Well, this is a surprise, a pleasant one. It's good to see you again, Katya. How are your parents?"

"Fine, Mr. Vronsky," she answered, giving him a friendly smile.

Valentin glanced at Laura, then looked at his father with hardened eyes. "We're not staying. Knowing how busy you are, I wanted to remind you about granddad's and grandma's wedding anniversary tomorrow."

"I appreciate the reminder," Anatol said, "but I hadn't forgotten."

"I can't go," Katya said, disappointment in her voice. "I have exams Monday."

"Is your mother going to be there?" Anatol asked his son.

The boy nodded, then asked, "Are you bringing Miss Walters?"

"I haven't asked her yet, but I plan to."

"Come on, Katya," Valentin said curtly, picking up her coat.

"Valentin," Anatol said, "there's no need for the two of you to run off."

"Sure there is. You must have business to discuss with your...associate."

Unceremoniously he pulled Katya from the apartment.

"Well," Anatol said, his voice bleak, "now that you've met my son, what do you think?"

"He reminds me of you."

His expression turned quizzical. "Really? In what way?"

"He seems concerned about problems here and he wants to do something about them."

Anatol chuckled. "He thinks that waving signs and shouting in the street will bring about instant change."

The relationship between father and son was strained, Laura reflected. "To be honest," she said carefully, "I think Valentin could use a little more support for what he believes in. Katya doesn't seem to give it to him."

"And I don't, either," Anatol remarked glumly, slumping onto the sofa. "Is that what you're really saying?"

Not wanting to interfere in family business, Laura changed the subject. "I didn't know you had plans for tomorrow."

"It's my parents' fifty-sixth anniversary. I'd planned to ask you to drive down with me. It'll give you an opportunity to see our countryside."

Laura would have enjoyed that, but she wasn't certain the rest of his family would appreciate her arriving unannounced. "I don't think so, Anatol," she said quietly.

"Does it bother you that Yelena will be there?"

"I've a feeling it would bother your son if I showed up."

"It would bother me more if you didn't, and don't be concerned about my son. Everything I do bothers him."

Laura took a few steps toward the window and turned. "Why ask for complications? Unfortunately when Valentin and Katya arrived, I had just gotten out of the shower and was wearing my robe. They probably think we're having an affair.''

Anatol smiled. "Now *there's* an idea! And since they already believe we're having an affair, what have we got to lose?''

She smiled slightly. "I have another idea. Let's not and pretend we did.''

"Not as much fun.''

"But sensible. I'm here to work, remember?''

"Not this weekend, you aren't.'' He rose from the sofa. "I'm going to shower, then take you out for a night on the town. Are you in the mood for our version of *Sophisticated Lady?*''

"Not really, Anatol. I saw the show in New York. While I'm here I'd like to explore things truly Russian.''

"A lady after my own heart,'' he said, unbuttoning his shirt.

As he did, Laura's eyes drifted to the spray of soft-looking brown hairs on his chest. Then she turned her head away, feeling the rush of frustration she'd experienced when he had left the apartment last evening. *So,* she told herself, *you're attracted to him physically. That's all. And that's healthy. Isn't it?*

"Laura.''

She moved her head a bit, still not looking directly at him, but when she felt his hand touch her shoulder gently, she almost sighed openly.

"Think about coming with me tomorrow. It would please my parents so much. They're good people, and I know you'll like them.''

"I'll think about it,'' she promised, feeling an abrupt coolness waft over her shoulder when his hand slipped away. Turning slowly, she followed him with her eyes as he sauntered into the bedroom, his shirt draped over a shoulder.

Alone, Laura again questioned the wisdom of her accepting Anatol's invitation to come to Leningrad. She already had reason enough not to become emotionally involved with him, and now she had another—his son. She couldn't blame Valentin for what he must have thought, but she hadn't been prepared for his hostile attitude. Had it been aimed at her, she wondered, or at his father? How would Valentin react if she did show up tomorrow? And what would Yelena think?

No, Laura thought, a pensive shimmer in her blue-gray eyes, she shouldn't have come to Leningrad. She should have stayed in Pavlovsk.

CHAPTER SEVEN

AT THE LENINGRAD Philharmonia the soothing strains of the adagio of Rachmaninoff's second symphony spun out over the auditorium. Listening intently, Anatol absently took hold of one of Laura's hands, resting his and hers on his thigh.

Her heartbeat quickened, enough to make her aware that Anatol's touch had become too potent. She had learned that he was a man who enjoyed touching, whether it was a casual motion as he passed her, or as he was doing now. There was no honesty in pretending she didn't enjoy it.

As the romantic melody soared, she felt his thumb move slowly over her fingers. She leaned closer to him, her shoulder touching his arm. His suggestion that they have an affair came to mind, and Laura wondered if she could handle it.

She was, as Anatol had said, "footloose and fancy-free," and so was he. But if they were to become lovers it wouldn't be merely because they were attracted to each other physically, nor would it be because their work had conveniently brought them together. It would happen because she cared for him deeply and because she believed he returned that caring. And he did care. She could see it in his eyes when he looked at her, hear it in his voice when he spoke with her, feel it in his gentle touches.

His hand tightening around hers brought her back to reality. No, she told herself firmly. She had to be sensible. Anatol would have little to lose when she walked out of his life. Not so for herself. She didn't take intimacy lightly, and already she knew he wasn't going to be an easy man to forget. How much more difficult it would be if she fell hopelessly in love with him.

Intermission in the foyer reminded Laura of similar intermissions at the Metropolitan Opera in New York—the same well-dressed crowd, excited chatter and bright laughter. Then Anatol nudged her. "You're about to meet the man who tried to steal your computers," he said quietly.

Laura followed Anatol's gaze to the Tom Selleck look-alike who was elbowing his way through the concert crowd.

"Dmitri Karnakov," Anatol whispered. "The man with him is his son-in-law, Pavel Krivtsov. He's Dmitri's right-hand man at the Ministry of Health."

Like his father-in-law, Laura thought, Pavel Krivtsov was an attractive man. He was stylishly attired and wouldn't look out of place in an executive office on Madison Avenue in New York. But there was an icy coldness in his gray eyes, a smug pout on lips, a rather haughty tilt to his dark-haired head.

"Anatol!" Dmitri gushed, taking hold of his shoulders.

Introductions completed, Dmitri's sparkling eyes bore into Laura's cautious gaze. "So this is the lovely American I've heard so much about. Comrade Director Chernov praises you to the heavens."

"I'm happy to hear that," Laura remarked, retrieving her hand. "But I suspect you may have turned around Mr. Chernov's remarks." *Because I'm sure he's actually been damning me to hell,* Laura added silently.

Catching her drift, Pavel tilted his head back and chuckled. "How refreshing. Miss Walters has a sense of humor, too." He assessed the royal blue dress Laura wore, then faced Anatol. "A beautiful woman with intelligence *and* wit is a dangerous combination."

"I would say an *interesting* combination," Anatol suggested. Then he asked Dmitri, "How's your wife?"

"Fine. She and my daughter are in Moscow. Ever since Estée Lauder and Christian Dior opened shops on Gorky Street, they commute weekly. Pavel and I are temporary bachelors." His eyes eased back to Laura. "Have the computers that were unfortunately misrouted reached the plant, Miss Walters?"

"Yes, thanks to Anatol." She saw the man's features cloud over.

"He is rather like a watchdog, isn't he?"

"It's a necessary part of my job," Anatol said with a smile.

"Chernov tells me you do it exceptionally well." He looked back at Laura. "He also tells me you're prejudiced against older workers at the plant."

"That would be his version of the conversation we had."

"Dmitri," Anatol cut in, "I've put through a request for an audit at the Pavlovsk plant. I'd appreciate your signing off on it as soon as possible."

"An audit? Why?" He guffawed heartily. "Have they lost something?"

"No," Laura said quickly. "I'd like to include the results of an audit in my report to Biomed."

"Biomed," Pavel repeated thoughtfully, stepping closer to Laura. When he did, she was assailed by the pungently sweet cologne he wore. "Ah, yes," he said, "the American company. Why would they want an audit now? If it goes ahead, the joint venture won't be operational until the first of January. That would be the time for an audit."

Anatol asked, "What do you mean 'if it goes ahead'? Preparations are already under way."

"Preparations don't make it a certainty," Dmitri cut in. "But good luck on meeting your deadline at the plant," he added with an insincere smile.

As the foyer emptied, neither Laura nor Anatol budged. "Should we or shouldn't we?" he asked.

"I'd just as soon not be in the same building with those two."

"They affect me that way also. Let's get out of here."

They returned to Anatol's apartment, and he opened a bottle of champagne.

"It's delicious," Laura commented, sipping out of the glass he had poured for her.

"From the Ukraine," he said, sipping from his own wineglass. Putting on a tape of soothing background music, he came and sat on the arm of Laura's chair. "I wasn't in the mood for Khachaturian, anyway," he told her, referring to the concert they'd left.

From the glow on his face, Laura was fairly sure of what Anatol *was* in the mood for. Easing herself up from the chair, she went to the table by the window and set her wineglass down next to the champagne bucket.

Anatol's eyes drank in the curves of the dress she wore, her slender legs and the way her golden hair shone like silk. The heaviness he felt in his groin teased him and magnified his need for her. He wanted desperately to tell her she was driving him crazy, that it was all he could do to keep his mind on work when he wasn't with her. But he had promised he wouldn't rush her, and as difficult as it would be, he was determined to be true to his word. Wondering at her silence, he asked, "What are you thinking about so hard?"

Laura looked back at Anatol over her shoulder. She had been thinking about him, but to follow a safer path, she answered, "My job. We have big problems on our hands with persons unknown who are going to put the Pavlovsk plant into bankruptcy if they aren't stopped."

"Don't you ever take a break from work?"

"Right now I can't afford to," she said, then stepped to the window overlooking Tchaikovsky Street. In the darkness she watched the moving headlights from the cars as they slunk by. The next thing she knew, Anatol was behind her, his hands skimming lightly over her arms.

"It's difficult," he whispered, "for me to be in the same room with you and not hold you. I like the way you feel, the way you make me feel." He chuckled softly. "I even like the way you walk and the way you smell. Does it bother you when I touch you like this?"

"No," she murmured. *I like it too much.* Desperately she tried to focus her thoughts on her job again. "If we can't put a stop to people just walking away with supplies at the plant, I won't be here much longer."

"Don't say that," he ordered, turning her around.

"But I'm obligated to report the theft, and Biomed isn't going to sink millions of dollars into this venture just to make some black marketeers wealthier. They'll pull out. We've got to do something, Anatol. I don't want to have to scoot home with my tail tucked between my legs."

"You have nice legs," he said, smiling. When she didn't smile back, he took hold of her hands and gave them a little shake. "Let's wait and see what the audit shows."

"Time, Anatol, isn't on our side."

"In more ways than one," he said, his voice cloaked with emotion. "I don't want you to leave, Laura."

"I don't want to go," she admitted, a tingling fullness settling in her breasts as Anatol drew her closer. She could feel the warm pressure of his hands around her waist.

"Laura—" he breathed, his face inches from hers.

The almost silent sigh she emitted gave way to his gentle kiss—a barely perceptible touch that seemed more passionate to her than a wild embrace.

Slowly she slid her hands up over his chest, sensing his wildly thumping heart that increased the beat of her own. A low moan filled her ears. Was it his or hers? She didn't know, she didn't care. She was too intent on his deepening kiss, his probing tongue and the feel of his strong arms around her as his hands stroked her waist and back. The pressure of his hips against hers and his obvious arousal made her feel light-headed. She felt as if she were floating, all the while held securely in his arms as her body drifted.

Desperate for air, she tilted her head back and struggled to get her bearings. Her breaths were coming hard, but not nearly with the effort of his.

Cupping her face with his hands, Anatol spoke quietly. "Say it again, Laura. Say that you don't want to leave."

"I don't," she said, attempting to move her head sideways.

But he held it firm. "Is it just the work here you'd miss?"

"What if I said yes?"

"I'd hope you were lying."

"Anatol," she said, averting her eyes, "I told you I needed time, and you said you wouldn't rush me."

"I'm not made of ice...not where you're concerned. You're the last thing I think about before falling asleep."

"I told you. I'm not good at—"

"I dream about you."

"At getting involved in brief affairs."

"You're the first thing I think about when I wake up."

"Don't, Anatol."

"Don't what?"

"Don't make this hard for me."

"Why not? I don't want to hide my feelings."

"That's all we're talking about here, Anatol—feelings, physical feelings."

"Mine or yours?"

"Both."

"Is the lady saying she's attracted to me?"

Laura eased herself back from him and clasped her hands nervously. "Yes, I am. Why shouldn't I be? You're an attractive man."

"That's the only reason?"

"Well...you're also intelligent."

"Two."

"Considerate and thoughtful."

"Three and four."

"And you set high standards for yourself in your work."

"You've got me falling in love with the guy you're describing. How come you're not?"

"I'm here on business, not to fall in love."

Crossing his arms, he leaned back against the wall. "Is this world of ours so filled with love that we can let it slip by when there's a chance to grab it? It's not just a physical attraction between us. A person can feel that without love, but with us—"

"There is no us," she interrupted, her words as steady as she could manage. "There's you, there's me, Anatol. In another time, in another place, maybe we'd have the luxury of falling in love...but not now, not here."

He let the finality of her words sink in before he crossed the room and retrieved his jacket and overcoat. Silently he started toward the door of the apartment. Then he turned. "That's something else I like about you—your honesty. I can't say I'm crazy about your self-control, but that's also part of you, isn't it?"

"For better or for worse," she said softly.

"Have you decided about the trip to the country tomorrow?"

"Still feel like inviting me?" she asked, moving in front of him.

Raising a hand, he gently ran the back of his fingers over her smooth cheek as he nodded. "I wish we could have met, as you say, in another time or in another place. But we didn't. All we have is here and now, Laura."

Then he left the apartment.

Slowly Laura traced his steps and drew the chain in place. Leaning back against the door, she attempted to congratulate herself for being so sensible. But why, she wondered, did she feel so damn miserable?

THE NOONTIME SUN melted the morning mist as Laura and Anatol drove southwest from Leningrad. For late October the day was an exceptionally warm fifty-two degrees.

"Are you sure your parents won't mind my tagging along?" Laura asked.

"They'll be thrilled. They're warmhearted people, in spite of having had so difficult a life. They've lived through political upheaval, famine and the German occupation." His voice lowered. "They lost their first three children during the war."

"I'm so sorry," Laura said sincerely. "How are they doing now?"

"Good, considering they're both in their seventies. My father still puts his shoulder to the grindstone. I'm sorry that your meeting my son wasn't more pleasant," he said, abruptly changing the topic.

"Considering the circumstances, it was understandable."

"Ever since the divorce two years ago, my relationship with Valentin has been going downhill. I have this feeling that he still thinks Yelena and I will get together again."

Laura was curious about Anatol's ex-wife, but she didn't want to pry. She didn't have to. Anatol continued.

"The decision to divorce was mutual. Yelena and I were making each other miserable. She complained that I traveled too much in my work. But when I was at home, she was always at the hospital or making evening house calls."

"House calls," Laura repeated lightly. "That's just about a thing of the past back home. Interesting to hear you're a workaholic, though, just as you claim I am."

"The problems Yelena and I had went deeper than my work habits. Over the years she put more and more distance between us. And slowly we became cold toward each other."

Reaching over, Laura clasped his hand in hers, and for some distance they rode in silence.

The terrain turned hilly and the copses of oaks and silver birches became more numerous. As they passed unpretentious square wooden houses, Laura saw women in print dresses and babushkas tending chickens, geese and pigs. Farther down the road she noticed a line of men and women passing concrete blocks, apparently building an extension to a wooden house.

After pulling onto a winding dirt road on a hillside, Anatol nodded to his left. "That's my parents' home."

Laura spied a grouping of whitewashed structures with brown wooden shingles. The two-story one was obviously the house, and as they neared it she guessed the largest of the other buildings was a barn.

Anatol parked next to the rustic wooden fence that enclosed a vegetable garden. Then he led Laura around to the back of the house where a long table had been set up buffet-style for the twenty-some guests who were milling around.

A stocky gray-haired woman in a rose-colored dress and heavy cardigan turned toward them, threw out her arms and cried, "Anatoliy Vasiliyevich!"

He met her halfway and kissed both her cheeks. "Mother, I brought a friend with me, an American business associate. This is Laura Walters. Laura, my mother," he said proudly.

Taking both of Laura's hands in hers, Anatol's mother eyed her and the burgundy suit she wore approvingly. "An American," she repeated, then turned to her other guests and waved her arms enthusiastically. "Come, meet my son's friend from America!"

Laura found herself surrounded by broad-smiling, curious faces, and one by one she was introduced to everyone. Some worked on the nearby state farm; others had their own small plot of land, as Anatol's parents did. And some were relatives who lived farther south in Luga.

"How wonderful!" Anatol's mother remarked, beaming at Laura. "You speak Russian so beautifully. You must call me Natasha." She studied Laura's face for several moments before nodding at her son. "It's in the eyes, just as I've always said."

Anatol grinned. "My mother reads eyes instead of tea leaves. What is it you see?" he asked, draping an arm around her shoulder.

"The intelligence is obvious, and there's a little ob-
stinacy in them, too. But lots of honesty and—" she
glanced up at her son and smiled "—a good deal of
passion."

When Laura blushed, he asked quickly, "Where's
Father?"

"He and Valentin are helping Yevgeni. His water
pump broke again." Natasha gestured toward a house
on the next hill and rocked her head. Facing Laura, she
added, "So, you have come so far just to help Vasili
and me celebrate our anniversary?"

Matching the woman's chubby-faced smile, Laura
said warmly, "I wish you both much happiness."

Natasha took hold of Anatol's hand and shook it.
Speaking to Laura, she said, "Having a son like this
one has given Vasili and me more happiness than we
ever dreamed we would have the day we were married." She laughed heartily, her ample breasts shaking
as she did. "That was some day. I cried and cried! I
was only sixteen then, and my parents had arranged the
marriage. That morning my mother unbraided my hair
and told me I was about to become a woman. I was
terrified! What did I know about being a woman? But
Vasili was so kind and tender, just like our boy Anatoliy."

"I see you made it."

Laura's head turned toward the attractive brown-
haired woman coming toward them. Instinctively she
knew it was Anatol's ex-wife. She was tall, slender and
wore a green wool dress.

"Yelena," Anatol said, his expression impassive,
"I'd like you to meet Laura Walters. She's coordinat-

ing the joint venture at the Pavlovsk plant. Laura, Yelena Shatalova.''

Not extending her hand, Yelena smiled pleasantly. ''Yes, the business colleague Valentin told me about.'' Her eyes examined the suit Laura wore. ''Business must be good.''

''It will be better,'' Anatol said, ''now that Laura's here.''

''I'm sure it will be,'' Yelena allowed, her eyes scrutinizing Laura. ''I'm a pediatrician. We have something in common, other than Anatol, that is. We're both involved in medicine.''

''You more so than I,'' Laura said, imagining what Valentin must have told his mother.

''I wish you success at the plant. We have adequate medical supplies at the clinic where I work, but that's not the case throughout the country.''

''Hopefully my company can be of help.''

Taking hold of her son's arm, Natasha said, ''Come, Anatoliy, bring my chair from the house and put it in the shade under the willow tree for Laura. Yelena, take our guest to the buffet table.''

Yelena guided Laura to the white-clothed table strewn with plates of salads, sausages, a variety of cheeses, brown bread and what looked like potato salad, with mixed vegetables in it. Handing Laura a china plate, she asked, ''How long have you known Anatol?''

''Approximately a month, just since I arrived.''

''I thought perhaps he had met you during one of his trips to New York. He's charming, isn't he? But he's a typical Russian male. They expect their women to run the home single-handedly, wait in lines all day to do the shopping, take care of the children and hold down a full-time job, as well. That can make for a long and aggravating day for a woman.''

''Many women in America find themselves in a similar situation.''

''Minus the long lines, I'm told. Are you divorced?'' Yelena asked, having noticed that Laura wore no wedding band.

''I've never married.''

''Pity. Anatol's a dear, but he's quite traditional by upbringing and rather rigid. He works hard to effect changes in society, but he's not willing to effect change in his personal life.''

In his defense Laura said, ''I imagine it's easier to be objective about change when it involves something other than oneself.''

''Being objective is a survival technique we women have to be concerned about, isn't it?''

''I doubt if you'll have trouble surviving, Yelena,'' Anatol said, coming up behind them and taking hold of Laura's arm.

''Not any longer, I won't,'' she remarked, patting his cheek before sauntering toward a group at the far end of the buffet table.

''There goes one extremely independent woman,'' he said.

''You're looking at another one,'' Laura reminded him.

Anatol smiled to acknowledge the retort, then led Laura to the shade under the willow tree where he had placed the chair.

Shortly Valentin and Anatol's father came walking over. Tall, barrel-chested and ruddy, Vasili Vronsky appeared robust for his age. He wore a blue shirt under denim overalls. His thick gray hair was still wavy and swept straight back over a high forehead. As he neared them, it was easy for Laura to see where Anatol had gotten his alert hazel eyes.

After Anatol introduced Laura to his father, Vasili's immense, callused hands encased one of hers and shook it enthusiastically. "Welcome to our home," he said in a booming voice. Then he embraced Anatol and kissed his cheeks. "I bought a new tractor with the money you sent. Wait until you see it!" Stretching both arms out, he called to a man sitting on the grass near the house. "Iosif, some music for our guests!"

Seconds later the sounds of a concertina filled the air, and an impromptu dance began, with Vasili and Natasha joining in.

Anatol sat down on the grass next to Laura's chair and balanced the plate of food his mother had fixed for him on his knee. He looked up at his son who stood mute, leaning against the tree trunk, observing Laura. "Valentin," he asked, "would it hurt your eyes to take off those dark glasses for a while?"

The young man obeyed and stuck one of the earpieces in the front pocket of his bleached jeans, letting the glasses dangle. He glanced down at Laura and asked, "Miss Walters, in America do seventeen-year-olds do everything their parents tell them to?"

After sipping her lemonade, she shrugged. "I doubt if teenagers anywhere do everything their parents tell them to."

"Did you?" he asked.

"Valentin!" Anatol barked.

Like father, like son, Laura thought, bemused by the
boy's bluntness. To answer his question, despite his
father's objection, she said, "As far as I can remember, I believe I was guided by my parents on important
issues."

"My father says that young people in America no
longer demonstrate in the streets for just causes. Is that
true?"

"Just causes," Anatol repeated glumly. "Instead of
demonstrating, you and your friends should be thinking about your futures."

Crouching down, Valentin leaned back against the
willow tree and hugged his raised knees. In a calm voice
he said, "That's what we're doing. The smog from
your factories is polluting the country." He tilted his
head toward Laura. "In some cities cars and trucks
have to drive with their headlights on in the day because of the smog."

He eyed his father again. "You should be demonstrating for the recall of deputies who are violating the
law. And what of the nuclear power plant they wanted
to build in Krasnodar! They would have gone ahead
with it if we hadn't demonstrated. Do we need another Chernobyl?"

"Valentin," Anatol asked, "could we please talk
about something else? How's school coming along?"

"So-so, but history's a joke. The teachers tell us one
thing, and the next day the newspapers tell us something else. It's getting so you don't know who to believe anymore."

"That's what *glasnost* is all about," Anatol said,
appreciating his son's confusion. "Why don't you
come by the apartment soon, and we'll talk about it."

The boy's eyes swept to Laura, then back to his father. "Sure you can spare the time?"

"I'll find the time," Anatol said, hurt by his son's remark.

Just then, Natasha came rushing toward them. "Laura, let me fix another plate for you."

"Thank you, no. Everything's delicious, but I'm stuffed."

"Some more lemonade, then?"

"This is fine," she said, holding up her tall, half-filled glass.

"Do you feel up to a little walk, Laura?" Anatol asked.

"Sure."

"Ah, but the wind!" his mother objected. "Wait just a minute."

Soon she was back with a floral scarf, which she handed to Laura. "Wear this, and keep it, please."

"Thank you again," Laura said, then folded the scarf in a triangle, draped it over her head and tied it under the back of her hair.

After slipping on her blue nylon coat, she and Anatol climbed hand in hand to the top of the hill. Spread before them in a panoramic view lay an untouched forest of pines and firs, with a small river snaking its way through the maze of trees.

"This is where I grew up," he said, more than a hint of pride in his words. "It's beautiful in the winter. The sunsets paint the snow in colors you wouldn't believe."

He crouched, plucked a little blue wildflower growing in the grass and placed it in Laura's palm.

She smiled her thanks and examined the little flower. When she looked back up at Anatol, he was again gazing out over the countryside. She could see the inner peace shining on his face. "It is lovely here," she said softly.

Spreading his coat on the grass, he took hold of Laura's hand, eased her down onto it and sat next to her. "Have you ever lived in the country?" he asked.

"No, I was born and raised on Long Island, and I've been living in New York ever since my college days." She took in the breathtaking view. "Except for Central Park, Manhattan is largely a cavern of buildings."

"Do your parents live on Long Island?"

"They divorced when I was still in high school. My father lives in Chicago now, but my mother and stepfather still live on the island."

Surveying the state farm far to their left, Anatol said, "In my grandfather's time the land was tilled with wooden plowshares, and the majority of people were illiterate. Today we send men and women into outer space. Here on earth, though, we still have much to do to make life happier and more secure for our people."

Laura's eyes drifted over his profile. "Our countries have a great deal in common."

Anatol turned toward her and smiled. "Do Americans realize that we Russians are a thinking people, a people who love, play with children and shed tears?"

"Yes and no. I mean, usually we're so busy coping with everyday problems, and the only time we think of people in other countries is when trouble erupts."

"The same here, I suppose." He reached over, took hold of her hand and traced a line in her palm. "When will you come to Leningrad again?" he asked quietly.

"I don't know," she answered, turning from him to look out over the forest below. "There's so much I have to do at the plant, Anatol. There are so many problems I hadn't foreseen. To be honest, before coming here I thought that this joint venture would open up enormous opportunities for Biomed. Now I'm not so sure."

Having wrestled again and again with her responsibility to her company and with the knowledge of how important the venture was to Anatol, Laura still wasn't sure just what to do. Already she had tempered her report to Biomed, kept back information that she knew she should have passed on. And she was aware of the main reason she had done so—Anatol.

"Don't give up on us," he said softly, "not yet."

"I won't," she promised.

After a protracted silence, he drew her hand to his lips, kissed her fingers and gazed up at her, his eyes reflecting the sunlight. "If you want me to, when I get back from Kiev, I'll move to the dacha and commute to Leningrad so that we can spend more time together."

"That would make me happy, Anatol, so very happy."

CHAPTER EIGHT

LENINGRAD'S INDIAN SUMMER was short-lived. The first week in November, arctic air swept over the city, bringing with it the first snow of the season. But at the same time Anatol returned from Kiev and moved into his dacha to be nearer Laura. With lifted spirits she doubled her efforts to work congenially with Chernov at the plant.

And her effort *seemed* to pay off. When she presented her plans for reorganizing his managerial staff and beginning training sessions for them, Chernov merely grunted, nodded and said, "Okay, do it."

"You approve?" she asked in surprise.

"Only so that your American personnel will be able to function. Anatol convinced me to give it a try."

Feeling as though she had just been handed some good cards in the game she'd been forced to play with Chernov, Laura smiled. "Both the American and Soviet managers will be able to function better if their jobs are coordinated. Your people just need to emphasize responsibility and contribution a little more than they do now."

Chernov reared up from behind his desk. "Both the American and Soviet managers will emphasize power and authority. George Hardcastle and I will take care of the responsibility and contribution. Inventory control, however, will remain entirely in Sergei's hands.''

"Why?" Laura demanded, standing to meet him eye-to-eye.

"What we produce here comes entirely from state-owned raw material and is manufactured by Soviet citizens. I'm not about to turn over half of its control to foreigners.''

"You realize that by insisting on complete control of even one department, you would be in violation of the agreement with Biomed. Joint managing of every department was stipulated.''

"Biomed will have its say in dispersing our products and in the sharing of profits, but while the inventory is here at the plant, I'll keep track of it.''

"Does that include an accounting of defective items not suitable for sale?''

"Of course.''

"Then perhaps now you can explain why fifty percent of the surgical instruments manufactured in September were deemed defective.''

"I'll have to get back to you on that.''

"Have you checked on the production reports for the blood-gas analyzers I asked you about?''

"I'll get back to you on that also. Now, if you'll excuse me, I have a meeting.''

Bluntly dismissed, Laura picked up the pad and pen she had laid on his desk and looked squarely at him. "Please get back to me before Friday when I send my report to New York. Biomed will take a dim view of equipment that just vanishes.''

"Biomed," he returned with a gaunt smile, "isn't entitled to a view of any kind until after the first of January."

"You're wrong, Yuri. Quite wrong," she said stiffly, then charged to Misha's office.

He was sifting through papers in his file cabinet when she entered. His head jerked around, and he pushed at the bridge of his wire-rimmed glasses. "Can I help you, Laura?"

"I thought I'd stop by and compliment you on the October quality reports you submitted. They were nicely detailed."

There was little heart in the smile her compliment brought to his face. "The new computerized forms make my job easier."

"You have Sergei to thank for them."

"Yes," he said quietly, glancing away. "Sergei is efficient. On top of everything, isn't he?"

His remark struck Laura as odd, but she dismissed it. "I hate to sound like a broken record, but I still haven't been able to locate the September quality-control reports on EKG machines and surgical instruments."

"I...I told you," he stumbled, his fingers twitching, "I processed them as usual and forwarded them to Olga. Why are those reports so important?"

"May I sit down?" Laura asked.

He motioned toward a chair at the side of his desk.

Seeing that he remained standing, and rather rigidly at that, she asked, "Do I intimidate you, Misha?"

"No, no...of course not."

That certainly wasn't the impression he gave her, she decided. "Are you having any problems you'd like to talk about, something that might be bothering you? Family troubles maybe?"

He glanced down, then raised his pale blue eyes to meet hers. "Family troubles . . . no."

From the way he responded she wasn't certain he was being honest. "Do they live near here?"

"No, in Irkutsk . . . in Siberia."

"And they're all right?"

"They're fine. It's kind of you to ask."

Again Laura smiled, hoping to put him at ease. "Problems with a young lady perhaps?"

"No, it's not that."

But something is wrong, she thought. "Maybe you've been working too hard. I'm sure Yuri would okay a few days off if you'd like a break in the routine."

"I'm fine, really."

"I'm glad to hear it. What do you do for relaxation?" she asked, trying to get him to loosen up.

"I like to listen to music, particularly Chopin."

"So do I. At home I have a tape of Horowitz playing his preludes."

His voice gaining a modicum of enthusiasm, Misha said, "I have a tape of his études. The third is my favorite, the one in E Major." He hummed a few notes of the opening theme.

"I think that's one of Chopin's loveliest melodies. Do you play the piano?"

"A little. I have one at home in Irkutsk, but not in my apartment here."

"That's too bad," Laura remarked, studying the young man's morose expression. Misha was obviously intelligent, fairly attractive and seemed to be in good health. His job at the plant was secure, and there was every reason for him to see his future as being bright. Yet, if eyes were the window to a person's soul, his looked rather dismal.

"Just remember," she said, lightening her tone, "if you ever want to talk to someone about the job or something that's troubling you, my office door is open. Or feel free to stop at my apartment if you'd rather talk away from the office."

"I'll remember that," Misha said, nodding.

"Now, about the September reports, do you recall why so many surgical instruments were defective?"

His facial muscles tensed again, and he crossed to the file cabinet, stroking his forehead nervously. "I think," he said slowly, "that it had something to do with faulty machinery."

"I guess that would explain it, but as far as I can tell, fifty percent of the sets were rejected for sale. That seems rather difficult to believe."

"Laura," Misha said, turning, "I've seen how hard you work around here, trying to get things in order."

"It has been a lot of work, but the cooperation I'm getting from the employees makes up for it."

"Take my advice, please." His words tumbled out as though his life depended on them. "Forget about the old quality-control reports. You said last month's were in good shape. They all will be from now on. I promise!"

Laura heard the desperation in Misha's voice and saw it in his eyes, and she wondered what was behind it all. "Well, if you should come across the September reports, I'd appreciate your letting me know."

"I will," he said in a monotone.

Taking note of his forlorn expression, she suggested, "Instead of working this weekend, Misha, maybe you should try to relax, do something you'd enjoy."

"Enjoy," he repeated, strangely, then chuckled. "There's very little I enjoy anymore."

Not knowing how to respond to that, Laura returned to her office to close up for the day.

BUNDLED AGAINST THE COLD AIR, Laura headed for her car in the parking lot. She was startled to see Anatol's son, Valentin, there, dressed in a leather jacket and leaning against a Honda motorcycle.

Remembering his cool attitude toward her, Laura concluded that he must be at the plant to see his father. She was about to tell him Anatol wasn't there when Valentin straddled his Honda, revved the engine and roared up beside her. Coming to a halt, he switched off the key and planted a booted foot on the ground.

"Miss Walters," he said, pulling off his dark glasses, "do you have a minute?"

"Certainly, Valentin. It's good to see you again. But if you're looking for your father, he's not here."

"I came to see you." Swinging his leg over the motorcycle seat, he hooked his thumbs on the front pockets of his jeans. "My dad said I owed you an apology for the way I behaved when I . . . well, you know, when I first met you in his apartment."

"Really, there's nothing for you to apologize for. You were surprised to find me there, that's all."

"No, I shouldn't have jumped to the conclusion that you and he were—well, I just figured that . . . Anyway, I'm apologizing."

Seeing how difficult it was for him to do so, Laura smiled. "I appreciate your coming all the way out here to tell me that."

"No problem. I like getting out on the highway on my bike. It helps me think."

From the way he said it and the troubled look on his face, Laura decided that Anatol's son had a great deal to think about. "If you're not in a rush to get back to the city, would you like to stop by my apartment? It's not far from here. We could talk a little…if you'd like to."

He took a moment to think about it, then shrugged. "Sure, why not?"

Laura took off in her car, and Valentin followed on his bike. Minutes later she pulled up across the street from the local Soviet headquarters and glanced in her rearview mirror. She noticed that the automobile that had been trailing her for the past few days had pulled up behind Valentin's Honda and parked.

It hadn't been the first time she'd been followed. Every trip she made to the stores two blocks away, or even when she took a brief walk in Pavlovsk Park, she'd had the feeling someone was watching her every move.

Getting out of her car, she locked it, then she and Valentin went up the side steps of the building to her second-floor apartment.

"Make yourself comfortable," she said as her eyes settled on the vase of red roses on the coffee table. She picked up the little card leaning against the glass vase and read it to herself: *Waiting for you at the dacha. Dinner will be ready whenever you are.*

Smiling, she slipped the card into her purse. "There's some cola in the refrigerator," she told Valentin. "I'll just be a minute."

In her bedroom she wondered if she should phone Anatol to see if he wanted her to bring his son along for dinner. A little voice in her head warned her that she'd probably wind up being a referee, so she decided against making the call.

When she returned to the living room, she saw Valentin holding the little wooden squirrel that Anatol had given her.

"My father carved this, didn't he?"

"Yes."

Wryly Valentin commented, "He's so damn good at everything he does. No wonder he's disappointed in me."

Laura's heart went out to him as she watched him move a thumb over the carved head before setting it back down on the little table.

"I can't believe your father's disappointed in you," she said firmly, sitting on the sofa.

Valentin slipped off his jacket and laid it across the back of a chair. Pushing the sleeves of his sweater up over his forearms, he said, "Just ask him . . . sometime when you have a few hours. He'll tell you all the things I do wrong."

"He happens to think you're very bright."

"Bright?" Valentin chuckled. "My grades the past two years don't back that up."

Laura recalled the slump her grades had taken in high school when her parents divorced and her mother remarried. "Everyone has periods when for one reason or another they don't operate at peak performance." Smiling at her choice of words, she said, "God, that sounds stuffy. My managerial training is showing."

"Laura..." he said, sitting on the sofa and propping a knee on it. "Do you mind if I call you Laura?"

"I'd like you to."

"Laura, was it your own idea to do the kind of work you do?"

Her thoughts swept back. "Yes, but it wasn't until my second year in college that I chose my career."

"That's one of the big problems my dad and I have. He thinks I should know what I want to do with my life. I don't! And he gets so damn mad at me. It's like...well, he wants me to get a degree in business, but I don't give a—I don't care about how much of what is sold or how fast I can make lots of money."

"Valentin," Laura asked, resting her arm on the back of the sofa, "what do you feel strongly about?"

He let loose a groan. "I don't know. Everything's so damn confusing. I feel like everyone else has got their life organized, and I'm on the outside looking in, like I'm kind of lost. I'm not even sure what I'm supposed to think. In school they give us a rosy picture of the future and tell us what a wonderful country we have, but I look around and see all the problems. Sure, we're great up there in space, but down here, everything's falling apart."

With both feet on the floor he leaned forward, rested his arms on his knees and interlaced his fingers. "My father tells me I've got to develop ethical values...be a credit to society. But look at him. He doesn't care about me or my mom anymore. All he cares about is his work. The only time he thinks about me is when he's afraid I'm causing problems."

Laura wanted to tell Valentin he was wrong, but she decided to give him the chance to talk out whatever was bothering him.

"It was different when I was a kid, though," Valentin said. "My dad and I used to have lots of fun together, and he seemed interested in whatever I was doing. I really looked up to him then. He was as big a hero to me as the cosmonauts were. But when I was about ten years old he became formal and stiff, as though he didn't like me anymore." He tilted his head, fixing his sad blue eyes on Laura. "I didn't know what I'd done. Now I know it wasn't me. It was him who changed."

"Maybe he hasn't changed as much as you think," Laura said softly. "He still loves you."

"He has a strange way of showing it. All he ever does is criticize me."

"He wants the best for you," she said, but she knew Anatol did criticize the boy.

"Next year I'm going into the army. If I'm old enough to fight for my country, why doesn't he realize that I'm old enough to have an opinion about what's good for it now?"

"If you'd give him a chance, I'm sure he would."

"Are we talking about the same man?"

"Your father," Laura clarified.

"But you see how he talks to me."

"I also see how you snap at him."

"He won't even take time to listen to what I'm saying. He's too busy flying all over the country."

"Do you think he enjoys that? I know for a fact that he doesn't."

"Then why *does* he?" Valentin raked his fingers through his hair and lowered his voice. "He could request a reassignment and stay in Leningrad."

At that moment Laura realized what was really bothering Valentin. Softly she asked, "You miss him very much, don't you?"

"No," he said quickly with too much defiance to be believed. "Why should I?"

"Because he's your father, and because you'd like the two of you to be close."

"He doesn't want anyone to get close to him."

"You're wrong. Anatol worries about you. Did you know that?"

"I don't want him to worry about me. I want him to be proud of me for what I am and what I believe in."

"If you give him a chance, I think you'll find that you both believe in the same thing. The two of you just go about it in different ways. As far as his claiming you should know what you want to do with the rest of your life, I think he is pushing a bit."

"That's one of the reasons we argue so much. He wants me to make decisions that I can't, and not being able to really eats at me and makes me feel guilty as hell. I really want to please him, but I have to be my own person, too. It hurts when I realize he's given up on me, because I . . . I want him to like me in the worst way." Valentin paused, then asked, "Am I making any sense at all?"

Laura smiled, recalling Anatol's having asked her the same question. "Sure you are. My guess is that sons and fathers have always been going through what you and Anatol are.''

"So you're saying we're normal, huh?''

"I'm afraid so."

"It must be different with girls, though. Look at Katya. She's known exactly what she wants to do for years now. That kind of bugs me, too, makes me feel like I'm just a kid.''

"Katya's an exception. At her age I wasn't even thinking of what I'd be doing the following month, and neither were most of my girlfriends. We were more interested in what David Bowie was singing and what our chances were for a date on Saturday nights.''

"Yeah, but now you aren't faced with heavy decisions.''

Laura chuckled lightly. "Valentin, I don't know anyone who goes through a day without having to wrestle with some pretty heavy decisions. God knows I do, and I don't always make the right ones. You'd be surprised how uncertain I feel at times and how I long for things to be different. Everyone does, even your father.''

"Do you think I'm being stubborn about not wanting to take advantage of his position? Katya does.''

"You have to be true to yourself, Valentin, or you'll regret it later on. But don't try to grow up too fast. This is a time for you to take a good look at the world you live in, see where you want to fit in and check out the options open to you.''

"I wish my dad was as easy to talk to as you are.'' Checking the time, he stood and picked up his jacket. "I'd better get on back to Leningrad. My mom will have the militia out looking for me.''

Going to the door with him, Laura touched his arm gently. "I'm glad we had this time to talk. Whenever you want, I'd be happy to do it again."

"Thanks," he said, offering her a smile that reminded her of Anatol. "It's easy to see why my dad likes you." Valentin took hold of the doorknob, then looked back at her. "You like him, too, don't you?"

"Yes...very much," she admitted quietly, taking his jacket and holding it for him. "It's cold outside. You'd better put this on now."

As he eased his arms into it, Valentin said, "Laura, there's something else I should explain. I kind of hoped my parents would get together again, and when I found you in my dad's apartment... Well, I guess I realized they weren't going to. Not that it's your fault," he added quickly. "And if he's going to be with someone other than my mom, I'm glad it's you."

Softly Laura kissed his cheek, then closed the door after he left.

From the window she watched him speed off on his Honda, thinking that Anatol was missing a great deal by not reaching out to his son. Then remembering that his father was waiting for her at his dacha, she flew into the bedroom to shower and change.

NESTLED AGAINST ANATOL as they relaxed on the braided rug in front of the fireplace, Laura concentrated on the flickering blue-yellow flames and listened to the hiss and crackle of the fire. The pleasant odor of pinecones he had laid over the wood mingled with the aroma of the coffee spiced with cognac that he had fixed for them.

"You're an excellent cook," she complimented, her voice little more than a whisper. "Dinner was delicious."

Nuzzling the side of her hair, he said, "I don't have a big repertoire, but it's a lot more fun to cook for two than for one."

A comfortable silence settled over the room, a quiet broken only by the soothing sounds coming from the fire. Perfectly content, Laura finally said, "It's nice knowing you're staying here."

"I'd live here permanently, but the Leningrad apartment is closer to my office and the airport."

Valentin's complaint about his father's traveling so much came to mind, and Laura decided it was time she told Anatol about his son's visit. Taking hold of his hand, she ran her fingers over the fine hairs on the back of it. "As I was leaving the plant, Valentin stopped by."

"Stopped by?"

"He thought he had to apologize for being a little abrupt when he first met me."

"Maybe he's finally growing up."

"Anatol," she chided, "maybe you have a little growing up to do yourself. Your son's only seventeen."

"Old enough to get his act together. You should catch a glimpse of his room."

"I didn't realize you had a fetish about neatness. Besides, the thought of a boy his age keeping his room in perfect shape is unnatural ... scary, even."

"Laura, he has to learn that there are more important things in life than ruining his hearing by listening to rock music and running around with those bizarre-looking friends of his.''

''Katya isn't at all bizarre-looking.''

''She's the one exception. Just how long do you think she'll go along with his indecisiveness?''

''He's not indecisive. He's confused. He feels alienated and thinks his world is falling apart. It's understandable that he'd join forces with friends who probably think the same way. He has to believe in something, something he feels may be solid.''

''A reasonable set of values would be solid.''

''What could possibly be of more value than his interest in the environment?''

Anatol lowered himself onto his stomach and rested on his forearms. ''I'm all for saving the planet, too, but I'm forced to set priorities, and food is high on the list. A quarter of this country's agricultural products rot in warehouses or on railroad sidings because we have an antiquated distribution system. Then there are little things like clothing and decent housing for everyone, not just for those living in urban areas. I don't have the luxury of listening to music and running around complaining about how bad things are.''

''Why don't you try explaining that to your son?''

''Because he won't let me get two words in without accusing me of being one of the bad adults who's destroying the entire world.''

''The two of you use the same argument. You're both saying the other won't listen.''

''You're the communications analyst,'' he said, smiling up at her. ''What do you recommend?''

"The first thing each of you has to do is agree to listen to each other. You, supposedly, are more mature. If anyone has to bend a little, it's you."

"Do I get a reward?"

"That's up to Valentin."

"I'm not talking about him now. I mean from you."

"That's up for negotiation," she said playfully.

"Let's negotiate," he suggested. He reached up, cupped the back of her neck and drew her lips to his. Within moments his arms were around her, molding her to him.

As always, when Anatol embraced her, Laura's body went limp, and she surrendered happily to his loving affection.

Reaching for a throw pillow from the chair by the fireplace, Anatol placed it on the floor for Laura to rest her head on it. As he stroked her shining hair, he gazed down at her face, amber-hued in the light from the fire. "You're so lovely," he whispered, "and so caring. You make me want to follow you around like a lovesick puppy."

Laura's smile evaporated. "If you're planning on following me around, you'll have to get in line."

"I've got competition?" he asked, his brow furrowing.

"I'm serious," she said, entwining her fingers in his. "People are following me. Sometimes they're men, sometimes they're women."

"It's nothing to worry about," Anatol said, smoothing a hand over her hair. "Before you accepted the job here, weren't you told you might be under surveillance? If you don't break our laws, they have nothing to report."

"I'm just not used to people watching my every move."

"Your position here is considered a highly sensitive one. If you applied for a sensitive job with your government, wouldn't you be thoroughly checked out by the FBI or the CIA? Wouldn't they dig deep, investigate your friends and talk to your neighbors? Here we're used to such things. It's a way of life for us."

Sitting up, she said, "I don't like it, Anatol. I couldn't live this way."

"Let's not think of the world out there, not tonight. This is our world in here." He kissed her lips gently, then asked, "Do you have any idea how relaxed and wonderful you make me feel?"

Laura placed a hand on his cheek. "You have the same effect on me," she admitted softly.

"At the same time, though, you make me miserable."

"How?"

"You make me realize what it is to be really happy. I'm afraid to get used to that, because I don't know how I'm going to handle your leaving." He glanced toward the flickering flames for long, silent moments before saying, "Laura, I—"

"No more talk," she pleaded, turning his face toward hers, not wanting to think of the future, forbidding herself to even think of tomorrow. All she wanted to think about was now—and about Anatol.

Drawing his head to hers, she kissed him long and hard.

His breathing ragged, he dragged his lips from hers. "I want you desperately, Laura. I need you. I want to please you, have you please me. Wouldn't that give us both memories worth holding on to?''

Laura realized she was on the verge of offering him everything that was hers to give, of taking from him everything he would offer. Her entire body was alive with wanting him, was racked with a desperate tension that only he could appease.

She heard her own voice, but in truth it seemed to her as though someone else were speaking. "We can promise each other nothing, Anatol. It has to be that way."

"Nothing and everything," he said huskily, taking hold of her and kissing her with an intensity that sent her senses spinning.

CHAPTER NINE

HER LIPS ON HIS, Laura slipped a hand under the hem of the white peasant shirt he wore. But her fingers met the resistance of the ropelike belt that gathered the material around his waist. She tugged at the belt and it gave way. This time her hand moved freely, sending a sensual shock wave through her as her fingers slipped over the warm, smooth skin at his side and the firm muscles of his chest.

Anatol's senses whirled. So many nights he had tossed in bed, imagining her touching him as she was doing, exploring his body just as he'd fantasized a slow exploration of hers. But this was no fantasy. It was actually happening! Her arms were around him now. He could feel her fingers digging into his back. He wanted more of her, all that she would offer him. He needed to give to her, all that she would accept.

Pulling his head back, he grasped her shoulders tightly and searched her vibrant face, seeking added proof that he wasn't dreaming.

"Larashka," he murmured, the affectionate form of her name a throaty moan that echoed in the fire-lit room. Easing his lips over the side of her throat, he pushed aside the collar of her silk blouse and trailed his feverish kisses along the curve of her neck and shoulder. He felt her skin shiver under his lips.

He felt his body tremble with anticipation, urging him to take her then and there, to make love to her until they were both exhausted. He wanted to, desperately, but he fought his need, disciplining himself as he never had before. He would be patient if it killed him, he determined. He would go slowly, gently, take time to please her first.

As Anatol knelt before her, Laura thought she could hardly breathe, yet her chest was rising and falling rapidly. She shivered again when he began to slowly unbutton her blouse. She wanted him to hurry!

The silky material slid from her shoulders, and she felt his fingers fumbling at the front clasp of her bra. She closed her eyes, each little brush of his fingertips on her skin making her want to rip the lacy thing off. The clasp gave, and she waited breathlessly for him to take hold of her, to ease the terrible tension tingling her nipples. Why didn't he? she wondered. Opening her eyes, she saw that he was pulling the folded quilt from the back of the sofa.

He turned toward her, locking on to her shining eyes. "I want you to be comfortable, love."

Spreading the quilt on the rug, he repositioned the throw pillow closer to the fire. His eyes lingered on her small, firm breasts. Then he swallowed hard and eased off her blouse and bra. Gently he lowered her to the quilt, carefully adjusting the velvet-covered pillow under her head, smoothing her lovely hair so that it flowed like strands of silk.

"You're even more beautiful than I imagined you would be," he whispered, his eyes roaming over her slender body before he leaned toward her and kissed her lips.

Laura's heart skipped a beat when she felt the warmth of his hand encase a breast, his thumb rhythmically grazing her turgid nipple. A breathless moan passed from her lips to his when he moved his tormenting hand to her other breast. Raking her fingers through his soft, wavy hair, she drew his head lower, guiding his mouth to her nipple, gasping when he took it in his mouth.

His soothing hands seemed to be everywhere, his fingers tantalizing her with whisper-soft strokes. As he removed the rest of her garments, his caresses became more urgent, and he left a trail of warm kisses where his hands had been.

"You're so perfect," he whispered, wanting to rip off his own clothes so that no barrier would remain between them. But he didn't dare. He knew he would lose the control he was fighting so hard to maintain.

Sighing, she opened her eyes, gazed up at him and slid her hands up over his loose-fitting peasant shirt. With a finger, she traced the rich embroidery round the collar. "You're not being fair," she chided.

"Why?" he asked, concerned. "Am I doing something wrong?"

She smiled softly. "Not at all, but—" she tugged at his shirt "—this, and these—" she tugged at his slacks "—have to go."

No longer able to think of maintaining a slow, easy pace, he crossed his arms and pulled his shirt up over his head. Tossing it aside, he stood and tore off the rest of his clothes.

Laura's breath caught at the magnificence of his athletic form that glowed like burnished gold in the firelight. Extending her arms, she whispered, "Come closer."

Lowering himself next to her, he rested on an arm and moved the other one over her, his hand caressing her side, then drifting downward over the graceful curve of her hip. "You feel like silk," he said quietly, overwhelmed by her loveliness as he tried to memorize each graceful curve of her slender form. Linking their hands, he drew hers to his lips, kissing each finger slowly as their eyes held.

Laura gazed up at him, almost afraid she was experiencing an illusion. He was being so gentle and so loving. But his gentleness was creating a hunger in her that grew stronger with each tender touch he offered.

She slipped her fingers through the soft brown hairs on his broad chest, dallying over a flat nipple. She felt his muscles tremble, sensed his heart thumping wildly against her palm. Her excitement heightened and she became bolder, trailing her fingers downward over the smooth skin of his waist and the arch of his hip, caressing his firm thigh before taking possession of his warm, throbbing erection.

Anatol shuddered, closed his eyes and tilted his head back, trying desperately not to give in to the pressure for release that racked his entire body. Her intimate strokes were driving him wild. He knew he couldn't take much more.

"Easy, love," he pleaded, covering her hand with his. "In my entire life I've never known a woman like you. You just touch me and I feel like I'm on fire."

Laura smiled. Brushing a gentle finger over his lips, she whispered, "I've never met anyone like you, either."

The soft weight of Laura's breasts against his chest and the sweet smell of her intoxicated him, but he was again in control of his reactions. He smoothed a hand over her warm back and caressed her soft, velvety buttocks. "I want to please you, Larashka," he said, his words soft and loving. "Tell me how I can."

Her heart beating wildly, she filled her hands with his wavy hair and pressed her lips to his in a long, drugging kiss. Easing him onto his back, she straddled his thighs and gazed at him with smoky eyes. "I want to please you, too," she said, her voice betraying the depth of her emotion.

Her eyes locked on his, she took hold of him and guided him toward her warm, moist feminine core, gasping as he entered her, feeling his hard heat uniting them, taking possession, completing her.

She took him deeper and deeper until she thought her body was more of him than of herself. Reaching behind, she grasped his muscular thighs and began slow, tantalizing undulations. She tilted her head back and closed her eyes, rocking over him, each sensual movement sending waves of delight and power coursing throughout her sensitized body. "Anatol... Anatol," she murmured.

He heard his name whispered from somewhere in the erotic void in which he floated. With closed eyes he slipped his hands up over her thighs and belly to her firm breasts, fondling them as she moved over him. All was sensation, pleasure. All was Laura. She was he, he was she. No fantasy he'd ever had about her matched the glory of the moment—the giving, the taking, the sharing.

His shadowy world began to sparkle, and he felt himself caught in a brilliant kaleidoscope of radiant light and tingling sound. She was sending him higher and higher, faster and faster. Gasps swirled about him, his and hers. He shuddered once, then again and again and again, crying, "Larashka . . . Larashka!"

She leaned forward, striving to follow him into bliss, thrusting her hips onto him. "Ahh!" she sighed, coming close to the pitch of pleasure he had already reached. Anatol arched his hips up, meeting her thrusts, his manhood still firm inside her.

"Ahh," she cried again, the sound a long, drawn-out sigh of pleasure. Then she soared after him into the special paradise created for lovers.

A world later Laura lay cuddled in Anatol's arms, her heart pounding so that it shook her entire body. Or was it his heart? she wondered, opening her eyes slowly.

He felt her long lashes brush against his chest and smiled. "That," he said hoarsely as he smoothed back a wayward lock of her hair, "was one hell of a revelation. When I first met you, I thought you were one cool, efficient lady."

"And now?" she asked, her hand gliding over his side as she realized she never wanted to be any farther from him than she was at the moment.

"You're definitely one very exciting, efficient lady."

"It's all your fault, you know."

"I like that." He tilted her chin up and kissed her tenderly before raising himself onto an arm. How could he possibly tell her how deeply he felt about her? What words could possibly say how much she meant to him?

There weren't any, he realized. "No one has ever made love to me like that," he said simply.

Blushing, she averted her gaze. "I've never made love to anyone . . . like that."

He placed a gentle hand alongside her face. "That pleases me more than you'll ever know." A log crumpled in the fireplace, drawing his attention. Rising, he added another, then said, "Don't move. I'll be right back."

When he returned, he was wearing a brown wool robe and carrying a blue one. "Slip this on," he said, holding it for her.

"I'll just dress, Anatol. I should be going home soon."

"You're not going anywhere." He thought a second. "Let me rephrase that. Please stay here tonight."

"All right." Still aglow from their lovemaking, she really had no desire to go anywhere.

"How about some hot tea or coffee?"

"Coffee for me," she said, turning up the too-long sleeves of his robe. "While you fix it, I'll straighten things up."

She gathered the clothes that were strewn about and folded the quilt and draped it over the chair by the fireplace.

"That quilt came in handy," he said, eyeing her mischievously. "Maybe you should leave it on the floor."

"If I'm sleeping here tonight, it's going to be in a bed."

"Another first for us."

"Fix the coffee," she ordered playfully, and carried their clothes into the bedroom.

After hanging their clothes, she washed her face and ran his brush through her hair, then returned to the living room. Anatol had set two brandy snifters on the coffee table.

"That's to take the chill off," he said, carrying their coffee cups. He gave her a quick peck on the cheek before setting the cups down. Relaxing on the sofa, he propped his legs on the corner of the coffee table and crossed his ankles. Then he patted the sofa next to him. "Let's cozy up."

Seated next to him, she drew her legs up under the robe. "Let's not cozy up right now. We have to talk business."

"Humph, you aren't the least concerned about my male ego, are you?"

She reached for the corner of his robe and covered his thigh. Meeting his steady gaze, she said, "There shouldn't be a thing wrong with your ego."

"Keep looking at me like that and talking business is out of the question."

"I'm serious, Anatol."

"You think I'm not?"

"Business first. I've got to report to Biomed that sometimes half of what the plant produces is being considered defective and junked."

"Won't that change when the American managers have a say in the operation?"

"It has to, but my company has a right to know how things are now. It's not ethical for me to withhold that information from them. And what if the products weren't defective? All I have is Misha's word that they were."

"Would it be so wrong to wait until the audit is done?" Sliding closer, he moved his arm around her. "Look at the bright side of things. Chernov's agreed to let you reorganize his managerial staff and work with them. That's a plus, isn't it? And you said Misha's quality-control reports for October indicated that only a normal amount of products had been rejected. Maybe they did have trouble with the machinery in September, and maybe the surgical instruments were really defective."

"And maybe I'm the queen of England."

"You're a queen to me," he said, slipping a hand inside her robe and caressing a breast. "How about we take our coffee and cognac into the royal bed?"

"Anatol, you have a habit of doing that."

"Doing what?"

"Changing the subject every time you're uncomfortable with it."

"I'm not uncomfortable with going to bed. Are you?"

"Right now I'm uncomfortable with the hard choices I've got to make."

After teasing her earlobe with the tip of his tongue, he asked softly, "Couldn't you make them lying down?"

"You're awful," she said, smiling.

"You're wonderful. Back to choices. Which side of the bed do you prefer?"

"The left. But remember, I've got to be at the plant bright and early tomorrow morning."

"I'll see that you get there early, anyway," he said, swooping her up from the sofa.

UNDER CHERNOV'S watchful eye Laura began daily afternoon sessions with his department managers in the plant's union room. To acquaint them with how their American counterparts were used to operating, she detailed American managers' training in organization, motivation, measurement and employee development. She was more than surprised when Chernov didn't interrupt to stress his own belief in managerial power and authority.

By mid-November Laura was ecstatic at the enthusiasm projected by the department heads. After one especially lively session, they surrounded her and plied her with questions for a full hour.

"This is enough for one afternoon," Chernov finally announced, breaking up the session. "You have a knack of making difficult concepts appear easy," he told Laura when the department managers had left.

Wonder of wonders, Laura thought, smiling to acknowledge his compliment. "Your people are to be commended. They're eager for new input."

"My people, or the ones you and Olga selected from the supervisory staff?"

"You have to admit that including them will give you a more balanced managerial team for the next decade."

"Yes," he said, much to her surprise, "I do admit that, and I also admit that I was highly suspicious of you when you first arrived."

"Suspicious? Why?"

"I wasn't sure what to expect in the way of interference." He glanced toward the organizational chart Laura had chalked in on the blackboard. "It's reassuring to see that my name remains at the top."

"You're the director, Yuri."

"Yes, and I particularly like the arrow you inserted that goes from me to George Hardcastle."

"I thought you would."

Chernov's usually stern features formed a smile, a bright one for him. "Will he and I get along as well as we have?"

"I'm certain George is wondering the same thing. He's not a suspicious man by nature, but people are always nervous when they begin working with someone new. You'll find that George is good with figures, especially production figures."

"He and I have something in common already."

Laura doubted that, but she didn't want to ruin Yuri's good mood by saying so. Instead she asked, "Any news of when the audit will take place?"

"It's scheduled for December."

She frowned. "Not until then?"

"The Soviet Union is a large country, and we have just so many auditors."

Thinking quickly, she said, "The computers that Biomed sent are operating. Could Olga and Sergei do an audit?"

"They have other work that I've assigned them."

"May I have one of Biomed's auditors come from New York to do one?"

"Why are you always in such a rush to get things done? What difference can a few weeks make in the long run?"

"The difference between finding out if everything this plant produces is actually being sold, for one thing."

"Laura," Chernov said in a stern tone, "don't overstep your authority, and that includes bringing in unauthorized personnel for unauthorized audits. Until January this plant is entirely under my supervision. Is that clear?"

"Perfectly clear," she replied, then hurried from the room, realizing that Chernov had reverted to his usual dictatorial attitude.

STANDING AT THE CREDENZA in her office, Olga cast a concerned look at Laura. "Calm down," she advised.

"I am calm. You should see me when I get angry."

"I don't think I want to. Here, take a drink of this." She handed Laura the cup of tea she had fixed for her.

"Thanks," she said, sitting rigidly in the chair next to Olga's desk. "The man is impossible to deal with! If it weren't for Anatol, I'd tell Yuri what to do with his plant."

"Yuri is one man. You've made great progress here, and a lot of people are depending on you to stick it out. If you pack up and go home, the morale here is going to dive lower than the temperature in February."

"It's cold enough now," Laura said, glancing at the snow falling outside the office window.

Stepping behind her desk, Olga sat down, and her expression turned serious. "Laura," she said hesitantly, "be careful where Anatol's concerned."

After taking a sip of the hot tea, Laura smiled softly. "I'm afraid it's too late."

"I'm not talking about your personal relationship. I'm talking about getting him too involved with digging into the . . . discrepancies here at the plant."

"You mean thefts, don't you?"

"I don't know for sure that anyone is stealing anything. What I do know is that the audit Anatol requested is making some people nervous."

"People like Yuri," Laura said flatly.

"Not just him, but others in the Ministry of Health. When they get nervous, they pass their anxiety on down to the local level."

Laura thought of the people who had been following her everywhere she went. "Are you saying that members of the local soviet are spying on Anatol and me?"

"Some of them are KGB."

Putting her cup down, Laura rose as she thought about that. Then she looked at Olga. "Maybe it's because I'm an American, but I don't find those initials awe-inspiring."

"As an American, you have a certain protection that Soviet citizens, including Anatol, don't. Laura, the KGB doesn't see gray areas. To them, things are either black or white. If you challenge the system, you're most likely seen as being black."

Concerned, Laura slowly sat down again. "You're telling me that I'm causing Anatol to challenge the system."

"Exactly. His position with the State Planning Committee gives him some security, but not enough that he can't be hurt."

Laura's concern escalated to worry, but before she could comment, Sergei rushed in.

"The plant's being shut down!" he said in a hushed but anxious voice, his eyes sweeping from Olga to Laura, who bolted from the chair.

"What?"

"Why?" Olga asked.

"Industrial waste was found in the river near us. An inspection team is being sent from Moscow to check out the source of pollution."

"How long will we be shut down?"

"For two weeks probably," Olga said. "It's happened before."

"Was the plant polluting?" Laura asked, her thoughts racing.

"No," Sergei said. "We were cleared."

Thinking about the January deadline, Laura groaned, then asked Sergei, "How did you find out? Did Yuri tell you?"

"Just now."

"Well, he could have had the decency to tell me also," she spit out, and tore back to his office.

"I TAKE IT none of the rivers in America are polluted by industries," Chernov said smugly.

"My concern right now is with one industry here in the Soviet Union. Are we polluting the river?"

"Of course not. Our industrial waste is disposed of according to law."

"We can prove that, I suppose."

Chernov nodded slowly.

"Well, that's something," Laura said, hoping it was true.

"You are a worrier, aren't you?"

"It's not just the temporary closing of the plant," Laura said defiantly. "There have been too many interrupting factors. First Biomed's computers were shipped to Siberia, then medical equipment apparently disappears, and now this. Obviously someone is trying to sabotage this joint venture.''

Chernov propped his elbows on his desk and began tapping his fingertips together. ''My guess is that you've been reading too many mystery novels.''

''There's no mystery about what's been going on here, Yuri,'' she shot back. ''You'd see that if you wanted to. Just why does it take two weeks to check this plant's waste-disposal records?''

''I don't draw up the investigators' schedule.''

Knowing that the quality-control department was also responsible for the records in question, Laura said, ''Then have Misha bring the files in here now, just to make certain they're available when the team from Moscow arrives. It shouldn't take them two weeks to verify that we've handled the waste properly.''

Chernov's eyes narrowed. ''Miss Walters,'' he said darkly, ''your status here doesn't give you the right to issue orders to the cleaning people, least of all to me.''

''You don't want to see this joint venture operational, do you?'' she asked, squaring her shoulders and maintaining her fixed stare on him.

His hands parted in a noncommittal gesture.

''Nor do you want an accurate accounting of plant production. Why not? Are you afraid of what it might prove?''

''I spoke to you once about overstepping your authority here,'' he warned. ''You don't know what you're getting involved in, Laura, nor what the consequences could be if you continue to create problems. This bravado of yours might work in America, but believe me—'' his stony eyes drifted over her ''—you'd be foolish to go on with it. Remember, you're a guest of the Soviet government only as long as you behave like one."

"When I came here—by invitation of the Soviet government—I came not only because it was my job. I believed my being here would help both our countries, and not just financially. I had hoped that our working together would help build trust between us. But I was wrong. With your attitude, I can see we have a long way to go before there can be any real trust between us."

Chernov lowered his eyes, and his voice took on a surprising quality of remorse. "I'm sorry you find my attitude lacking."

"It's not only *your* attitude, Yuri. Ever since I started working here, I've had the feeling that just about everyone knows something odd is going on—something they won't talk about. It's as though they're afraid to, just as you seem to be. What is it?"

A look of despair settled on his features, his troubled eyes seemingly asking for understanding, but then the softness left his face and he said quietly, "Please don't slam the door on your way out, Miss Walters."

IN HER OFFICE Laura lifted the phone receiver, ready to make reservations for the first flight home. Then a vision of Anatol floated before her mind's eye, and she hesitated. It was so important to Anatol that the joint venture be a success, and Olga had told her that many at the plant were depending on her to stay. Besides, she'd hate to return to New York in defeat.

"Damn it!" she muttered, slamming the receiver down. "Chernov's not going to drive me away."

Rising, she paced, trying to organize her thoughts, wondering what to do next. *If you had any sense,* she told herself, *you'd make that plane reservation.*

"Okay," she muttered, ordering herself to calm down, "deal with this pollution business first."

Quickly she went to Misha's office, but he wasn't there, and his door was locked. She hurried down the hall to Sergei's office, hoping the waste-disposal records had been put in the computer by now. His door was open, but he wasn't there. She went directly to the computer and requested the disposal records, but the message on the screen informed her none was available.

"That's not surprising."

She thought for a moment, then took the opportunity to check the sales status of the high-tech medical equipment Biomed had shipped recently. Laura had requested the equipment after Olga had told her of the desperate inquiries she'd had from Leningrad hospitals.

Minutes later Laura sank back in the chair, having discovered that seven high-power microscopes and five autoclaves hadn't been sold, but they weren't listed as available inventory, either. They'd just gone missing.

"Oh, Sergei," she whispered, realizing he would have to be aware of this latest disappearance.

CHAPTER TEN

A LITTLE AFTER 6:00 p.m. Laura was pacing nervously in her apartment, waiting for Anatol to return from Leningrad. Over and over again she thought of the so-called defective sets of surgical instruments and EKG machines and the now-missing microscopes and autoclaves. Sergei had to know they were unaccounted for. But she also knew how protective Anatol was of his friend.

She stopped dead in her tracks when she heard steps bounding up the wooden stairway. The second Anatol opened the door, she said, "We have trouble, big trouble."

"No welcome?" he complained, closing out the wind when he shut the door behind him.

"The plant is being closed down." As he peeled off his overcoat, her words flew out, bringing him up-to-date on what had happened at the plant.

"It's being shut down is problem enough," he said grimly, sinking onto the chair by the radiator, "but I'm more concerned about the microscopes and autoclaves. They'd bring a good price on the black market."

Slumping onto the sofa, Laura's voice became as dismal as her expression. "They've probably gone the same path that the surgical instruments and EKG machines went. God only knows what other supplies are missing. Only an audit would tell us." Slapping the arm of the sofa, she asked, "If Karnakov is delaying the audit, why is he doing it? The man supposedly works for the Ministry of Health!"

"He could have his own reasons, but it could be that other ministries are putting pressure on him."

"So much for idealism," Laura remarked, shaking her head.

Anatol sighed deeply. "Resources, money and real power are in the hands of the ministries. Their main concerns are their own interests, not those of the people."

"Certainly we have problems back home with toxic waste and political power plays...and with bureaucracy, but it pales in comparison with what I've seen here." She paused, then said, "Speaking of bureaucracy, isn't that exactly what your son is demonstrating against? You ought to applaud his efforts."

"Should I applaud the possibility of his being sent to a camp in Siberia?"

"What?"

Anatol crossed to the sofa and sat down beside her. "For all the new openness here, I still worry that the door to change could slam shut anytime. The hardliners in government could take over and crush dissenters. Demonstrators like Valentin would be the first to be picked up by the KGB."

"He's only seventeen!"

"Laura, he's been organizing demonstrations! Last week he and some of his friends were waving their signs in front of the Winter Palace. That's where the czar's police used to shoot dissenters in cold blood."

"I'm sorry," she apologized. "I've no business interfering in your family affairs, and now I can appreciate your concern as a father."

"I'm not just concerned, I'm worried sick," he said, standing and shoving his hands into his trouser pockets. "Next year Valentin goes into the army. What if he's sent to one of the republics to restore order? He would no more shoot anyone than I would. I've a pretty good idea what they'd do to him for disobeying orders."

Considering the reports from the republics that she'd heard nightly on TV news, Laura realized that Anatol's fears for his son were justified. Not knowing what to say to him, this time she was the one who changed the subject. "I tried to tell myself that the plant could be open again in a week or two, but I'm not so sure."

"Why?"

"I tried to check waste-disposal records in the computer, but none have been entered."

"Maybe Sergei's people just haven't gotten that far yet."

"And maybe someone doesn't want those records to be handy so that when the investigators come, it will take them twice as long to do their job."

"Misha handles the waste-disposal reports, doesn't he?" Anatol asked, sitting sideways on the sofa.

"Yes, I tried to check with him, but he wasn't in his office. I think he's ready to have a nervous breakdown about something. The last time I talked with him, he seemed terrified."

"I don't know much about him, other than that he's the quiet type. Sergei always speaks highly of him, though. In fact, as I remember, Misha was made manager of quality control on Sergei's recommendation."

"Your friend Sergei seems to think Misha's on top of everything in his department. If he is, why is the man so anxious, and where are the September quality control reports and the waste-disposal records?"

Anatol shook his head. "This country is drowning in paperwork. The fact that Misha can't locate a few records isn't surprising. Also, if anyone at the plant *is* working with black marketeers, we can't be sure it's the same person who's orchestrating the other problems."

"Anatol," Laura said, placing her hand over his, "I have to admit that at times I thought you were dragging your feet about helping me at the plant, but now I see how overwhelming the situation is, and I realize there's little you could have done."

"I could make a lot more noise, but I'm not that thrilled about the prospect of spending long winters as an exile in Siberia."

"Don't say that!"

"It's a reality, Laura, one that I can't afford to forget."

"I've no intention of letting you spend a minute in Siberia. It's Dmitri Karnakov who should be sent there."

"And be careful who you point a finger at, at least until we have some proof."

"I've got to do something. Right now I have only two options. I can either stay here and fight it out or give up and return home."

He eased an arm around her and drew her close. "It looks like I'm in a no-win situation. I don't want you to leave, but I'm afraid for you to stay."

"Anatol," she said quietly, "I've never been any good at just looking the other way. If I stay, I have to protect my company's interests. But now I'm afraid for you."

Wishing he hadn't mentioned the possibility of being exiled to Siberia, he tried to put her concern to rest. "Don't worry about me. I have contacts in the government."

"I hope they have contacts, too, lots of them."

He kissed her forehead, then said, "I have to fly to Moscow tonight for a morning meeting at the State Planning Committee. Come with me. The plant is closed, so there's no need for you to sit here all alone. I'd like us to talk to a friend of mine in Moscow, Mikhail Debabov. He investigates crime for the Ministry of Internal Affairs."

Laura looked up at him, concern in her eyes. "Maybe I'm getting paranoid, but are you sure it's safe to tell him about the problems at the plant?"

"Mikhail's a longtime friend. I've known him since we were boys in school. Nothing we tell him in confidence will go any farther. But he'll be able to advise us."

IT WAS COLD, windy and dark when Laura and Anatol completed the hour-long shuttle flight from Leningrad to Moscow. After checking into the National Hotel, he tried to phone Mikhail at his apartment, but there was no answer.

During their late supper at the Uzbekistan restaurant, Laura turned the conversation to Valentin. "Have you spoken with your son lately?"

"Uh-uh. I have this uncomfortable feeling of being a failure as a father. I'm not sure he'd want to have a serious talk with me."

"That's nonsense," Laura countered. "How many teenagers confide in their parents routinely? It's an age when kids are sure they're being misunderstood by anyone over twenty-five. I think that all Valentin wants is an opening to talk to you."

"I do talk with him."

"You talk *at* him, Anatol. Give him a chance to speak his piece and let you know how he feels about things. Even if it kills you, be quiet and listen to him."

Silently he gazed across the table at her, then he said, "If things work out at the plant, would you think about staying here? You'd make a great governess."

His suggestion—even made jokingly—took her by surprise. Smiling the idea away, she said, "My wings aren't quite large or experienced enough to take a seventeen-year-old under them."

"How about a forty-year-old Russian who thinks you're one terrific lady, even though you're a capitalist?"

"Hands across the ocean, that sort of thing?"

"It's not hands I'm thinking of at the moment."

"You'd better. Your right one is sitting in the gravy."

Anatol looked down and saw that his pinky was smudged à la carte. Wiping it with his napkin, he smirked at her. "I wouldn't say that you completely unsettle me, but you're well on your way to doing so."

"Serves you right for checking us into one room."

"Are you objecting?"

"Not at all."

WHILE ANATOL ATTENDED his morning meeting at the State Planning Committee, Laura browsed through the shops on Gorky Street, then waited for him in Pushkin Square. Near the entrance to the park she noticed that a crowd had congregated by the bronze statue of Pushkin. Curious, she ambled toward them, seeing that they were listening to a group of young people, some carrying signs protesting pollution. One of the young men turned her way and raised a clenched fist as he spoke.

"Valentin!" Laura murmured, certain that Anatol had no idea his son was in Moscow.

She waved to him, and when he finished speaking he left the gathering and ran to her.

"Laura, what are you doing in Moscow?"

"What are you doing here?" she asked. "I'm expecting your father any minute."

"He's with you!"

"Yes. Shouldn't you be in school?"

Standing tall, Valentin said, "Someone has to speak out against the destruction of our lakes and rivers."

Laura took hold of the sleeve of his parka and waltzed him just inside the park entrance. "You should be more concerned about the destruction of your rear end if Anatol sees you."

"He wouldn't care."

"You're wrong. He does care. I told him about the conversation we had, and he realizes the two of you have to talk . . . calmly and like adults."

"He said that?"

"Yes, but my advice to you right now is not to let him find you here."

"Good advice, but a little late," Anatol said, looming up in front of them. "Why the hell aren't you in school, Valentin? Does your mother know you're here? If she does, I'm going to tell her—"

"Sure you will," Valentin cut in. "You're so busy telling people what you think, no one can get a word in."

Anatol glanced over at the crowd surrounding the young demonstrators who were jerking their signs up and down. His eyes shifted to Laura as though to express his fears for his son's safety. Then he asked Valentin, "Where are you staying here?"

"Nowhere, I'm going back to Leningrad this afternoon."

"Are you with that group?"

"They're my friends."

"Well, I'm your father, and I want you to come with Laura and me now."

"Why? What would we do, sit down and have a long man-to-man talk?"

"Don't you think it's time we did?"

"Sorry, but now that you've finally found time for me, I'm busy."

"I'm not asking you, Valentin," Anatol said, taking a firm grip on his son's arm. "I'm telling you."

"My friends are waiting," Valentin snapped. Pulling his arm free, he rushed back to his fellow demonstrators.

Glaring at Anatol, Laura said, "Open mouth, insert foot."

"What should I have said? 'Oh, I see you've decided to skip school. How nice.' What kind of a father would sanction that?"

"You know, Anatol, as a lover you're great. As a father, you stink."

She stalked toward Gorky Street, and he caught up with her, grasped her arm and spun her around.

"What am I supposed to do...just ignore that he's making a public nuisance of himself?"

"And ignore that he might get arrested?" she added.

"That, too," he admitted, glancing back toward his son, who was speaking and waving his arms.

Laura saw Anatol's worried expression and hated having lashed out at him. "I'm sorry I said what I did. Again I'm butting in on family matters."

"No, you're right. I shouldn't have gone at him that way. I'll talk to him as soon as we get back to Leningrad. I mean I'll *listen* while he talks to me." He noticed the McDonald's sign across the street. "Can I interest you in a hamburger?" he asked, unable to keep his eyes from drifting back to his son again.

Laura's gaze followed his. She nodded, and soon they were seated at a small round table in the Soviet Union's first McDonald's restaurant. Anatol put his hamburger down and wiped the corners of his mouth with a napkin. "Valentin doesn't think I know how hard he took it when Yelena and I divorced," Anatol told her. "He tries to act so independent and so tough, but inside I think he's still the little boy I taught to play soccer."

"You might try telling him how you feel about him. He thinks you don't care."

"Of course I care. I'm his father. But every time I open my mouth, he's ready to argue."

"Oh, Anatol," Laura said, her voice a gentle complaint, "we all need to be reassured that we're loved every now and then. Valentin's no different. Right now he's confused. He feels you've given up on him, and that's killing him. He misses you and thinks you've deserted him.''

"I don't know what happened between us," Anatol said thoughtfully. "We used to be close. Maybe I let my work make too many demands on me. Maybe it was the problems Yelena and I began having. Or maybe it was just that he was growing up and it was time to let go.''

"Letting go shouldn't have meant cutting him off completely.''

"Cutting him off? He's never wanted for a thing. When he was fifteen, I could have gotten him into the Nakhimov Naval Academy, but he wanted no part of it. Now he'll have to go into the army. For two years I'll hardly see him. After that he'll want to marry Katya. Then there'll be children. And he's too stubborn to let me help him financially, so he'll have to work at whatever unskilled job he can get to support his family. That's not what I wanted for my son.''

"Anatol," Laura said softly, "you're talking about what *you* want again.''

Picking up a french fry, he chewed on it thoughtfully. "You're sounding like the voice of my conscience.''

"At times you need one.''

"It would be a lifetime job.''

Laura didn't want to read more in Anatol's offhand remark than a joking comment, but something in his tone told her he was half-serious. Uneasily she said, "I already have a job, remember. And so do you—making things right between you and your son.''

"My conscience speaks," he said, taking hold of her hand. "I could get used to that."

"Neither of us can afford to get used to...anything. I'll be leaving next month. In fact, if possible, I'd like to be home for Christmas."

A pained expression reshaped his features. "Are you in that much of a hurry to leave?"

"Whether I am or not has nothing to do with it."

Seeing her determined expression, Anatol stifled his objections. "I called Mikhail at his office," he said, his voice flat. "But I didn't want to say much on the phone. We're having dinner with him and his wife."

"A RUSSIAN MAFIA?" Laura repeated, staring across the dinner table at Mikhail.

"They have connections abroad," he explained, "especially in drug trafficking and antique dealing, particularly icons. Furs are a big item, too, but the crime rings are also engaged in racketeering, robbery and extortion. You name the crime and they're involved in it."

"They're definitely well organized," Anatol added. "They have their own accountants, hit men and a host of informants."

"And that goes on under the noses of the police?"

Galina, Mikhail's wife, rolled her green eyes toward the ceiling. "The crime rate here in Moscow is up seventy-one percent over last year. The militiamen are overworked and understaffed. Tell her, Mikhail."

He shrugged. "It's true. One-third of our crimes go unsolved. Of course," he said, running his fingers through his thinning black hair, "it doesn't help that the syndicates pay off some government officials."

Laura thought of the recent hearings in Washington where ties between politicians and organized crime were investigated. "I guess bureaucracies are vulnerable wherever you go."

Galina chuckled as she started to clear the dinner plates. "We have our own special brand of bureaucracy here. No offense to you, Anatol, but the State Planning Committee does little to solve the problem of food shortages and our having to stand in endless lines for just about everything."

"Some of us are attempting to correct that. But it's like wading through molasses, trying to get anything done." He faced Mikhail. "From what Laura and I have told you, do you think organized crime is involved at the Pavlovsk plant?"

"It's possible. Even likely, I'm afraid."

Disheartened by what she was hearing, Laura said, "Even if we're able to up production at the plant, continued thefts would eat up the profits. We've got to do something. Increase security maybe."

Mikhail laughed, his ample torso shaking. "If the police and the KGB can't put a stop to thefts, how could a guard or two more do it? The people in the syndicates are cold-blooded gangsters, willing to do anything for money."

Thinking of Chernov, Laura asked, "What kind of things?"

"I've got cases piled on my desk now where cars and houses have been set on fire. Children have even been kidnapped. Businessmen are being threatened and blackmailed to force them to look the other way while the black marketeers help themselves to whatever they want. Usually they don't run off with everything a business manufactures. They just skim off the top, so as not to destroy the source of the goods.''

He leaned back in his chair. ''It's all part of a very lucrative protection racket, and decent people work with them. Usually out of fear. But sometimes the syndicates snare a naive employee with money, drugs or sex, then terrorize him into cooperating with them.''

Anatol turned to Laura, ''That's why we have to be careful. We can't be sure who we can trust.''

''We have to at least try to stop the thefts,'' she insisted. ''Does the Criminal Investigation Department have any idea what happens to stolen goods?''

''Some are sold nationally on the black market,'' Mikhail explained. ''But it's believed that most of them are exported via the Black Sea to Western Europe. From there, who knows?''

''I'm not interested in tracking down everything that's being stolen in the Soviet Union, but I would like to find out where my company's medical equipment went, and who at the plant made it possible for it to be taken in the first place.''

''It's not a job for one person,'' Mikhail warned, ''particularly a foreigner in your position. Your movements here are probably being followed. If you start asking the wrong questions, you could find yourself in big trouble.''

''The Pavlovsk plant isn't the only problem I'm concerned about,'' Anatol said. ''I'm having trouble with thefts at other plants and factories. If I could trace the medical equipment, I might find the route a lot of stolen goods take when they're smuggled out of the country.''

Galina overheard him as she returned to the dining area with a plate of little cakes. "Anatol, you'd be foolish to go up against the syndicates. They're brutal people."

"She's right," Mikhail agreed. "One more life wouldn't make a bit of difference to them."

"I can't believe that people high up in government know this is going on," Laura said.

"The syndicates pay off the government. They buy protection from the law. In the criminal cases I've investigated, one out of five involves corrupt officials. It's not all black, though. In the past two years we've confiscated some 350 million rubles' worth of valuables and cash from racketeers."

"I'm only interested in seven high-power microscopes and five autoclaves," Laura said, her expression grim.

"Do you have any idea where the stolen goods are stored before they're shipped out of the country?" Anatol asked.

"Right now we believe a lot of it is shipped from Odessa."

"In the Ukraine," Anatol said pensively. "Can you give me the name of someone in Odessa who might be dealing in black market goods?"

Leaning forward, Mikhail shook his pipe at him. "You're asking for trouble, Anatol. You could get killed if you go snooping around the syndicate."

"I've put my life on the line before for my country. And these syndicates are a much bigger danger to the Soviet Union than Afghanistan ever was. Besides, I'll be careful."

"It would be worth some risk if we could just stop the drain on the Pavlovsk plant," Laura said.

"*We?*" Anatol repeated. "If I go to Odessa, you're *not* coming with me."

"Yes, I am. Two heads are better than one." She faced Mikhail. "*Is* there someone we can contact in Odessa?"

"Laura," Galina said, touching her shoulder, "your being an American won't matter to these people."

"Exactly," Anatol chimed in, thinking the matter closed. Then he asked Mikhail again, "Can you get me the name of someone in Odessa that you suspect is handling stolen goods?"

"It's not a city I'm working on now, but I can ask around. Come to my office in the morning. I'll see what I can do."

In Gorky Park the amber glow of lamplights shimmered on the leafless silver birch trees as Anatol and Laura meandered down a pathway, his arm over her shoulder. The lightly falling snow had stopped, and nighttime ice skaters, bundled in heavy coats and fur hats, glided around the rink to recorded music coming from speakers that edged the pond. In the distance Laura saw now-closed children's rides backed by a Ferris wheel.

"It doesn't make sense for you to come with me," Anatol said again. "Mikhail told us how brutal those people are. I'd spend all my time worrying about you."

"I'm not heroic, Anatol," Laura argued, raising the fur collar of her coat with her gloved hands. "But I just can't sit by idly and let you take all the risks to find out what happened to my company's equipment. With the plant closed, what would I do—play tourist while I worried about you? And it's not just that I want to trace the microscopes and autoclaves. The entire joint venture is at risk. I've never failed in an assignment for Biomed, and I don't plan to fail at this one, either."

Anatol stopped, took hold of Laura's shoulders and turned her to face him. "I've got a lot at stake, too. Finding Biomed's microscopes isn't the only reason I'm going. I'm also looking for electronic equipment that's been stolen from another factory I look after. But, Laura, I'd rather we both failed in our jobs than have anything happen to you. You mean a great deal to me."

"And you to me," she said quietly, appreciating his concern. "But I haven't come five thousand miles to pack it all in without giving it my best."

"Is your job as important to you as your safety? You heard what Mikhail said the syndicate was capable of doing."

"Are you saying you'd be immune to danger?"

"I'm saying you're not going with me."

Waving a hand in front of his eyes, Laura asked, "Hello? Are you in there? Are you listening to me? I *am* going."

"Has anyone ever told you how stubborn you are?" he asked with little humor in his tone.

"Has anyone ever told you how stubborn *you* are? You want everything done your way. You're treating me just as you treat Valentin."

"I *know* how to treat Valentin—better than you do."

"Do you? How come you jumped all over him before even asking why he was doing what he was doing this afternoon? I'll tell you why. You were too preoc-

cupied with sounding like a dictator. You want everyone to snap to it when you decide what's good for
them. Then, if anyone stands up to you, you get your
feelings hurt and expect the world to stop and take notice.''

"Are you finished?"

"Yes, I'm finished," she tossed off, and stomped
back toward the park entrance.

CHAPTER ELEVEN

LAURA STOOD AT THE WINDOW of their darkened hotel room, wearing her robe and staring down at the lights of the Kremlin. Perhaps Anatol was right, she thought. Maybe she was getting in deeper than she had a right to. Tracking down stolen equipment was a police matter, and Anatol's relationship with his son was none of her business. But as she'd told Anatol, she wasn't good at just looking the other way when problems arose.

As long as she could remember, she'd charged forward, tackling life with zest, commitment and hard work. And she'd always planned ahead, never simply trusting things to work out by themselves.

As soon as she'd been given this Russian assignment—long before leaving the States—she'd tried to conceive of possible difficulties that might lie ahead of her. But never in her wildest imaginings had she thought she'd come up against the problems that now faced her: Chernov opposing her every move at the plant, powerful Communist Party officials hijacking her computers, the KGB following her every move, and now she had to take on the Russian Mafia!

At least she had Anatol on her side. Back in the States, she'd never anticipated meeting a man like him, either, she thought, glancing back to where he was lying in bed. He was every bit as willful and obstinate as his son, and every bit as likable, usually.

Likable? No, he was more than likable. In fact, she was desperately in love with him. So much for planning, she thought, slumping against the window frame.

As she stood in the quiet semidarkness, hailstones began clicking against the window. Again she gazed absently at the lights of the Kremlin, thinking how ludicrous it was that she could possibly be in love with a card-carrying Communist. It was totally insane.

"Larashka," Anatol called quietly.

She didn't respond or move, having said few words to him since they arrived back at the hotel.

"Please, come to bed," he said, his voice low and husky.

"In a while," she answered softly.

Raising himself on his arm, he studied her silhouetted figure, hating the tension that had grown between them ever since they'd left Gorky Park. "Larashka, have you ever wanted something, someone, so badly that at times you almost forget everything else in your life?"

Turning toward him, Laura nodded silently.

"It's scary, isn't it? I mean, the feeling of losing control of your life, of handing that control over to someone else."

"Yes," she agreed. "That's why you frighten me at times."

"Frighten you? How?" he asked, drawing back the covers and rising from the bed.

"I never planned to get so involved with you, Anatol."

"And I didn't plan to get involved with you," he told her, leaning against the wall on the other side of the window. "And I didn't choose to fall in love with you. I just did."

A rumble of thunder echoed through the room, and Laura clasped her arms as she stepped away from the window. She hadn't expected to hear Anatol say those words, and she didn't want to believe them. But she did, and that frightened her more than the storm that was brewing outside.

She had convinced herself that she could handle a brief romantic interlude with him. She'd known all along that she'd have to leave eventually. And she'd imagined there was an element of safety in that knowledge. How foolish she'd been.

"Love comes with time, Anatol, not in a rush," she said quietly, not looking his way.

"It isn't something you can schedule, Laura. It's something you feel deeply."

"You're confusing love with deep friendship," she insisted, her pulses racing.

"You're denying what we feel for each other." He moved behind her so that she could feel his warmth caress her back. "Why are you afraid to call it what it is?" he demanded, taking hold of her arms and pulling her against him. "Tell me you don't love me."

"Anatol, I—"

"Tell me honestly," he insisted, "and that will be the end of it." Again she was silent, but he felt her trembling. Gently he eased his arms under hers and crossed them over her breasts. Kissing the side of her neck, he murmured, "Tell me you don't love me."

Hardly able to breathe, Laura gathered all her emotional strength. "I don't love you," she lied, breaking free from his arms.

For a few silent moments Anatol examined her profile in the semidarkness. He saw a distraught woman, uncertain and confused. But he saw something else—a vulnerability that caused him to hesitate at the same time that it gave him reason to believe the truth he so wanted to hear.

Another emotion shot through him, a strong one: his own vulnerability. And he didn't know how to deal with it.

His eyes drifted aimlessly, then returned to her. "I've been honest with you," he said, her aloofness making him feel more desperate by the second. "I hadn't expected to fall in love with you. I've gone over it in my mind time and time again, trying to convince myself that I wasn't in love with you. But you're unlike any other woman I've ever known. You've . . . you've gotten inside me, taken possession of me until I'm nothing without you."

Dragging his fingers through his hair, he let the words pour out, as if he were talking to himself, trying to understand his feelings for her. "You're fiercely independent, unafraid to take risks for what you believe in. Your intelligence is more than obvious. You walked into the plant, took one look and knew what was wrong. And yet you're also so feminine, so soft and caring. I would have fallen in love with you even if you weren't so lovely."

Slowly Laura turned away completely, her back to him again. She didn't know how to respond. He pleased her and frightened her at the same time. He made her feel she was responsible for his happiness. But at the moment she couldn't even take responsibility for her feelings.

Laura's silence gnawed at Anatol like a steel drill. Having opened his heart to her, having admitted that he loved her—only to be rejected—Anatol turned hard inside. He felt an urgent need to cover his feelings.

"Perhaps you're right," he said, his voice rough with anxiety. "Perhaps love only comes with time. For now, though, we have what you call our deep friendship."

When her head turned toward him, he jerked open the buttons of his pajama top and moved closer. "You can't deny we have that." The top fell to the carpet as did her robe seconds later.

"Anatol," Laura whispered, her head tilted back, "we're not making any sense doing this."

"I don't want us to make sense," he said, easing the straps of her silky gown off her shoulders. "I want us to make love."

Lowering his head, he covered one nipple with his lips, then the other, bringing them to instant hardness as he pushed the silken garment from her hips. Hearing her deep sigh, he raised his head and gazed at her flushed face. He ran his hands down over her sides, then back up slowly, feeling her shiver when his thumbs stroked the underswell of her breasts. "Say you want me as much as I want you, Laura. Say it."

Not able to deny that she did, her hands encircled his warm neck, and she slumped against him. "I want you," she murmured in total defeat.

With a flourish he swooped her up in his arms and placed her down on the crumpled bedclothes. Tossing aside the bottoms of his pajamas, he knelt between her legs and braced his hands on either side of her.

"To our deep friendship," he said, his brooding eyes holding hers as he plunged into her moist warmth.

SNOW FELL OUTSIDE the duty-free Beryozka shop on Kutuzovsky Prospekt as Laura sauntered through it, looking for a gift for Anatol. She stopped at a display of crystal animals and recalled the white swans she had seen gliding over the lake by his dacha. Picking up a small crystal swan, she thought he would like it. She also hoped he would keep it on his desk at his office and think of her long after she had returned home.

Leaving the shop, she went to the taxi stand and instructed the driver to take her to Sofia, a restaurant on Gorky Street, where she was to meet Anatol after he spoke with Mikhail.

Anatol had arrived first and was seated at a table when she entered. After he ordered a red wine to go with the Bulgarian cuisine he recommended, Laura reached into the bag she'd placed next to her purse and handed him a little box.

A violinist began playing Gypsy music as Anatol carefully opened the package. Withdrawing a crystal swan, his eyes sparkled his sincere thanks. "It's beautiful," he said, setting the gift on the table and raising his wineglass, "just as you are."

Over the rim of her wineglass Laura's smiling eyes met his for a long moment before she sipped, still thinking of their nightlong lovemaking.

At first Anatol had been rough and hasty, but very quickly he became the gentle and tender man he usually was when they made love. And sometime during the night they had both forgotten they had ever had harsh words.

Looking at him now, she asked, "What did you learn from Mikhail?"

Anatol glanced around furtively before saying, "He gave me the name of a man in Odessa, a Taras Luryn. He's suspected of handling black market goods for a crime syndicate working out of Kiev. But he's not to be alerted that he's being investigated. I promised Mikhail that we wouldn't do or say anything that would make Luryn suspicious."

"If the man's being investigated, who's watching the investigators?" Laura asked, only half in jest.

"You're starting to think like a Russian now. That's exactly what Mikhail is concerned about. He thinks it's possible that Luryn or someone else might be bribing the investigators." Reaching over, Anatol placed a hand over hers. "Please, for my sake, change your mind about coming with me."

He was unsuccessful.

THE NEXT DAY Anatol and Laura checked into the Odessa Hotel, which overlooked the Black Sea. From the moment they'd deplaned and walked into the afternoon sun, Laura realized it was some thirty degrees warmer than it had been in Moscow. After changing into a white suit, she and Anatol headed for Luryn's shop on the docks to put the plan they had formulated into operation.

From a distance the patchwork of pleasure boats, ships and freighters moored in the busy port gave the appearance of a mammoth traffic disaster. Huge hydraulic cranes loomed up like ancient oil rigs, their mechanical arms dipping and raising as they loaded and unloaded massive crates of cargo.

The cacophony of horns, whistles and shouting voices reached a deafening crescendo as they walked along the dock. Laura scanned the rows of sleek hydrofoils and larger passenger ferries that they passed. Farther down, burly bare-chested dockworkers loaded cargo onto freighters with Soviet, Cuban and Italian names.

"His shop's got to be along here somewhere," Anatol said, taking a firmer hold on Laura's arm as he edged their way through the longshoremen, sailors and people on holiday.

Laura inhaled the strong odors of saltwater skimmed with oil. A more pungent aroma of cooking oil came from the vendors' carts siding the long wharf.

"There it is," Anatol said, nodding to his left.

Outside, the shop was weather-beaten and sorely needed a coat of paint; inside, it was even more unkempt. Laura glanced around the repair shop quickly, deciding it looked suspiciously like pawnshops she'd seen in movies.

A short, stocky man emerged through a tattered gray curtain that hung over a narrow passageway to a back room. "Can I help you?" he asked in heavily accented Russian.

"Taras Luryn?" Anatol asked.

"And you are?"

"Viktor Makarov." He gestured toward Laura. "This is Anne Stuart."

"You have something to be repaired?" Luryn asked.

"Miss Stuart would like to purchase a high-power microscope."

The man's eyes narrowed. Then he sputtered a squeaky, breathy laugh, emitting a rancid aroma of garlic from between thick pink lips. Raising his arms sideways, he grinned, exposing bad teeth. "This is a repair shop, not a medical supply establishment."

Taking out his wallet, Anatol removed two American hundred-dollar bills and spread them out on the smudged glass countertop. "We were told by a friend who lives in Kiev that you were diversifying your business."

Bug-eyed, Luryn stared at the money, and the tip of his tongue slid slowly over his thick lower lip. Looking back up at Anatol, he smiled unctuously. "Whoever told you that has me confused with someone else. I'm only a poor shopkeeper. I can hardly make ends meet now."

He followed the movement of Anatol's hand as he placed another hundred-dollar bill over the other two. Then his eyes wandered over the white suit and the white pumps Laura wore. "Why do you want a microscope?" he asked her.

"I'm doing biomedical research in Sinop," she replied, referring to the city in Turkey just opposite Odessa across the Black Sea.

"The Turkish government can't provide you with a microscope?"

"I use my own equipment," she said, her voice even. "I'm engaged in independent research in Sinop."

"You're an American?" Luryn asked.

"Yes," Laura said, taking note of the balding man's bloodshot eyes and greasy complexion.

"Perhaps we do have the wrong shop," Anatol said, starting to collect the money on the countertop.

Luryn's pudgy hand quickly covered his. After an indecisive moment, he said, "Microscopes are expensive. One could run—" his eyes switched to Laura "—as much as a thousand dollars."

"That's a lot of money," Laura said.

"Not for an American-made high-power microscope."

Her pulse quickened, and she glanced at Anatol.

He asked Luryn, "Is the microscope in good condition? New maybe?"

Jerking the three bills from under Anatol's fingers, Luryn pocketed them. "All I can do is ask around. Perhaps I will find someone who has one to sell."

Anatol asked, "How soon could we pick it up?"

"Come back at ten o'clock tonight."

"If you don't find one," Laura said, "you'll return our downpayment."

He raised his hands, palms upward. "I'm a struggling shopkeeper. Inquiries are expensive. Is there anything else you'd be interested in?"

Thinking of the thefts at his Sverdlovsk plant, Anatol said, "We might be interested in some tape recorders."

Luryn grinned, then bent down, grunting as he did. Straightening, he placed one on the counter. "German-made, good quality."

Anatol studied it briefly. "Do you have any smaller ones, Russian-made perhaps?"

After leaning down behind the counter again, he handed another tape recorder to Anatol. "How many would you like?"

Examining it, Anatol recognized the Sverdlovsk code number. Poker-faced, he said, "A dozen."

Casually Laura asked, "If the microscope is what I'm looking for, would you be able to get two of them for me?"

Luryn's fuzzy black eyebrows lifted. "At a thousand American dollars each there shouldn't be a problem," he assured her.

"Good," Anatol said. "We'll be back tonight with the money to collect everything."

Heading back down the pier, Laura asked Anatol, "Do you have that much money?"

"No, but Luryn doesn't know that."

"What then? Do we notify the police?"

"Uh-uh. I'm after more than two microscopes and some tape recorders. The one he showed me was from the Sverdlovsk plant. Having one could be a fluke, but if he comes up with a dozen brand-new ones and two of your microscopes, I'll find out how he got them...one way or another."

"But Mikhail said Luryn wasn't to be alerted that he's under investigation."

"He won't be, not if I convince him the syndicate he's working for is operating in my syndicate's territory."

THAT NIGHT THE DOCKS were inhabited by different types of people than in the daylight. A colorful assortment of buxom ladies of the evening were draped over the iron railing that ran along the edge of the wharf. Mixed in were a few questionable young men in tight jeans who seemed more interested in Anatol than Laura. Along with Soviet sailors who had been on a binge, she spotted some dreamy-eyed folk who had obviously been playing in the medicine cabinet. The eerie wail of a foghorn did little to lift Laura's spirits, and she tightened her grasp on Anatol's arm.

When they neared Luryn's shop, it was dark inside. Whispering, Laura asked, "Do you think he's in there?"

"From the way he drooled over the money this afternoon, I'd guess he would be." Anatol tried the doorknob, and it turned. "If he's not, why would the door be unlocked?"

Entering, he closed the door quietly behind them, then called, "Luryn?"

There was no response.

Laura went to the curtain over the narrow archway that led to a back room. "Mr. Luryn," she called softly, drawing it aside.

She gasped, jerked her hand away from the tattered material, and it swung back in place. Her back flat against the wooden wall, she stood stiff, her blood running cold, her eyes wide with terror.

Anatol pushed the curtain aside and peered in. A yellowish glow from a streetlight coming through a back window streamed over Luryn's body. He lay in a heap on the floor, a red circle of blood at his right temple.

Stepping over him, Anatol searched the room in vain for the microscopes and tape recorders. Returning to the store area, he checked behind the counter for the Russian-made tape recorder he'd been shown earlier. It was gone.

"C'mon," he told Laura, "let's get out of here. Maybe we're being set up."

Quickly they exited and retraced their steps on the pier.

By the time they reached the park at the end of the docks, Laura was able to speak. "I don't think he committed suicide."

Anatol stared at her. "I didn't think you had that much of a sense of humor."

"I don't. I just can't seem to get that other word out."

"Murder?"

"That's the one." Suddenly she felt chilled, and overlapped the lapels of her nylon coat. "Now do we notify the police?"

"No," he said quickly. "We'd have too much explaining to do. For one, they'd want to know why we were there at this time of night."

"But we're respectable."

Anatol chuckled dryly. "So are half the people in Siberian labor camps. I'm getting you back to Pavlovsk now." He stopped by a park bench and took hold of her shoulders. "Not a word about this or stolen microscopes to anyone until I return from Sverdlovsk."

"Sverdlovsk?"

"Where the electronics factory is. I've got to tighten security there. Just keep your eyes and ears open at the plant. I'll arrange to spend several days there after I get back."

"You'll be careful, won't you?" she asked, placing a hand on his arm.

"We had both better be careful from now on. Very careful."

CHAPTER TWELVE

IT TOOK THE TEAM from Moscow less than a week to discover that the pollution in the river was coming from a collective farm upstream. Laura was doubly grateful when the plant reopened. Being busy at work again not only helped to mute memories of Odessa and her concern for Anatol, but she could once again focus her energies on meeting the January first deadline. When the plant was in operation again, even Chernov seemed relieved.

He leaned forward and rested his hands on his desk, smiling at Laura, who had just remarked on the Moscow team's having cleared the plant of polluting charges quicker than she'd expected. "So," he said rather smugly, "sometimes things are handled quite efficiently here."

"I agree," she said, wondering if Chernov had paid off the inspectors. "It's good to be back at work, Yuri. There's a great deal to do before George and his people arrive."

"Yes, but you're not to brainwash my managers into thinking that power and authority aren't effective management tactics."

"Will it be all right if I suggest they aren't in first and second place?"

"You'll just confuse them."

"It's a risk I'm willing to take," she said.

"You're willing to take a lot of risks in your work, aren't you?"

"What do you mean?" she asked, suddenly thinking of Taras Luryn.

Several strained moments passed before he said quietly, "I only meant that you go at your job as though little else mattered to you."

She smiled weakly, relieved at his reply. "My job is my life."

"Then you'd better do your work carefully, hadn't you?" he advised her, standing to let her know the conversation was over.

Laura headed down the corridor toward Sergei's office. "Would you run off a printout for me on the disposition of the medical equipment Biomed shipped here?" she asked as she entered.

Sergei was opening his mail with the opener she'd given him, and he held it up so that she could see the shiny replica of the Empire State Building. "I think of you every time I use this."

Laura smiled at his childlike enjoyment. "When I get back to New York, I'll find a foot-high statue of the building and send it to you."

"Don't be so nice to me, or I'll fall in love with you the way Anatol has. By the way, where is he now?"

"He had to go to Sverdlovsk on business."

"Well, he'd better get back soon. If he wasn't my best friend, I'd chase you from here to Vladivostok."

Easing herself onto the chair next to his desk, Laura crossed her legs and plopped her clipboard on her lap. "I take it that Olga isn't the jealous type," she quipped.

"I'm the jealous one, not Olga."

Laura's smile diminished slightly as she remembered the way he had taunted Olga that evening in his apartment. "A little jealousy can be flattering, but you're also a nice guy."

"I'd rather be Tom Selleck," he remarked, unconsciously running his fingers over the scar on his face. "You know, the tall American TV star with the bright smile and the mustache like mine. Olga glues her eyes to the television whenever we watch his series."

"She's not alone. Now how about that printout?"

Sergei's fingers flew over the keyboard, and in moments the printer came to life, rapidly spewing out lines of Cyrillic letters and numerals. Tearing off the pages, he handed them to Laura.

Her eyes darted down to the listing for the high-power microscopes, then to the autoclaves. She rechecked, seeing that every one was accounted for now, the records indicating the date they were shipped and that appropriate receipts were on file.

Hiding her surprise, she asked, "Who receives the signed receipts when they arrive here?"

"Olga does, and she passes them on to me."

"And she controls the records of when purchase payments are received," Laura said pensively. After a moment, she asked, "Is payment information in the computer now?"

"Sure."

"Would you get the status on payment for the microscopes for me?"

"No problem."

Laura checked the printout when he gave it to her. Everything seemed to be in order. "Sergei, have the waste-disposal reports been computerized yet?"

"They were processed this morning. Do you want copies?"

"Please."

When he produced them, Laura saw that they indicated the plant had handled waste material appropriately.

"Come to dinner Friday evening," Sergei said. "I'll make you *golubzi*."

Cabbage rolls not high on her list of culinary delights, Laura begged off and returned to her office, the printouts clutched in her hand.

"ANATOL!" SHE EXCLAIMED, surprised and more than pleased when she found him waiting for her. "I'm so glad you're back."

After she closed the office door, he said, "Things are worse than I thought they would be at the Sverdlovsk factory. Not only are crates of tape recorders missing, so are hundreds of VCR machines."

"Look at this, though," Laura said, showing him the printouts. "All of the microscopes and autoclaves are accounted for now."

Glancing at the printout, Anatol said, "On paper they are. Chernov could be doing some innovative accounting just as the director at the Sverdlovsk factory was doing."

"But Sergei said he has receipts for every piece of Biomed's equipment that was shipped from here, and Olga has verified payment."

"How nice that everything's in order now," Anatol commented dryly. "How about Chernov? How has he been treating you?"

"All right, but I'm never sure what to expect from him next." She was about to tell him of Chernov's comment that she was willing to take a lot of risks in her job, but she decided not to, thinking she was just becoming paranoid.

"Is he still cooperating with you on the retraining of his managers?"

"Yes. The talk you had with him seems to have changed his attitude."

"Good." He and Laura turned when the office door opened and Chernov entered.

"I was told you were in the building, Anatol," he said smoothly. "Times are changing, aren't they? Even a representative of the State Planning Committee used to stop by my office first." He glanced at Laura. "Not that I blame you. Our American friend has made quite an impression on everyone here, particularly the women. They're wearing their holiday clothes and doing strange things to their hair."

"Content employees are productive employees," Laura remarked.

"We'll be able to tell more about that when the October production reports are finalized. So, Anatol, what brings you back to Pavlovsk so soon?"

"A routine visit. I'd like to go over your quality-control records."

Chernov's eyes flicked to Laura for an instant. "They're not all computerized yet. Is there a problem?"

"Just a routine check for the State Planning Committee."

"You realize," Chernov reminded him, "that I'm entitled to a written request before anyone goes through plant records."

"You've nothing to hide, have you?" Anatol asked.

"No doubt Laura has told you that I warned her about overstepping her authority here. In friendship, I'd also advise you against doing that. Our local soviet would be disheartened to learn that her capitalist ideas were rubbing off on you."

Hearing his not-so-veiled threat, Laura stepped forward. "I asked Anatol to check the records with me, Yuri. My company is willing to take great financial risks here at the plant, and it's entitled to know what it's getting into."

"Is that what the two of you believe—that I'm hiding things from Biomed? That I'm a thief perhaps?"

"Maybe you are and maybe you aren't," Anatol said, "but we both know that bribery and corruption are eating away at our country's resources. I just came from Sverdlovsk. The factory director there was being terrorized by a crime syndicate and was forced to look the other way as black marketeers hauled off merchandise. If there's anything you want to tell me, say it now."

"Let things be, Anatol," he said, his words more of a plea than an order.

"You know I can't."

Chernov flashed Laura an accusing look. "What is the saying you have . . . something about people making their own beds and having to lie in them?" The office door slammed behind him.

"Let's take a look at those files," Anatol said, re-opening the door.

"JUST AS I TOLD YOU," Laura said in the file room, "the September quality-control reports on surgical instruments and EKG machines are still missing." She flicked a finger across several other folders. "I'm not even sure we can believe what we'd find in these."

"Misha should be able to clear that up for us. I'm going to have a talk with him now."

"I already asked him about them. He said he gave the September reports to Olga, and she told me she sent them here to be filed."

"I'll talk to him, anyway."

Laura noted the hardness in his eyes, and she knew how easily Misha could get upset. "No, Anatol, let me check with him again, please. Wait for me in my office. I won't be long."

She went directly to Misha's office and was told he had gone to the plant cafeteria. There, she saw him seated at a table in the corner by himself, hunched over a glass of tea.

"Misha," Laura asked, taking note of the drawn look on his face and his glassy eyes, "do you mind if I join you?"

He half rose, then shook his head.

Sitting across from him, she hesitated, then asked, "Were you able to locate the September reports?"

"You have a fixation about those, don't you, Laura?"

Even though Misha had his hands cupped tightly around his glass, she could see his fingers shaking. She hated pressuring him this way, but she firmly believed that the unaccounted for surgical instruments and EKG machines might just be the tip of the iceberg, that probably there had been other thefts at the plant.

As kindly as she could, she said, "Misha, I suspect that some of our records have been falsified, and it's my obligation to either prove or disprove that before Biomed begins operating here. I need your help to do that."

His eyes narrowed as if he were trying to focus on her, then he chuckled quietly. "How can I help you when I can't even help myself?"

"If you're in some kind of trouble, tell me and I'll do whatever I can."

"No one can help me, not even you."

"Maybe I could, if you'd tell me what's wrong."

"It's too late for help. It's too late for anything."

Deeply troubled by his depressed mood, Laura placed a hand over his. "Don't say that. It's never too late to put things in order."

After a few silent moments, his words seemingly forced out, he asked, "You really believe that, don't you?"

"Yes, I do. Now tell me what's gotten you so worked up."

He let out a short, harsh laugh. "You won't like it."

"Let me decide that."

His expression mirrored mixed inner emotions that made Laura suspect he was arguing with himself. Then he slowly nodded. "All right, but I won't discuss it with you here."

"I'm available whenever you like."

"I'll come by your apartment tonight, if that's—"

"Don't make it tonight," a man's voice said. Laura's and Misha's heads swung toward Sergei, who stood smiling down at them. "Laura and Anatol are having dinner with Olga and me."

Misha sprang up so quickly that Laura thought he was going to stumble over his chair. Standing, she told him, "We'll talk tomorrow, Misha, all right?"

"Yes," he said quietly, not taking his eyes from Sergei.

THAT EVENING at Olga and Sergei's apartment, Laura again brought up the issue of the missing reports.

"So," Olga said, "the reports must have been misfiled. They'll turn up as the rest of the files are transferred into the computer."

"I hope so," Anatol remarked, taking another swallow of his vodka before looking over at Sergei, who was sitting next to Laura on the sofa. "It's not just the missing files that I'm concerned about. I think someone at the plant may be stealing inventory."

"I would know," Sergei objected forcefully.

"That's exactly what everyone will think if it turns out plant supplies are missing," Anatol said.

Olga placed a hand on Sergei's shoulder. "That's ridiculous! Sergei wouldn't take a bottle of aspirin from the plant."

Laura said, "We aren't suggesting that you would steal anything, Sergei, but someone could make it look like you were involved."

"Sergei," Anatol said, sitting on a chair across from him, "there's going to be an audit done at the plant, a thorough one that will review every major transaction for the past year. We'll know if listed sales were actually made to the recorded recipients and if products declared defective were disposed of properly."

Holding a small silver tray of after-dinner mints toward Anatol, Olga said, "All the departments at the plant would have to be checked on, not just inventory control."

"But," Sergei reminded her, "the accuracy of information stored in the computer is my responsibility. I'm supposed to cross-check department reports."

"Now that they're computerized," she said. "But in the past it was an impossible job."

"Sergei," Laura said, "when I first checked the files, I found that seven of Biomed's high-power microscopes and five autoclaves were unaccounted for. Suddenly they are. Why did you change the records?"

"He didn't," Olga admitted. "I did. My computer ties into the main terminal. I found an error had been made and corrected it."

Sergei looked up at her quizzically. "I didn't know you did that."

Olga smiled and ruffled his hair. "If I took time to tell everyone at work what I was doing, I wouldn't get half of it done." She glanced over at Anatol. "It seems to me you're making a mountain out of a molehill with this investigation of yours."

"It's only an audit," Laura said, "something that should be done periodically as a matter of routine."

Olga ran a hand over the side of her dark hair. "If the audit does show that supplies are missing, you'd be wiser to check on the people in the shipping department, not Sergei."

"This is crazy," Sergei insisted. "Here we are pointing accusing fingers at people, and there's no proof of any wrongdoing."

"We almost had proof," Laura said.

"What proof?" Olga asked warily.

Anatol leaned forward. "We traced what we believed was some of Biomed's equipment to Odessa."

"A man offered to sell them to us," Laura added, "but before he could he . . . he died."

"He was murdered," Anatol clarified.

"Murdered?" Sergei repeated, rising from the sofa as Olga placed a hand over her mouth.

Anatol nodded. "The man was suspected of being involved with a crime syndicate that deals in stolen state-owned property."

"Olga," Laura asked, "can you verify that Biomed's microscopes were actually received and paid for by the purchasers listed in the records?"

Obviously shaken, she was slow to reply. "Certainly, but it . . . it would take some time. It's not a simple matter of just picking up the phone."

"It can't be all that difficult," Laura said.

"Getting photostats of financial transactions has to be requested in writing by Yuri. Most plant and factory directors guard their records as though they were state secrets."

Sergei added, "They're all suspicious of each other or are trying to hide their economic failures."

"If Yuri does have something to hide," Anatol said, "he could manage a complete cover-up by the time the audit is done in December."

Still upset, Olga blurted out, "If he was doing anything illegal, don't you think I'd know about it?"

Laura's eyes shifted from one person to the other, then settled on Olga. "Anatol and I can't be the only ones who believe something illegal is going on at the plant. We've got to do something. If Yuri or someone else is involved with organized crime, that person might even be able to pay off the auditors." To Anatol she said, "I think you should report what we suspect is going on to the Foreign Economic Commission."

"Be careful, Laura," Olga warned. "Some powerful people could be involved, even the ones Anatol might report his suspicions to. It's not inconceivable for a person to disappear here without a trace."

"Olga's right," Anatol agreed. "We've got to think carefully before reporting anything without sufficient evidence."

Exasperated, Laura said abruptly, "I don't see how the three of you can just sit by, knowing that something is wrong. I can't prove it, but I'd swear the man in Odessa was killed because he was going to give us the proof we needed. And from what I've seen in comparing the plant's overall production figures and recorded profits, something is wrong there, too. If the sales are correct, the plant should have more money in the bank than it does."

Tempering her voice, she said to Olga. "You handle the financial records. Haven't you noticed any discrepancies?"

A look of consternation on her face, Olga replied, "No, I haven't, but Misha did tell me how you've been nagging him, and I don't understand why. He didn't lose the September quality-control reports, and neither did I. And I've already explained the problems he has with the other two inspectors. Why do you keep looking for problems where none exists?"

Sergei sat next to Laura and placed a hand on her shoulder. "Listen to Olga and Anatol, please. Here, people are normally suspicious of each other, and we've been taught to be extra cautious where foreigners are concerned. If you continue to stir things up, the authorities will think you're trying to make us look bad."

Not wanting Laura to say more just now, Anatol stood up. "Laura won't mention this talk to anyone, and I hope the two of you will keep this talk confidential, as well."

"You're forgetting that I have an obligation to my company," Laura said.

"Are you going to report what you've told us to Biomed?" Olga asked.

"I will report that there could well be a lack of adequate security at the plant. How they follow up on that is for them to decide. But I wouldn't be surprised if they choose to contact the Foreign Economic Commission."

"I think it's time we left," Anatol suggested.

At the door, while Anatol thanked Olga for her hospitality, Sergei lowered his voice and asked Laura, "What did you say to Misha in the cafeteria to shake him up so?"

"Nothing. I just asked if he had found the September quality-control reports."

"Did he say what he wanted to talk to you about tomorrow?"

"No," she said, slipping into the coat that Sergei held for her.

Anatol thumped Sergei's back. "Thank you, too. You're a first-class cook."

Opening the apartment door, he grinned. "That comes from liking to eat. Now that you're living at the dacha, don't make yourself a stranger around here."

The moment Sergei closed the door behind Laura and Anatol, he spun around to face Olga. "Why did you think it was necessary to defend me the way you did? Do you really think I'd be involved in criminal activity at the plant?"

"Of course not, but you heard what Laura said. It could look like you were."

"Why...because the inventory files are a mess right now? As soon as my people finish computerizing them, I'll be able to pinpoint any irregularities. If there are any, they won't be in my department."

Olga started to clear the buffet table, then stopped and looked over at Sergei. "What if Misha's quality-control reports show irregularities?"

"Why should they?"

"What if they don't agree with the quality-control reports filed by the inspectors from Leningrad and Moscow? Will you report it?"

Sergei stared at her, confusion in his eyes. "Why shouldn't they agree? What's going on in that head of yours? First you think it's necessary to defend me, and now you're worrying about Misha. Has he said anything to you that I should know about?"

Carrying some plates to the kitchen, she said, "I just asked what you would do if Misha's reports weren't in order."

"What would you expect me to do?" he asked, following her.

"I don't know," she answered irritably, "but I do know that Misha wouldn't do anything illegal unless he was forced to."

"Forced to? Olga, why would you even suggest something like that?"

"I'm not suggesting it. It's just that all this talk about black marketeers and someone at the plant working with them has me upset."

"Is that why you're going into Leningrad Friday—to get calmed down?"

Rinsing the plates at the sink she said, "I told you. It's plant business."

"Yes, at the Ministry of Health. Who knows? With any luck you might bump into Dmitri."

As her head jerked toward Sergei, Olga's expression changed from concern to defiance. "I'm not going to apologize for anything I do. You knew from the beginning that I want more out of life than to be stuck here in Pavlovsk. I want to live and work in Moscow. Dmitri can help me."

"He's not going to help you. He's using you."

"Maybe I'm using him," she said defiantly, sweeping past Sergei and returning to the living room.

Silently he watched her place a bowl of imitation fruit on the table. Then his voice became even more surly. "His being handsome doesn't hurt, I imagine, not when you've been stuck with someone who looks the way I do."

Olga's eyes flashed up at him. "I've loved you as much as I can love anyone. But this—" she scanned the apartment "—isn't enough! I'm still young. I want as much from life as I can get. I want nice clothes and furs and jewelry, like Dmitri's wife has. I want a reserved seat at the theater and the opera on opening night. Those things are important to me. Can't you understand that?''

Sergei's dark eyes narrowed. "Can't you understand that I've been as generous to you as I can afford?''

"I've paid my share of our expenses here.''

"With Dmitri's help," he snapped. "It doesn't bother you a bit that you've been using me just the way he's using you, does it?''

Lowering her voice, Olga said, "Be honest, Sergei. Haven't you been using me, also?''

She lifted her chin defiantly when Sergei started toward her. Then with relief she watched as he grabbed his coat and stalked out the door.

"I'M TEMPTED TO GIVE UP on this assignment and go home," Laura confessed to Anatol as he drove her to her apartment.

"I wouldn't blame you if you did. But I'd miss you.''

"I'd be leaving soon, anyway," she reminded him.

"Not until the end of next month.''

"I'm not sure I can last that long. Back home, the world of business can get pretty rough, but nothing like this.''

"We see news reports of how organized crime operates in your country. It's probably the same everywhere.''

"At home it's never touched me the way it has here, Anatol.''

After a painful silence, he asked, "Is it the plant...or me that you want to get away from?''

"You know better than to ask that.''

"Then don't talk about leaving until you have to. Who knows? You might decide to stay on for a while longer. You could do wonders at the plant if you did."

"That's George Hardcastle's job. I'm an advance person for Biomed, and I'm already scheduled to be at three plants they're taking over in the States next year."

"You're obsessed with your work, aren't you?"

"Aren't you?"

Ignoring her question, he said, "Your fluency in Russian makes you extremely valuable right here. I don't understand how you'll be able to abandon the work you've started at the plant."

"It's not just my career that I'm thinking about, Anatol. You've taught me that there are more important things in life other than work."

"Like what?" he asked, pulling onto the street where she lived.

"Like my personal life. When I get home, I'm going to do some serious thinking. I have to. Time is running out for me if I want to have a family."

"Are you going to marry Roger?" he asked curtly.

She frowned and looked at the dark road ahead. "No, not Roger. But I do want to get married. You should marry again. In spite of the problems between you and Valentin, I think you're basically a family man. You'd be happier with a wife."

"You and I could be happy together."

"Please, Anatol, don't talk like that. Your life is here. Mine is in New York."

Parking in front of her building, he twisted his body toward her and extended his arm over the back of the car seat. "You know I love you. Doesn't that make any difference?"

"Are you so sure it's love that you feel and not just need?"

"Oh, I know the difference. I've made love to women out of need," he admitted. "But as soon as it was over I was satisfied. That's not the way it is with you, Larashka. After we make love, I want to hold you so you can't get away from me. I want you beside me when I go to sleep, and I want you there when I wake up. That's not need. That's love."

Biting her lip, Laura looked away. "It's late. I should go in."

"Come back to the dacha with me," he pleaded.

"Anatol," she said quietly, her head bowed, "it just can't work, not for us."

"You could move in with me, and we could try to make it work. You might even decide you want to stay here permanently."

She raised her head and stared at him in disbelief. "You say that as if I'd just be moving from one city to another. Don't you realize what you're asking of me? Would you consider moving to America?"

"What would I do in America? Drive a bus? Besides, you know I can't leave."

"Why not? Wouldn't the government let you?"

"They might. But you can't expect me to forget about my son or my parents. And I have important work to do here."

"I have family back home, too, remember? And my work is as important to me as yours is to you."

"Laura, your job is to make money for Biomed. What I'm doing is fighting for my country's survival. If people like me can't improve the way things are run here, then pretty soon, there won't be a Soviet Union anymore. Maybe, as an American, you don't care about that. But I do.''

"Ah," she said, nodding. "So your work would come first, and I would come second. Isn't that how it was with you and Yelena, and isn't that exactly what you found so blamable in her, that her work came first? And your son, where would he fit in . . . a distant third?"

"Valentin has nothing to do with you and me."

"That's something else we'd never agree on. He's your son, and you have a responsibility to make him feel loved. You do love him, don't you?"

"Of course I do," Anatol insisted.

"But you just don't like the way he thinks."

"I don't want him putting himself in danger."

"You don't want. That's exactly the way you talk to Valentin. No, let me correct myself. You don't talk to him. You lecture him. And if I were to stay in the Soviet Union, you'd be lecturing me, too."

"Is that what you really believe?"

She despaired of making him understand how impossible it was for her to stay. "Anatol, please, let's not hurt each other like this."

He chuckled softly. "I thought I was the one who was bleeding."

Laura glanced toward the Soviet headquarters on the first floor of her building and saw that a light was on. Her eyes drifted up to the dark windows of her apartment. She looked back at Anatol when he touched her shoulder.

"I wish you'd change your mind and come back to the dacha." She shook her head. "Then let's plan on having dinner in Leningrad tomorrow night,'' he suggested, wanting to smooth things over between them.

"Yes, I'd like that,'' she answered, then quickly got out of the car, afraid she might change her mind.

CHAPTER THIRTEEN

LAURA WATCHED SADLY as Anatol's car disappeared around a corner. Again she glanced up at her dark windows, knowing that if she went directly to bed she would toss and turn for hours. Too many disturbing thoughts were running through her mind: her feelings for Anatol, his for her, the warnings thrust at her by Olga and Sergei, Misha's desperation. Pulling up the fur collar of her coat, she started walking toward Pavlovsk Park, her fur-lined boots crunching in the light snow that had fallen earlier.

A half hour later she was deep into the park, staring down a steep stone staircase leading to the Slavyanka River. Absently she ran a gloved hand over the side of a huge white stone lion, then glanced at his companion on the other side of the top step.

Her head jerked to the right suddenly. Did she imagine it, or had someone moved between the white birch trees in the distance? Was it someone from the Soviet headquarters following her again? she wondered. Not wanting to find out, she hurried back down the pathway, glancing back over her shoulder.

Yes, someone was following her!

She raced over a small wooden bridge, the heels of her boots clacking, giving her away. On the other side she darted off the path into the soft snow. Reaching a copse of fir trees, she braced her back against a trunk to catch her breath and to listen.

The syncopated pounding of footsteps running over the bridge sent a surge of terror rushing through her, and she scanned the area, wondering which way to run.

In the distance, through the night haze, she spotted the park's circular Greek-style temple and ran to it. Her heart thumping, she raced up the steps and hid behind one of the tall columns, covering her mouth to muffle her gasps for breath.

A cloud drifted under the half moon overhead, cutting off the meager light. Straining her ears, she heard what sounded like slow footfalls mounting the circular steps of the temple. Stifling a cry, she backed away to the next column, then to the next, listening as the click of footsteps on the marble came closer.

When she reached the other side of the temple, she didn't know what to do. If she continued around, she might even bump into whoever it was.

Suddenly it was quiet, deathly quiet.

She looked to her right, then to her left, her pulse pounding in her ears. The cloud slipped from under the moon, which rayed enough light for her to see an elongated shadow moving toward her on the curved marble floor.

Noiselessly she moved backward toward the steps of the temple, turned and darted toward the fir trees and froze. Again she listened. Was she imagining it, or were there now two people at the temple? Yes, and they were arguing. Of that she was sure, but she couldn't hear well enough to recognize the voices, never mind understand what they were saying.

Laura jumped when an ear-piercing sound like a car backfiring cut through the night air!

Then, deadly silence.

Her heart in her throat, she edged her way around several trees, wanting to get out of the park as quickly as possible. Then she heard someone running back over the bridge. Only one person, she decided.

And the other?

Against her better judgment she cautiously retraced her steps toward the temple. Reaching the edge of the trees, she paused and peered through the haze that hovered over the snow-covered ground.

The silence was terrifying.

As she approached the temple, a night bird swooped low, startling her. Gathering her courage, she moved closer, taking one step up, then another, placing a hand on a column. Slowly she walked around to the front of the temple.

Suddenly she froze. There was something on the ground! As she moved closer, her eyes widened. Black boots jutted out from behind one of the columns.

Forcing herself on, Laura raised her hand, prepared to silence the scream that was gathering in her throat as she moved closer and saw more of the prone body that lay across the temple steps.

"Ohh!" she gasped, covering her mouth.

Staring at her blankly, a gun clutched in his right hand, lay Misha Vinokurov, a circle of blood on the right side of his forehead.

Laura turned and ran. By the time she reached the street at the edge of the park, her lungs felt ready to burst. Gasping for air, she staggered down the road and at last reached her apartment. Swinging the door shut behind her, she slammed the dead bolt in place, dragged herself to the phone and called Anatol.

THE MOMENT the Leningrad militiamen left Laura's apartment, Anatol took her in his arms. "I'll stay here with you tonight," he said, massaging her back with comforting strokes.

"Thank you," she whispered, still in a daze from the horrifying experience and the questions of the investigators, who Anatol had phoned.

"Are you certain you heard Misha talking to someone else?"

"Talking? He was arguing with whoever it was. Then there was that awful sound." Pacing, she asked, "Why didn't the officers believe me? Why are they so certain that Misha committed suicide? Yes, he was high-strung, maybe on the brink of a nervous breakdown, but when I spoke with him today, it seemed as though he had finally decided to confide in me."

"I wish he had told you then what was bothering him." Anatol paused briefly. "Misha was always so mild-mannered that it's hard to think of him making enemies, never mind one who would kill him."

"Anatol," Laura asked quietly, "why would Misha have followed me into the park and then...do what he did?" She shook her head. "It doesn't make sense. I'm certain someone else was there with him."

"The gun could have belonged to whoever it was," Anatol said darkly. "That someone could have wanted to stop Misha from talking to you."

"It had something to do with the plant," Laura said, sinking onto the sofa. "I'm sure of it."

Wishing he could relieve the worry he saw on Laura's face, Anatol eased her legs onto the sofa, slipped off the afghan that was draped over the back of it and covered her legs. "Are you feeling better?" he asked.

"Yes," she lied for his benefit.

Lowering himself to the carpet, he rested an arm on the sofa seat and placed his hand on her afghan-covered leg. Silently he traced one of the knitted geometric patterns, desperately wishing he could shut out the terrifying events that Laura had gone through in recent weeks.

Laura covered his hand with hers and said quietly, "You should get some sleep. You have to be in Moscow tomorrow."

"I can't leave you at a time like this," he said, shaking his head. "I'll postpone the meeting."

Laura smiled weakly as she ran her fingertips through his hair. "You know you can't do that. The people from Amtorg have come all the way from New York to consult with you."

"Investigators will be at the plant tomorrow, asking all kinds of questions about Misha. I don't want you to have to go through that alone."

"I won't be alone. Sergei and Olga will be there." Laura thought a moment. "Do you think we should call them and tell them what happened?"

"May as well let them sleep," he suggested. "I'll phone them in the morning."

"Before you leave for Moscow," Laura said to emphasize that he was going.

"Are you so anxious to get rid of me?"

"You know I'm not. But we both still have jobs to do. I'll be fine. Honest."

"You're sure?"

"Uh-huh."

"All right," he said, taking hold of her hand and giving it a tug. "I'll get back here as soon as I can—by Friday at the latest."

He became pensive, then raised himself, slipped onto the sofa and braced a hand on the back of it. "This weekend I want you to move into the dacha with me," he said, his tone leaving little room for argument.

Laura pondered that, deciding that doing so had great appeal. After what had happened in the park, she wasn't looking forward to being alone in her apartment night after night. Equally appealing was the prospect of falling asleep every night, secure in Anatol's arms. After all, he had moved from his Leningrad apartment so that they could have more time together. And time for them was running out.

"Will you?" he asked, his gaze unwavering.

"Yes," she said softly, wishing with all her heart that they had met in another time, in another place.

IT WAS DIFFICULT to get much work done at the plant the next few days as the investigators from Leningrad queried everyone about Misha's business and personal life. Laura was prepared for Sergei, Olga and Chernov to be shocked, but she sensed another emotion, particularly in Olga and Chernov, a reaction that she thought was more akin to fear. But each time Laura tried to get the two of them to talk about Misha, they clammed up. Sergei was the only one who let Laura see his personal grief. An uneasy routine gradually returned at the plant after Misha's death was formally declared a suicide.

In her office Laura stared at the confidential report to Biomed she had just signed. It clearly outlined the difficulties she was having and those she foresaw for the company if it proceeded with the joint venture. Silently she struggled with her obligation to send it and her hopes that the venture might yet be saved somehow—for herself, for Anatol and for the people at the plant who were depending on Biomed to make changes for the better.

She picked up the envelope and stared at the New York address. It seemed a world away. Dropping it facedown, she searched desperately for a reason, or some excuse, not to send the report as she had written it.

What could she prove that was wrong, really? she rationalized. Chernov was at best ambivalent, fighting her one day, supporting her the next. And the missing supplies were no longer missing—according to the computer.

As usual, thoughts of Anatol's deep concern for the venture's success came to the fore. She knew he had laid his career on the line for it. And if the venture were a success, other medical supply plants would also be opened for cooperative ventures. Biomed could profit from them, as well.

Distracted from her thoughts, Laura looked up when Sergei entered. She smiled at his wide-eyed grin and the dark brown hair that usually looked as though someone had worked on it with an eggbeater.

"I've found the quality-control reports for September," he said, obviously pleased with himself.

Taking the documents from him, Laura scanned the three reports that Misha and the representatives from

Leningrad and Moscow had submitted. Laura noted that half of the sets of surgical instruments and EKG machines had indeed been rejected that month. The reason given: defective production machinery. The finalized report was signed by Misha Vinokurov.

"Where were they?" Laura asked.

"Mixed in with Misha's analysis of performance standards reports."

"Well, that seems to clear that mystery up," she said dubiously, handing the papers back to Sergei.

"Olga wants to go to Moscow this weekend to see Vladimir Nemakhin's new exhibit of paintings and bronze sculptures. Why don't you and Anatol come with us?"

"We'll pass this time, but thanks for the invitation. I doubt if he'll feel like going back to Moscow right away, and I've got a million things to do on the weekend." *Moving into his dacha, for one,* she added silently, smiling at the thought.

"This busy weekend of yours," Sergei asked teasingly, "could it have anything to do with my friend Anatol?"

"Possibly," she returned, leaning back in her chair.

"You two are very good for each other," he said warmly. "I've never seen Anatol so happy, and you glow like the northern lights whenever he walks into the room."

"Is it that obvious?"

"It's that wonderful." Sighing deeply, he added, "I used to have that effect on Olga, but—" he shrugged and started toward the office door "—people's feelings change, don't they?"

Yes, they do, Laura thought. But she knew in her heart that her feelings for Anatol would never change, not even after she returned home. Not wanting to think of that, she turned her attention back to the report in her typewriter.

She scanned it once more, jerked it from the machine and tossed it into the wastebasket. Inserting a blank sheet of paper, she quickly retyped a more optimistic report to Biomed, then took the envelope to the reception desk, wanting to get it out in the day's mail.

"Lydia," she asked, handing her the envelope, "any news on who the new quality-control manager is going to be?"

"It's not definite, but word has it that the director wants Sergei to take charge of quality control as well as inventory control."

"Sergei? That's really piling the work on him."

Lowering her voice, Lydia commented, "Wasn't it terrible about Misha? And poor Sergei."

"Why poor Sergei?"

"The argument they had the day Misha died. Didn't you hear them? Everyone else in the plant did."

"No, I didn't. What were they arguing about?"

"I don't know, but Sergei must be feeling awful. You know, if you have a quarrel with a good friend, and he's suddenly hit by a car or something, you regret not having made up before it happened. I still can't believe we won't see Misha again." She picked up a water globe from her desk and tilted it. Little snowflakes fell over a cabin in the woods. "He brought this back from Odessa for me. He said it reminded him of Siberia."

"Odessa," Laura repeated. "When was Misha in Odessa?"

"A few weeks ago when the plant was closed." Her phone rang and she answered.

Misha was in Odessa the same time that Taras Luryn was murdered, Laura thought as she returned to her office. But that didn't mean they saw each other or even knew each other. And it certainly didn't mean that Misha had killed Luryn. Laura had a difficult time imagining Misha killing himself, never mind someone else. "Coincidence," she mumbled.

Closing her office door, she continued mulling over what Lydia had just told her. But if Misha was silenced because he knew that something illegal was going on at the plant, and if Taras Luryn was killed because he'd gotten hold of the plant's medical equipment, maybe there was a connection between the two men. But what?

Going to the window, she stared out blankly, wondering what Anatol would have to say when she told him.

ANATOL WAS IN THE MIDDLE of shaving when he heard a knock on the apartment door. Opening it, he was surprised to see his son.

"Can I come in?" Valentin asked.

"Sure," his father said, wondering what the problem was. The few times his son had come to his apartment in the past was because the boy had had deep trouble he couldn't handle himself. "Take off your coat and stay awhile," Anatol suggested, then returned to the bathroom to finish shaving.

Valentin tossed his fleece-lined jacket on a chair and followed his father. Propping a shoulder against the doorframe, he lowered his head and studied his shoes. From the corner of his eye, Anatol examined his downcast expression. "You look like you just lost your best friend."

"I have. Katya says we should cool things off for a while."

"Any particular reason?" Anatol asked, surprised and pleased that his son wanted to talk to him about it.

"She keeps throwing Nikolai in my face. We were at his and Tatyana's apartment last night, and after we left, Katya started nagging me about not having plans for my life."

"The way I nag you," Anatol said, running water over his razor.

"Yeah."

Anatol's lips parted, but, remembering Laura's advice that he listen to his son for a change, he asked, "What do you think about her suggestion?"

"I think it stinks. So do the guys I talked to."

"The guys with the spiked hair and metal jewelry?" Anatol asked, then clamped his jaw shut to keep any other negative words from slipping out. "Your friends, I mean. What advice did they give you?"

"They weren't much help. They think she's stuck-up, anyway."

"What do you think?"

"I like her just the way she is."

"I do, too," Anatol agreed as he dried his face and patted on some after-shave.

"Dad," Valentin said, following his father to the bedroom.

Hearing his son call him *Dad,* Anatol almost tripped over his feet. Usually he addressed him with the impersonal *you*.

As his father reached for a shirt from a dresser drawer, Valentin continued. "You were young once. Were you always so sure of what you wanted to do?"

Anatol turned, gaping at his son. "As long ago as that was, I do remember that I had very few choices."

"But if you'd had, would you have known what you'd be doing today?"

As he buttoned his shirt, Anatol thought hard about that. "No," he said, shaking his head, "I wouldn't have. In fact, I would have been surprised as hell if I could have foreseen that I'd end up where I am now." Shoving the shirttails under the waistband of his pants, he asked, "Are you wondering what you'll be doing when you're forty?"

His son chuckled. "God, no. I'm just trying to get through this year." He glanced at the suitcase on the bed. "Off on another business trip?"

"No. I'm spending some time at the dacha."

"Oh . . . with Laura. I like her. She's pretty cool."

"Cool? Yes, I guess you could say that." Snapping the suitcase shut, Anatol tugged a tie loose from the rack behind the closet door and started putting it on. "Valentin, I want to talk to you about your going into the army. No," he corrected himself, "I want you to tell me how you feel about it."

Plopping onto the bed, Valentin let his body fall backward and rested on his arms. "I've got to go. It's the law."

"You don't have to go. You have choices now. You'd be exempt if you'd attend a university instead. You could stay right here in the city, see Katya, your mother...and me if you wanted to. What do you think about trying that?''

Valentin eyed his father suspiciously, not used to being asked for his opinion.

"Well, what do you think?" Anatol repeated.

Valentin sat up and crossed his arms on the wooden footboard. "What would I study?"

"Study music, join a rock band if that's what you want to do."

Testing his father, Valentin asked, "Could I get a punk cut and dye my hair three different colors? Maybe I should have it all shaved off and get a tattoo?"

Anatol winced, biting his tongue before turning. He leaned back against the dresser and braced his hands on it. "If that would really make you happy—" he had to force the words out "—that's what you should do."

"Naw. I'm only kidding. I'd look like a mess. Besides, rock music is just something I like at times. I wouldn't want to spend my life screaming and jumping up and down on a stage."

"Any ideas about how you might want to spend your life?" When his son hesitated, Anatol went on. "How about majoring in environmental studies? You want clean air for your kids to breathe, don't you? God knows, we could all use a better water supply here in Leningrad."

"I doubt if I could get into a university. My grades haven't been all that good this year."

"You've got time to bring them up. Do that and I guarantee you'll be accepted."

"I don't want to get in on your pull."

"Why not?" Anatol asked as calmly as he could. "If everyone's going to accuse me of being a bureaucrat, I'm going to get some benefit out of it. Besides, look at it this way. You'll be able to do a hell of a lot more as a trained ecologist than by demonstrating."

"School would be expensive," Valentin said tentatively.

"I'm not a pauper. So," he asked, ruffling his son's hair, "want to give it a try?"

Valentin turned it over in his mind a few times. "It'd make Katya happy."

"It would make your mother and me happy, too, but don't do it for that reason. Do it because it would make you happy. Once you're at the university, you might even find that you'd rather pursue some other course of study. But whatever you decide, I want you to know you'll have my support."

"Dad," Valentin asked suspiciously, "you're not on anything, are you?"

Anatol stared at him, then chuckled. "No. It's just that at my age the mind tends to go, and sometimes it takes me a little longer to see the light." Slipping into his jacket, he picked up the suitcase and went into the living room. "Tell Katya what you've decided, and I'll bet she'll want things between you to warm up again. Also tell your mother. She'll be pleased." He reached for his overcoat. "And let's continue this conversation real soon. Why don't you ask Katya if she'd like to have dinner with us, and Laura. We could go to the Astoria. I doubt if Nikolai takes Tatyana there."

"That'd be neat," Valentin said, his eyes lighting up as he picked up his father's suitcase. "I'll carry this down to the car for you."

"Thanks. Us old folks have to avoid any unnecessary strain."

Valentin gave him the once-over. "I don't know. You're in pretty good shape." He opened the apartment door. "Oh, say hi to Laura for me."

LAURA WAS SITTING in front of the fireplace at Anatol's dacha, listening to a music tape of Russian folksongs. Her eyes drifted to the clean white snow falling outside the window. Soon she would be back in Manhattan, she thought, trudging through the brown slush on Madison Avenue.

Giving in to a flight of fancy, she wondered if remaining in the Soviet Union for just an extra week or two would cause the earth to stop spinning.

You're entitled to a vacation, she rationalized. *All work and no play makes Laura a dull girl.* But if she stayed, she wouldn't be playing. And she wouldn't be making things any better, either. She'd only be postponing the inevitable.

With an effort she shut off that train of thought and went to the kitchen to prepare the chicken she planned to fry Kentucky-style for Anatol.

Just as she finished, she heard the apartment door open and hurried back into the living room. Anatol was there, smiling, with snowflakes dotting his muskrat hat and the black fur on the collar of his overcoat.

Her heartbeat racing, she rushed to him. "You must be numb from the cold."

Anatol stomped his feet on the throw rug by the door and set his suitcase down. "Cold? It's only twenty-five degrees outside. That's practically summer weather."

He hung his muskrat hat and his coat on pegs and pulled off his overshoes. Then before he could budge from the entryway, Laura snuggled against him, her arms around his warm sweater. "I'm so glad you're back," she whispered.

Pressing his cheek against the side of her hair, he asked quietly, "Is the lady saying she missed me?"

"She is."

With a gentle finger, he tilted her face up. "I thought of you all the time I was gone, and of this." He kissed her with a hunger that warmed her toes and made them tingle.

Flushed, she took hold of his arm as they walked into the living room. "How did your trip go?" she asked.

Anatol crossed to the fireplace and raked his fingers through his hair. "There's good news and there's bad."

"The good news first," she suggested.

"We're going to increase the size of the Soviet trade delegation in New York. The progressive elements in our government are eager to do more business with America."

"That's wonderful," she said, wondering about the frown that settled on his face. "What's the bad news?"

"The government's refused to let me go ahead with a joint Soviet-American venture for a factory in Minsk that manufactures construction materials."

"Why not, for heaven's sake?"

"Heaven has nothing to do with it. It's the hellish power struggle going on in the Kremlin. While half the people in our government are all for Soviet-American business, the other half hates the idea."

"I guess that puts you in a difficult position."

"Yes, it does. And the worst of it is that now I've got to be in Minsk on Monday."

"Oh," she said, her disappointment obvious.

"I wouldn't go if I didn't have to," he said, massaging the back of his neck. "God, sometimes I feel like I'm beating my head against a brick wall."

Moving to the sofa, she sat down slowly. "If you have to go, you have to go."

Anatol sat next to her and took one of her hands in his. Smiling he said, "Guess who came by the apartment while I was there."

His smile brightened her mood. "Male or female?"

"Male, young."

Laura beamed. "Valentin?"

"Uh-huh. He actually wanted advice from his aged father. We had a good talk. No challenging each other. Just an honest, open talk like we used to have. I think he'll decide to attend Leningrad University next year."

Laura rested her head on Anatol's shoulder. "I'm so proud of you, of both of you," she said softly.

Anatol brought her hand to his lips and kissed it. "It's all your doing, you know. You made me see what should have been obvious to me all along."

"That Valentin loves you?"

"Maybe. But I'll settle for him needing me and wanting me to be part of his life." As he tilted Laura's chin up, Anatol's voice took on a velvety softness. "I didn't realize how important it was to feel needed and wanted, not until I met you."

"You make me feel needed and wanted, too, Anatol."

"Then," he said easing his thumb across the corner of her chin, "don't leave. Stay here and marry me."

CHAPTER FOURTEEN

LAURA'S SMILE DISAPPEARED. She drew back from Anatol, too startled to say a word. Disoriented, she crossed her arms and stared across the room before glancing back at him for an instant.

Her negative reaction brought Anatol down to earth fast. He suffered through Laura's silence for as long as he could, then, with staid calmness, said, "I take it the idea of marrying me doesn't hold a great deal of charm for you."

Hardly able to believe what he was saying, Laura's eyes swept back to him. "You talk as if it would be easy for me to stay here."

"It doesn't have to be difficult."

"Not for you perhaps. But for me it would mean restructuring my whole life."

"I'd help see you through it. I love you, Laura."

Dear God, but she was tempted to say yes, to think about nothing except the soothing comfort of being so close to him, so wanted, so loved. But by training she always looked beyond short-range gains to long-range needs. The realization that she would eventually have to pay the piper was crystal clear to her. Standing abruptly, she asked, "Would you like something to drink before dinner?"

"That's quite a departure from what we were talking about."

His tense expression made her feel even more unsettled. "Even discussing my staying here is crazy. Don't you realize the problems I'd have?"

"You knew there'd be problems when you took on this assignment for Biomed. That didn't stop you."

"Anatol, three months in this country is a lot different from relocating here for the rest of my life. And be honest, just how much do we really know about each other?"

"We respect each other and our work, and we are, to say the least, compatible."

"What about our basic beliefs, our backgrounds? I honestly don't believe I could make the adjustment."

"It would be a risk for you, I know, but you're not a woman who's afraid to take risks. If you were, you wouldn't have come here in the first place."

"How much do you expect me to risk for loving you, Anatol? What price should I be expected to pay, with only the hope that things would work out for us?"

"Larashka," he said enthusiastically, jumping up and taking hold of her shoulders, "you can have a career anywhere in the world. You can even fall in love anywhere. But if you can have those two things and spend your life making a real difference, wouldn't that be worth taking a risk?"

"If I thought I was up to it, it might be," she said, feeling more trapped by the second, "but I'm no Joan of Arc. There are no voices driving me on to a mission."

"Except in your work," he remarked quietly, letting his hands fall to his sides. "Maybe you're right. Maybe I am asking too much of you."

"Anatol," she said softly, not able to look at him, "We agreed we wouldn't promise each other anything."

"We did, didn't we?" he said, his voice husky. "But what if I've changed my mind?"

Hurting for him and for herself, she went to him, slipped her hands around his waist and rested her head on his shoulders, feeling his arms embrace her. "Ours is a joint venture, too. We both have a say on how it moves along."

"And you insist on fifty-one percent of the control," he said, his voice resigned.

Through the soft wool of his sweater she could feel the pounding of his heart, feel the rise and fall of his chest with every breath he took. "Right now it would be so easy for me to give in to you completely, Anatol, so very easy. But to do so I'd have to think only of the present, not what would lay ahead for us."

"Laura, I—"

She lifted her head and placed her fingers over his lips. "No more talk, not now. Love me, Anatol, just love me as though the present was all that mattered."

A heaviness centered in his chest, he gazed deeply into her glistening eyes, then kissed her long and hard.

HOURS LATER, as they lay in bed, Anatol's arms wrapped around her possessively, Laura forced their earlier conversation from her thoughts by thinking of the plant. Adjusting her head on his shoulder, she said quietly, "Sergei found Misha's September quality-control reports. They indicated that the surgical instruments and the EKG machines weren't sold because they were defective."

"And what was done with them?" Anatol asked, quite alert now.

"Supposedly they were taken to the dump."

"Supposedly," Anatol repeated, not believing it any more than Laura did.

Raising herself onto an arm, she gazed at him with anxious eyes. "I also learned that Misha was in Odessa the same time we were. Lydia showed me a water globe that he brought back to her."

"Misha?" Anatol pushed himself up and leaned against the headboard. "I would have guessed he would have visited his family while the plant was closed. But they live in Irkutsk. It's nowhere near Odessa."

"The first thing I thought about was our finding Taras Luryn in his shop. But what connection could there be between him and Misha?"

"It could be that Misha was working with black marketeers. He could have been the one at the plant who let them haul off medical supplies."

"That could explain why he was always so tense and upset."

"It's also possible that someone was afraid he would talk, and killed him to make sure he wouldn't."

"Don't think less of me, but considering what happened to Luryn and Misha, I'm frightened."

"I'm frightened for you. It could be we haven't heard the last from the black marketeers."

A chill ran through her, and she tightened her arm around Anatol. "I'd rather believe that we have.

Maybe we should stop thinking about what might have happened at the plant in the past. Couldn't we just concentrate on its future?"

"I can't," Anatol said, stroking her hair. "It's not just the Pavlovsk plant that's being attacked by a crime syndicate. But that's my problem, not yours. I don't want you getting any more involved."

"I'm deeply involved now. I represent Biomed, and I've made friends at the plant who trust me to deal with problems there." Tilting her head up toward him, she asked, "Isn't there any way of getting the government to do something about the thefts?"

"I'm afraid the Pavlovsk plant isn't at the top of their priorities right now. Their attention is focused on the uprisings in the republics, the spiraling deficit and the power plays in the Kremlin."

"I guess that does make the security of one plant's medical supplies rather insignificant," she said quietly, and lowered her head back onto Anatol's chest.

As Anatol held her, moving his hand over her shoulders in soothing strokes, Laura closed her eyes and tried to convince herself that everything was insignificant, everything other than their being locked in each other's arms.

THE EARLY-MORNING SUN sparkled on the icicles dangling from the leafless trees around the frozen lake as Anatol tried to teach Laura to skate backward. He'd wanted them both to forget—for the weekend at least—the myriad problems facing them.

"Open your eyes," he yelled, holding her hands and laughing with her.

"I'll get dizzy," she protested, then screamed when one of her skates hit his, knocking him off balance.

Swiftly his arms went around her protectively. Smiling at her red nose and cheeks, he said quietly, "I told you I wouldn't let you fall."

Secure in his embrace, Laura looked up at his compelling eyes. "But you did let me fall. You let me fall in love with you."

"So what are we going to do about that?"

"We still have a few weeks together," she said sadly, digging her gloved fingers into his padded jacket. "We'll do what lovers do."

"That's not enough time."

"But it's all the time we have." She skated back to the wooden bench by the edge of the lake and began removing her skates.

Anatol joined her and removed his skates, as well. "I make two trips to New York each year. Will you want to see me, or when you leave, is that it for us?"

"I have a friend back home who's having a miserable time trying to cope with a long-distance romance. She's in New York and he's in Boston. That's only a couple hundred miles. We'd have five *thousand* miles between us, Anatol. I'm not sure I could handle that."

"You won't even think about staying here?"

Her eyes flashed to his. "We've been over that. You know I can't."

"If it's your career, your work wouldn't have to be limited to the plant. I've given this a lot of thought. With your experience and knowledge of the language, you'd be extremely valuable doing liaison work with various joint ventures across the country."

Her skates slung over her shoulder, Laura trudged through the snow toward the cottage.

Anatol caught up with her and matched her pace. "You were the one who said that Valentin and I would be better off talking things out. Why can't you and I do the same?"

"Because it's pointless. It's not a matter of what kind of a job I'd have here. I just couldn't live here permanently. So many things are too different from what I'm used to."

"Such as our lack of perfumed toilet paper?"

Her eyes flared at him. "I'm not that shallow, Anatol. Although I don't like having to wait in a long lineup every time I want to buy something. Nor do I like not knowing if the electricity will go off whenever I use a hair dryer in my apartment. These endless annoyances *do* bother me, but they're not the reason I can't live here."

"I didn't mean to offend you," he apologized. "You know I don't think you're shallow."

"No offense taken," she said calmly. "We both have a right to be a little edgy about saying goodbye."

Leaning back against a birch tree, Anatol forced a halfhearted smile. "Other than long lines and undependable electricity, what else worries you about staying here and marrying me?"

His tentative smile was enough to make Laura realize how much she did love him. She did want to be with him always, and she couldn't keep herself from toying with the idea of staying. "Considering your position with the State Planning Committee, are you sure it would be so easy for you to get permission to marry a foreigner?"

"I wouldn't let it be a problem," he answered, a dim hope growing in his eyes.

"Even if I insisted on retaining my American citizenship?"

"It could be arranged."

"There are so many things we'd have to talk about."

"Let's talk about them," he said. Now hope was surging through his heart, and he wanted to take her in his arms. But he pinned his arms to his sides.

"For one thing, I have family and friends back home. I'd miss them."

"Aeroflot jets land in New York every day. You could visit whenever you wanted to."

"Also, I'd want children, two probably."

"We'd have beautiful, healthy children."

"I don't think I'd want to raise them here. They'd be Soviet citizens. I'd have little control over how they were taught to think."

"They'd be our children first. Our educational system hasn't exactly brainwashed Valentin or crushed his ability to challenge authority. Things are changing here, Laura, and they're changing quickly. But if you'd like, we could go on vacation to New York when you were due, so you could have your children there. Then they'd have American citizenship."

"I'd plan to keep on with my career."

"I'd want you to. You wouldn't want for work here, not with your managerial skills. The world's economy is becoming more closely tied together day by day, and this country desperately needs people with experience like yours." Unable to restrain himself any longer, he reached out and drew her against him. "You and your ideas are like a breath of fresh air here, invigorating and necessary."

The closer Anatol's face came to hers, the more indecisive Laura felt. "You'd have to understand that I don't like housecleaning."

"We'd have someone come in to take care of that and the children later on."

"That would be expensive."

He grinned. "I'm a bureaucrat, remember?"

"Yes," she said, frowning, "and I'd be a bureaucrat's wife with all the privileges **you** and Valentin speak out against."

Coming to her senses, Laura started toward the cottage again.

Anatol met her stride and asked, "Would that be so different from being a successful capitalist's wife?"

"Don't confuse me. I'm thinking."

"I like the way you're thinking."

"What about Valentin? He's warmed up to me, but is he ready to accept me as a stepmother?"

"He is," Anatol assured her as he opened the cottage door and they went in.

"What makes you so sure?"

"You're loving and intelligent, and my son thinks the world of you."

"I think a great deal of him, but I don't know. I have a feeling I'd wind up being a referee most of the time."

"Valentin and I have settled things between us...thanks to you," he added. "Everything will go smoothly from now on."

"You paint a pretty picture, Comrade Vronsky."

"You bring out the artist in me," he said, slipping his arms around her waist. "Let's celebrate."

"Celebrate what? I haven't said I'd stay here," she reminded him.

"You haven't said you wouldn't."

Laura tensed in his arms, realizing they both had to face the truth. "We need to be realistic, Anatol," she pleaded, averting his eyes. "Right now relations between our countries are warming, but what if that changes . . . for the worst?" She met his intense gaze. "What would happen to us then?"

"Nothing! I love you too much to let anything bad happen to you."

She grasped his arms with her hands and forced her words through the constriction in her throat. "If the cold war started again, I'd have to return home, Anatol. Would you love me enough to leave your country and come with me?"

The look of pain that crossed his face almost broke Laura's heart. But his downcast expression foretold what his response would be.

"No," he admitted in a choked voice. "I'd be needed here more than ever." He paused for disquieting moments as his eyes drifted over her tortured features. Then he managed a weak half smile. "You're right, Larashka. We do need to be realistic. I can't ask you to stay here with me, can I? Forgive me for being so selfish. I never thought—" A sob caught in his throat, cutting off his words.

"No, Anatol, forgive *me*. I never should have let you hope, even for an instant. It's just that I want it so badly, too." She placed her hands alongside his face and gazed up at him through tearful eyes. "There's nothing I want more . . . nothing. Except to stay here with you. But it just isn't possible."

His arms tightened around her, and his lips came down on hers fiercely. And their tears mingled with their kisses in a desperate embrace.

ON MONDAY MORNING Laura leaned back in her office chair, reflecting on the weekend she and Anatol had spent together. The certainty that they had no future lent a new intensity to their relationship.

On Sunday they'd gone to Leningrad to attend a ballet and have dinner with Valentin and Katya at the elegant Astoria Hotel. The new closeness in the relationship between father and son warmed Laura's heart. At least Anatol would have Valentin when she left, Laura thought.

And the nights had been heaven. Anatol had lulled her to sleep with soft caresses and soothing words. And he'd awakened her with gentle kisses and loving touches. Everything had seemed so right, so comfortable, so perfect. Her lips still tingled from the goodbye kiss he'd given her this morning before leaving for Minsk.

Laura's smile was bittersweet as she thought of his many trips and how often they'd had to say goodbye. Rehearsals for their final parting, she mused sadly, recognizing that her momentary weakness in even considering to stay in the Soviet Union had been foolish. She looked up when Olga opened the door and stuck her head in.

"Got a minute?"

"Sure, come on in."

"I just came from a meeting at the local soviet, and I need to talk to you," Olga said, her expression dour.

"What now?" Laura asked, clasping her hands on the desk.

"As a friend, I've got to tell you that you're causing trouble for Anatol."

"How?"

"I found out that the chairman of the local soviet is filing a complaint about his interference here at the plant."

Laura's jaw tensed. "This is Chernov's doing, right?"

Olga nodded. "Anatol could get into a lot of trouble if he continues to stir things up."

"He's trying to straighten things out."

"I know, but—Laura, you believe good work should be rewarded. But it doesn't always work that way. Let's face it. Anatol's spending an unusual amount of time searching for problems here."

"There *are* problems here. And I've a responsibility to protect the millions of dollars Biomed is going to be pouring into this plant." Her expression darkened. "What could they do to him?"

"He could lose his position and have difficulty finding another job...except as a day laborer maybe."

"But he has friends in high places, doesn't he?" Laura said hopefully.

"So do the people who might wish him ill." Sitting on the chair next to Laura's desk, Olga placed a gentle hand over hers. "Anatol has worked hard all his life to get where he is. With just one stroke of a pen, everything he and his family has could be taken away from them."

"In spite of all the talk about reform here?"

"It's not just talk, but changes won't come overnight. Laura," Olga added quietly, "I'm worried about Sergei, too. If the audit does show irregularities, it could look bad for him. And I know he's not benefiting from the missing supplies."

"You know supplies are missing?"

"*If* they're missing, I should have said. But supposing some are? If you continue to goad Anatol on the way you're doing, even innocent people could be hurt, sent to prison perhaps."

"Olga, I can't believe your judicial system is that blind or corrupt."

"A chain is only as strong as its weakest link, and there are a few weak links in our court system." Olga lowered her eyes. "Look how quickly Misha's death was ruled a suicide."

Laura searched Olga's drawn expression. "You don't think it was?"

Her eyes flicked up. "I didn't say that."

"But you do think it."

Olga remained silent, and Laura suddenly felt deep concern for her. Olga had become a friend, a confidante even, and she could understand Olga's wanting to protect Sergei. If the audit did indicate that inventory control was lacking, Sergei would be held accountable.

"Olga, do you know what Sergei and Misha were arguing about the day...the day Misha died?"

"No," Olga said quickly, obviously shaken. Regaining her composure, she added, "But if it had been something serious, Sergei would have told me about it. Surely you're not suggesting he had something to do with Misha's death?"

"Of course not. I'm just wondering if you knew what they were arguing about."

"You would do anything to protect Anatol, wouldn't you?"

"You know I would."

"Then you understand that I won't let anyone hurt Sergei if I can help it. He's been good to me, and I owe him for that."

"Good God, I don't want to hurt him or anyone else. I'm just trying to figure out what's going on around here."

"Laura, things aren't always what they seem. You don't know the kind of trouble you're asking for if you and Anatol keep prying."

"Trouble is the last thing I want, but I'm not going to sit by idly and watch this joint venture go down the drain because someone around here has sticky fingers."

"You're going to pursue the issue, aren't you?"

"Things aren't going to get any better unless someone does. If I have to, I'll go directly to the press to focus attention on the criminal activity at this plant. And I'm sure they'd be interested in Dmitri Karnakov's antagonistic attitude toward the venture here."

Amazed, Olga asked, "Why drag Dmitri into this?"

"Because I don't think equipment could be stolen from this or any other medical supply plant in this country without him or someone at the Ministry of Health being aware of it. Why else would Karnakov be making it so difficult to have an audit done here? And why would Yuri—"

Just then Yuri Chernov himself rushed into the office, his face beet-red.

"The audit has been rescheduled for next week," he said almost hysterical.

Olga paled. "Next week?"

"Karnakov just phoned me."

Laura's eyes swept from the dismal look on Chernov's face to Olga's shocked expression. "What are they going to find?" she asked grimly.

"Nothing," Olga said quickly.

"Oh, what's the point?" Chernov moaned, shutting the office door. "Laura's going to find out sooner or later. If she doesn't, the American managers will when they arrive."

"Yuri," Laura asked as she rose slowly from behind her desk, "what are they going to find out?" Neither he nor Olga responded. "I want to know what's going on, and I want to know now!"

"Poor Misha," Olga said, her fingers covering her lips.

"Misha?" Laura repeated.

Chernov slumped back against the closed door. "Misha was helping the syndicate steal supplies from the plant."

Laura's eyes widened. "You both knew that!"

Chernov glanced at Olga, then said quickly, "Sergei discovered it."

Olga propped her elbow on the desk and braced her forehead with a hand. "That's what he and Misha were arguing about the day he died."

"When the police were here investigating," Laura asked Olga, "why didn't you tell them what Misha had been doing?"

"There would have been an immediate audit, and we weren't ready for that."

"No more than we're ready for the one next week," Chernov said dismally.

Still stunned, Laura moved slowly to the window, thinking how convenient it was for the two of them to blame Misha now that he couldn't defend himself. But whether or not he was solely responsible for the missing supplies, she realized that the upcoming audit she had wanted so badly would probably be the death blow for the joint venture.

"But," Chernov said, "now that Misha's . . . gone, supplies shouldn't just disappear anymore."

Laura whirled around. "There's not likely to be an 'again,' once the auditors go over the books. Unless they're idiots, they're bound to discover that you haven't been selling everything the plant's been producing."

"Maybe and maybe not," Olga said weakly. "They may not notice anything unless you give them reason to really search the records."

Laura stared at her. "You not only expect me to lie to my company, but also to the Soviet government?"

"Not saying something," Chernov insisted, "isn't the same as lying."

"Just a little sin of omission, is that it, Yuri?"

"Do you want this venture to become a reality?" he asked.

"Anatol does!" Olga pitched in.

"I know that," Laura agreed.

"Laura, you mustn't tell him about this conversation, at least not until after the audit. He's having enough trouble with problems at other plants and factories."

"That's true," Laura said uneasily.

"Anatol's really dedicated to increasing the number of ventures we have in this country," Chernov added, "particularly with the Americans."

"Laura," Olga said, standing close and placing a hand on her arm, "Sergei and I have done everything we could to help you here. If the auditors discover what Misha alone was responsible for, it's not only Yuri who will suffer. I, as his assistant, and Sergei, as inventory-control manager, will pay severely. Right now the government is making examples of people who are even suspected of being involved in corruption. Their savings are being confiscated and they're being given long prison terms or sent to labor camps in Siberia. Is that what you want for Sergei and me?"

The thought of Olga and Sergei in a Siberian labor camp shook Laura to the core. "Of course not," she said. "What do we do about the auditors, though?"

Chernov moved to the front of the desk. "We'll meet with them before they begin their inspection. They'll be impressed when they learn you've sent enthusiastic reports to your company."

"Fortunately that's true, in spite of the misgivings I've had." Laura thought a moment, then said, "I can give them copies of my reports, but what if they check the records thoroughly?"

"Then we're in deep trouble," Chernov admitted.

"Just how much trouble?" Laura asked.

Olga glanced anxiously at Yuri, then told Laura, "I've created false account-payable files to cover our losses."

Laura swallowed hard, but still had to struggle to get the words out. "How much?"

"The plant's bank account is short ... ninety thousand rubles."

"Ninety thousand!" Laura gasped.

Collapsing onto a chair, Yuri groaned. "We're finished here if they find out. If I had any way of getting the money, I'd replace it."

"So would I," Olga chimed in. "Do you think Biomed would help?"

Laura glared at her. "Not likely."

"Not even if we—" Yuri began.

Lifting a hand, Laura cut him off. "Let me think a minute." Sitting behind her desk, she began tapping with a pen. After discounting several ideas, she looked up at them. "There might be a way of temporarily getting the books in order." She raked her fingers through the sides of her hair. "I can't believe I said that. Back home I'd be fired for even suggesting we doctor the records. But maybe, just maybe, it would get us through the audit."

"What would?" Olga and Yuri asked in unison.

"Employee profit sharing," Laura said with reservation.

Chernov's jaw dropped. "If the plant goes bankrupt, there won't be any profits to share with anybody!"

"We won't go into bankruptcy if we can get through the audit! And if the employees invest some of their savings in the plant." She leaned forward, clasping her hands. "Our employees have a definite self-interest in the survival and prosperity of this company, but we've got to be honest with them about the present financial mess. If enough will invest in the plant, all employees would have job and income security."

"But," Yuri said, "our workers expect profits to go for better housing and to enlarge our day-care facility."

"If the plant is closed, they won't have anything," Laura reminded him. "Let the employees decide, through their council, how much of a dividend to issue and how much should go to building. Anatol told me that employees at other factories and plants are investing their savings in the development of their enterprises and are receiving interest on those investments. Is there any reason we can't do that here?"

"Now that the plant's on a self-financing system, we could," Olga said.

Chernov became more nervous by the second. "You're both assuming we'll survive and have a high profit margin."

"We will if we give employees a good reason for increasing productivity. As it is now, most of them don't care whether or not the plant generates any profits. Why should they? They're paid the same wages whether it does or doesn't. Give them a financial interest in the plant, and I guarantee production figures will go up. The market for quality medical supplies is enormous in this country. All we have to do is take advantage of it."

"I don't know," Chernov said, shaking his head.

"Do you have a better idea?" Laura asked, then turned to Olga. "If we're able to raise enough money, it's not going to solve all our problems. But if we do, can you get rid of the phony accounts payable and use whatever investment money we get to make our bank records pass the audit?"

"I'll find a way. You really think it would work?"

"I don't see that we have any other choice but to find out. But we have to act fast."

Wiping his forehead with a handkerchief, Chernov nodded. "I'll call an emergency meeting of the plant council right now and tell them of our financial situation. You, Laura, will explain this profit-sharing business."

"All right, but first I want to have a little chat with Sergei."

CHAPTER FIFTEEN

LAURA'S HEELS CLICKED on the linoleum in the hallway as she charged to Sergei's office. There, she closed the door behind her with more force than usual, causing him to stare at her, confusion written all over his face.

"How did you find out what Misha was doing?" she demanded.

Startled by her bluntness, Sergei realized Olga must have told Laura everything. "With the new computer," he said, putting a hand on the machine on his desk. "I was cross-checking Misha's September quality-control reports against shipping's. They didn't match. Misha's figures showed that only four hundred sets of surgical instruments were available for sale, but the shipping department records indicated that eight hundred sets had been crated."

"Didn't the shipping department manager think that was strange?"

"He told me Misha wanted the defective sets crated and said a truck would pick them up to take them back to the factory that produced the raw material. When I couldn't find a receipt from the factory, I asked Misha about it. He broke down and admitted that there had been nothing wrong with the surgical instruments and that black marketeers had picked them up. He said they'd threatened to harm his family if he didn't go along with them.''

"Who's 'them'?'' Laura asked.

"Misha wouldn't say. He claimed I'd be in danger if I knew."

"Sergei, why the hell didn't you tell me this before?''

Slowly he shook his head. "You don't know how terrified Misha was. He swore he'd never do it again, and I promised him I wouldn't report him or tell anyone." Leaning forward, Sergei covered his face with his hands. "I never thought he would commit suicide over it.''

"Don't blame yourself,'' Laura said, calmed somewhat by Sergei's remorse. "I'm still not convinced that he did.''

Lowering his hands from his face, Sergei stared up at her. "What are you saying?''

"He could have been murdered.''

Sergei rose slowly. "Murdered? By whom?''

"The syndicate he was working with. What has me so angry is that you, Olga and Chernov knew what was going on and covered up for Misha.''

Laura's nerves tingled as she tried to get her thoughts and suspicions in tow. She wasn't sure who to believe anymore. Certainly she didn't want to see Olga and Sergei shipped to Siberia unjustly. And with Misha gone, so were the plant's problems.

George Hardcastle and his people would arrive in two weeks. Nothing got by George, not a missing pencil. She had only two shoulders. George would come with twenty-four more. The managers at the plant, whom she had been working with the past weeks, were enthusiastically looking forward to the Americans arriving. Yes, everything would work out, she told herself, desperately wanting to believe it.

Forcing aside her ruminations, she looked directly at Sergei. "The auditors are arriving next week."

"What!"

"Are all the plant's records in the computer now?"

He nodded.

"Olga may have to adjust some of them temporarily." Having said that, Laura groaned inwardly. Never in her working career had she gotten involved in anything that had been the least bit unethical. But the situation she found herself in now was anything but normal. And the joint venture had to be saved!

Seeing the pained expression on Laura's face, Sergei asked, "Are you all right?"

"No. I'm not used to playing games with auditors."

Sergei's eyebrows lifted. "Our auditors are used to playing all kinds of games. If they do find out that state-owned property has been stolen, they have to know that it was Misha's doing, not Yuri's or Olga's." Thrusting his fingers through his hair, he said, "What I don't understand is how Misha thought he could get away with it. I hate to say it, but I actually felt sorry for him when he admitted what he'd done. When your parents are threatened, what's a person supposed to do?"

"I can't understand why neither Yuri nor Olga realized what Misha was doing before you told them."

"They did know, but they had to cooperate by saying nothing. Misha told them the syndicate would take care of them if they didn't keep quiet."

"All three of them were terrorized," she said, thinking out loud.

"That's why Olga and Yuri didn't want you and Anatol to get so involved in digging through the records. Neither of you is any safer from the syndicate than anyone else here at the plant is."

"Damn!" Laura said, banging the top of the desk. "All I want is for this one plant to succeed. But if George Hardcastle does increase production, the syndicate could just haul off more equipment. And if they do, George will know it in a minute."

Sergei shook his head. "Being an American won't protect him if he goes up against the syndicate."

Laura stood and began rubbing her hands together. "I can't let George and the others walk into a no-win situation like this." She took a few steps, then turned. "Surely if the right people knew what was going on here, some kind of action would be taken by the authorities."

"*If* we knew who the right people were. It's normal for many of our bureaucrats to be paid off. It's a way of life here."

"I am *not* going to give up on this venture," Laura said decisively. "As soon as Anatol gets back from Minsk, we're all going to sit down and thrash this out."

"When is he due back?"

"Not until next week. After the audit . . . I hope."

But, she wondered nervously, how would Anatol react when he eventually did find out about her plans to save the venture?

THE WEEK FLEW BY as Laura, Chernov, Olga and Sergei worked furiously to prepare for the upcoming audit. Employee reaction to the profit-sharing plan Laura outlined was overwhelming. More than half of the plant's six hundred employees invested portions of their savings, giving Olga twice the amount she needed to put the plant's books back in order—temporarily.

The morning of the audit Laura sat rigidly across from Olga in Chernov's conference room, more worried than surprised when Dmitri Karnakov and Pavel Krivtsov, his son-in-law, arrived with the auditors. She was positive that Dmitri would have the accountants dig deeply into the records and use their findings as a means of destroying the joint venture. Her prayers that Anatol wouldn't return in time to attend had been answered, but now, as she stared at Karnakov, she wished with all her heart that Anatol had returned.

After a nervous Chernov gave a glowing report on the plant's operation, Laura fielded Karnakov's pointed questions and supplied him and the auditors with copies of her reports to Biomed.

A pleased smile worked its way on Karnakov's face as he read them. Then he turned to Chernov. "I wish all our medical supply plants were in as good a shape as this one, Comrade Director. The employee profit-sharing plan you initiated is ingenious. It could be a model for our other plants to follow. Do you have copies of your production figures and financial statements?"

"Certainly. I thought I'd hand them out after the audit."

Dmitri's eyes raked across the three auditors. "I don't see any point in spending hours poring over computer printouts, do you?"

They turned to one another, then shook their heads. "No, Comrade Karnakov," the head auditor agreed.

"Good, then I suggest you three return to the ministry, so you'll be back in time to get some productive work done."

As soon as the auditors left the conference room, Dmitri smiled at Yuri. "Congratulations. You'll receive a copy of the audit report shortly."

He glanced briefly toward the end of the long table where Olga was sitting, then said to Yuri, "There are a few personnel changes I want you to make. Pavel—" he gestured toward his son-in-law "—is your new assistant director."

Laura's head jerked toward Olga, whose face paled at the news. Her eyes widened in amazement and her lips parted in protest, but she remained silent.

"Olga will assume Sergei Angizitov's position, and he will be in charge of plant finances."

"But—" Chernov sputtered.

A wave of Dmitri's hand silenced him. "We're living in a period of change, and like all good citizens we'll adjust. You agree completely, don't you, Comrade Director?"

Chernov glanced at Olga soulfully, then lowered his eyes and nodded.

Rising, Dmitri smiled at Laura. "If we don't meet again before you return home, have a safe journey."

Stunned, Laura said nothing as Dmitri sauntered out of the conference room. Olga tore out after him.

Laura scanned the dismal look on Yuri's face and Pavel's passive expression. "That's it?"

"The audit's finished," Yuri said, slumping back in his chair.

Pavel leaned forward, rested his arms on the edge of the table and clasped his hands. His voice betraying little emotion, he fixed his gray eyes on Laura. "Miss Walters, you seem to be having a problem with Comrade Karnakov's orders."

"What I'm having a problem with is the wisdom of his removing a highly successful assistant director for—" she chose her words carefully "—someone unknown."

"So," he said, smoothing a hand over his slick black hair, "I'm reduced to being 'someone unknown.'" He checked his watch. "I'll see you in your office promptly at three o'clock. You may go now."

Summarily dismissed, Laura glanced at the helpless expression on Yuri's face. Stiffening, she rose, her lips pursed as she left the conference room.

Immediately she went to Olga's office, intent on offering her friend all the support she could. At the door she raised her hand to knock, then froze when she heard Karnakov speaking in a hushed voice.

"It's not necessary for you to know why. Pavel's the new assistant director, and that's that. I'll make it up to you if I can."

"That's not good enough, Dmitri," Laura heard Olga say. "You're not going to get away demoting me like this. You promised me a better position in Moscow, and I'm holding you to it!"

"Right now I'm having real problems at the ministry."

"You don't know what problems are. You said you'd help me get out of this place, and now you've given Pavel my job. Do you think I'm just going to accept that?"

"Don't threaten me, Olga."

"I'm not threatening you. I'm promising you."

"What can you do, tell my wife? She's just as greedy as you are. She's not about to give up the life she leads because of anything you'd say."

"Even if she learns you haven't been the perfect husband while she's out of town?"

"Hardly," Dmitri said, laughing.

"Stop it! No one laughs at me, not even you. I may know more than you think about your involvement here at the plant."

"Shut up," he warned.

"I'll be quiet . . . if you get me a position and a good apartment in Moscow. If you don't, I'll—"

"All right! I'll see what I can do."

Stunned, Laura backed away from the door, realizing that Sergei's jealousy wasn't unfounded. Moreover, it appeared Olga knew something that Dmitri Karnakov wanted kept secret. What was the involvement she had just alluded to? Laura wondered. Was his involvement the reason Dmitri had derailed the audit? The reason he had replaced Olga with his son-in-law? Was some other unforeseen problem about to surface?

So many questions, Laura thought, but so few answers. Well, she'd get some answers right now! Retracing her steps to the office door, she knocked, then opened it. Two heads swung toward her.

"Miss Walters," Dmitri said casually. "I was just leaving."

"Remember what I said," Olga warned him.

"I'm blessed with a good memory," he remarked dryly, then strode out of the office.

Seeing that Olga was on the verge of tears, Laura temporarily postponed asking the questions she wanted answers to. "I'm sorry about your being replaced," she said sympathetically. "It's not fair."

"These things happen," she said stoically, squeezing her hands tightly. "It's just a temporary assignment. Dmitri's offered to find me a better position in Moscow."

"Olga, I accidentally overheard the two of you talking before I came in."

Olga blanched. "Are you going to tell Sergei?"

"Of course not. It's none of my business."

"Then why are we discussing it?"

"If it was anyone other than Karnakov, we wouldn't be." Laura paused, then said, "Olga, we've become friends. I'd like you to tell me that you're not involved in any kind of subterfuge with him, that you're not doing anything that would hurt this plant."

Slipping her hands into the side pockets of her smock, Olga asked, "Just how much of our conversation did you hear?"

"Enough to make me realize you know something about his involvement here, something he doesn't want known."

Olga's eyelashes flicked nervously as she studied Laura's firm expression. "My relationship with Dmitri has nothing to do with the plant." She laughed bitterly. "I'm not sure we could even be considered friends, but he's in a position to help me. Yes, I know he's married and has a family, but I don't care." When Laura lowered her eyes, Olga said, "You think I'm insensitive, don't you?"

Quietly Laura said, "That's for you to decide, not me."

"Perhaps I am insensitive to other people's feelings," Olga admitted in a strained voice. "I wasn't always that way, though. When I was younger and naive, I met a young man at Tashkent University. His name was Konstantin. He was my reason for living. Like Sergei, he was going to make a career for himself in the military. And like Sergei, he was sent to Afghanistan, but Konstantin...didn't come back. All my sensitivity died with him."

"I'm sorry. I didn't mean to open up old wounds," Laura said softly, hearing the deep pain in Olga's voice.

"You mustn't tell Sergei what you overheard, Laura. He's insanely jealous. Part of him died in that damn war, too. That scar of his has twisted something in his thinking. He can appear comic on the surface, but inside he's filled with anger and self-pity. When the right time comes, I'll tell him I'm leaving him, but for now I'd rather you didn't mention this conversation."

"Of course I won't say anything to him. How you and he handle your relationship is your affair. But I want to know what you meant by Dmitri's involvement here at the plant."

"Nothing actually. That's the kind of threat that would shake up any of the higher-ups in the ministries. They all have something to hide. I just assumed that Dmitri does, too."

"I see," Laura said before she left the room, not convinced that Olga was telling her the entire truth.

AT TWO-FIFTY-NINE, having decided to fight fire with fire, Laura waited in her office, poised for Krivtsov's arrival. The door opened and he entered, glancing up at the wall clock.

"It's a minute slow, Miss Walters," he announced, then settled in a chair in front of her desk and crossed his legs. "I'll have the timekeeper adjust it."

Laura met his steely eyes spiritedly, again catching a whiff of the overly sweet cologne he wore. "Already you're making my job easier for me, Mr. Krivtsov."

"I prefer that you call me Pavel."

"If you'll call me Laura," she countered, thinking she saw the corners of his lips quiver as though he were fighting a smile.

"A lovely name, Laura. My grandmother's name was Larissa."

"One of my grandmothers was named Phoebe, the other, Jenny Rose. Now that we've drawn our family trees, let's get down to business...Pavel."

"All right," he responded, never taking his eyes from hers. "Comrade Chernov informed me that you were instrumental in coaxing the workers to invest their money in the plant."

"I doubt if he used the word 'coaxed.' I did explain the benefits the employees would have if they chose to join a profit-sharing plan."

"Did you happen to mention the risk they would be taking with their hard-earned savings?"

"Of course I did. I also pointed out that at times interest on their investments would go up and at others it could go down, depending on plant productivity."

"Apparently you were quite persuasive."

Laura rose and moved to the other chair in front of her desk. "Pavel, are you in favor of this joint venture?" she asked bluntly.

"Let's say my enthusiasm lies somewhere between Anatol's and Dmitri's."

His frankness surprised her. "An honest answer," she commented before continuing. "The time I've spent here has been filled with problems I hadn't anticipated, but this plant can be a stunning success if it's allowed to function without outside interference."

"And you think I'm here to interfere?"

"At this point I'm not certain what to think. Your father-in-law hasn't exactly been a pillar of support. I have no way of knowing if your attitude will be a carbon copy of his, or if you plan to back this venture wholeheartedly."

Appearing unruffled by her remarks, Pavel said, "I am my own man. Does that answer your question?"

"Not really. Are you going to work with us or against us?"

"I don't plan to be an assistant director the rest of my life. A success here would look good on my résumé."

His answer came as another surprise. But Laura remembered Anatol's saying that Pavel was an ambitious man. Perhaps, she thought hopefully, if his own interests were served, he might be a help rather than a hindrance. Or maybe he was just trying to put her off guard.

He stood, leaned back against Laura's desk and crossed his arms. "I was impressed with your reorganization of the plant managers. Do you think they're ready to work with their American counterparts when they arrive next week?"

Standing so he wouldn't be looking down at her, Laura replied, "They're ready and enthusiastic."

"And we'll be able to begin joint operation by January the first?"

"Yes," Laura said.

"Sooner?"

"How much sooner?"

"As soon as possible."

Laura took several moments to ponder that. "I'd like the American personnel to have a week to observe the procedures here at the plant. During that time I'll schedule seminars to acquaint them with governmental rules and regulations. After that, I'd say they'd be prepared to work harmoniously with the present managerial staff."

"Then they can begin serious work by the second week in December."

"Yes," Laura answered in a subdued voice, taken aback by his suggestion, "but the joint venture won't be in place legally until the first of the year."

"I realize that. Chernov told me why the two of you initiated the employee profit-sharing plan...and of Misha Vinokurov's involvement with black marketeers."

Laura tensed. "You don't seem to be as shocked as I was."

"The West is more advanced than we are at many things, but not in crime. Black marketeers are the only true entrepreneurs we have in this country."

"Now that you're here, I'm hoping this plant will be immune to criminal activity."

"Hope is essential, isn't it? With your managers and ours working together, I'm hoping that before January first we'll be able to make up the ninety thousand rubles that Misha gave away. Do you think we could?"

"If you and Yuri work with George Hardcastle and not against him, it's a possibility."

"We will." Starting toward the office door, he said, "I'll see you in the morning. Oh, yes." He turned, adding as if an afterthought, "Arrange your schedule so that you're free between eight and nine each morning. I'd like to meet with you in my office to discuss plant progress."

"Fine. When George arrives, I think he should join us."

"I don't. He can hold Chernov's hand. It's your opinions I'm interested in."

"As you like," Laura said, following him with her eyes as he departed her office.

"What a difference a day makes," she mumbled, trying to put the pieces together, but still suspicious of Pavel's motives.

Why the sudden team-player attitude? she wondered. Why the rush to get the joint venture operational? And why had Dmitri ordered changes in personnel?

Her troubling questions were interrupted by the jangling of her phone. Answering it, relief washed over her when she learned it was Anatol calling from Minsk.

"One way or the other I'll make it back by Thursday evening," he said, a smile in his words. "Things are going much smoother here than I expected."

Laura had to bite her tongue to keep from telling him immediately about the shake-up at the plant and everything else that had happened in his absence. "I can't wait to see you again," she said.

"Same here. I've missed you terribly. How are things going there?"

"We'll talk about it when you get home."

"Home," he repeated, his voice wistful. "I wish we really could have a home together. I've got to go now, love. See you soon."

"Soon," she repeated softly as she put the receiver down, mentally reviewing the things she had yet to buy for their reunion dinner. She'd hoped Anatol would be back on Thursday—Thanksgiving Day.

AFTER BASTING THE GOOSE she'd bought in lieu of the turkey she usually cooked, Laura returned to the living room in the dacha.

"Something smells delicious," Anatol complimented her, sniffing the pleasant aroma coming from the kitchen.

"It's the candied yams and dressing," she said, accepting the glass of red wine he offered.

He raised his wineglass and touched it to hers. "My first Thanksgiving dinner," he said, grinning. "I'm thankful that I'm having it with you."

"Better hold off on your thanks," she suggested. "This is the first goose I've cooked."

Anatol lowered himself onto the easy chair near the fireplace and leaned back. "I'm beat," he admitted, "but the trip was worth it."

"You deserve a rest," she said, again thinking how tired he looked. She had first noticed the dark circles under his eyes the moment he had walked in the door. "Do you ever take a vacation?" she asked, moving next to the chair and running her fingers through the side of his hair.

"I'd take a few days now, but all I'd do is sleep." A teasing grin reshaped his lips. "Of course, if you could manage some free time from the plant, we could spend it together—resting in bed.''

"Maybe you're not as exhausted as you think you are," she quipped as she set her wineglass on the table next to the chair.

"I said I was beat, not dead."

Easing herself down onto the braided rug, she rested her hands on his thigh, laid her cheek on his knee and listened to the hiss and crackle of the fire. Her eyes drifted to the snowflakes piled high on the sill outside the window, and she wished with all her heart that she and Anatol could retreat from their daily work problems and remain cloistered in the comfortable warmth of his cottage—just the two of them alone, forever. Just as they were now, close and touching each other. But wishing was one thing. Reality was another.

She had yet to bring him up-to-date on the events that had taken place at the plant. He had been so exuberant when he'd first come home, telling her about how he'd saved the joint venture in Minsk, and then being excited about her having planned a Thanksgiving Day dinner for them. But now she knew she had to spoil his mood.

Leaving out nothing, she told him about Misha's involvement with black marketeers, the profit-sharing plan, the audit and Pavel's having assumed Olga's job.

Astonished, Anatol said, "You've had a busy time."

"To put it mildly, but Pavel has me guessing. He sounds too good to be true."

"Are we speaking about the same man? Dmitri's son-in-law?"

"Yes. His attitude is not only positive, it's enthusiastic. He wants the joint venture operational by the second week in December."

She caught a warning whiff from the kitchen and jumped up. "The yams!"

Anatol followed her to the kitchen, watching as she grabbed the pan from the top of the stove.

Using a spoon, she tested the bottom of the sweet sauce for signs of burnt sugar. "Just in time," she said, turning off the gas.

Anatol braced a shoulder against the doorframe, more concerned about what he'd just learned. "I don't trust Pavel any more than I trust Dmitri."

"I suppose I shouldn't," Laura said, lowering the temperature in the oven. "But I certainly want to. Why would he come on like a cheerleader if he has something else in back of his mind?"

"I wish I could ask him. Not that I'd get a straight answer. I can't understand why either he or Dmitri would change so much overnight, nor can I see Pavel not following Dmitri's orders. Unless—" Anatol broke off, lost in thought.

"Unless what?" she asked, switching on the flame under a pot of broccoli.

"Unless Dmitri's in trouble. There's talk about an investigation of corruption at the Ministry of Health. Dmitri's included. He might need a few financial successes at medical supply plants to prove his value."

"I don't care who gets the credit for the success of this venture, as long as it gets off the ground."

"I'm just supposing," Anatol said, leery of putting too much hope in suddenly receiving Dmitri's sincere cooperation.

Laura returned to the living room, reached for her wineglass and handed Anatol his. Thanking her, he said, "Yuri had best keep a close eye on the plant's financial records. I've heard that Pavel has a knack for creative accounting."

"That's something else I wasn't prepared for. Dmitri appointed Sergei manager of the financial department."

Anatol thought about that for a moment, then said, "Now I'm really worried."

"Maybe we've had so much bad news lately, we've forgotten how to accept the good."

"I wish that were true, but it's possible that Pavel could be setting Sergei up to take the blame for the plant's financial problems if there's ever more trouble."

"He wouldn't do that to Sergei!"

"Unless Pavel has suddenly gained a conscience, I wouldn't put it past him. I should talk to Sergei about that. Do I have time to call him before dinner?"

"No," Laura said adamantly. "You'd be on the phone for an hour, and our goose would look like a Cornish hen. You relax while I put the finishing touches on the meal."

"That's another thing I like about you," Anatol said, smiling. "You're decisive."

"And hungry," she said, returning to the kitchen.

As she removed the goose from the oven, Laura realized that Sergei had more problems than she had told Anatol about: Olga's relationship with Dmitri, for one. But, she decided, Anatol had had enough bad news for one evening.

SERGEI POUNDED the bedroom door with his fist and glared at Olga. "Dmitri hands your job to his son-in-law, and you still think the man isn't a snake!"

"It's a matter of politics," she said, sweeping past him as she carried a laundry basket of lingerie to the kitchen.

Following her, Sergei leaned back against the sink. "It's a matter of his dumping you."

Ignoring his outburst, Olga pressed the start button on the washing machine for a third time. "This damn thing is broken again."

"So much for your great gift from Dmitri."

"At least we can still show guests that we *have* a washing machine," she declared, grabbing the laundry basket and heading back to the bedroom.

"Face it," Sergei said, hard on her heels, "he used you, and what have you gotten from it besides some clothes and a lousy washing machine that doesn't work?"

"He's going to get me a job in Moscow."

Sergei let loose a shrill laugh. "He'll be lucky if he can keep his own."

Dropping the basket onto a hamper in the bedroom, Olga whirled around. "What are you talking about?"

"He's being investigated for bribery and corruption."

"Who told you that?"

Hooking his thumbs on the waistband of his corduroy pants, Sergei's expression turned smug. "You're not the only one who has friends at the Ministry of Health. You might as well forget your fairy-tale dream of high life in the capital."

When Olga slumped down on the bed, the spiteful look evaporated from Sergei's face. Crouching in front of her, he gathered her hands in his and pressed his cheek against them. "Why can't we go back to the way it was for us? You said you were happy when we moved in here."

"Nothing stays the same," Olga said quietly.

Sergei raised his head and smiled up at her. "Sometimes they can get better. Look, I'll get you a new washing machine, one that works, a German-made one. And this Christmas we'll go to the Crimea again and enjoy the beach at Balaklava. Remember the room we had and how we watched every sunset together? At Christmastime it will be like summer there. We could go to that little restaurant you liked so much, the one with the garden of roses and the magnolia and palm trees."

A vacant smile on her face, Olga reminisced absently. "We did enjoy ourselves. Except you drank too much wine."

"It wasn't the wine that made me drunk. It was you, Olga. Without you I'd be less than a man. I need you desperately. Forget Dmitri."

His name dragged her back to the present, and she looked down at Sergei. "Dmitri will keep his word to me," she whispered in a dull monotone.

Slowly Sergei rose, stretching and curling his fingers to release the aching tension he felt. "Stay away from him," he warned between clenched teeth. "He'll drag you down with him."

"He can't be in real trouble. He's too powerful."

"Not for long. Times are changing, and his days of power are numbered."

"That's what you'd like to believe."

"The Criminal Investigation Department believes it, too. They think Dmitri is taking money from the syndicates. If you get too close to him, you may wind up in the same labor camp he does."

CHAPTER SIXTEEN

LAURA HAD NEVER RIDDEN in a horse-drawn sleigh before, let alone a troika. On Saturday morning, sitting next to Anatol on a cushioned board as the sleigh flew over the fresh snow, she huddled closer under the felt blanket over their laps, feeling the cold air seep into her lungs.

Bells dangled from the trio of Arab horses, steam clouding up from their rumps as the fur-hatted heavy-set driver guided them. Six reins streamed from his immense gloved hands. Ice crystals dotted his broad mustache.

The horses followed a curve in the road and broke free from the forest of snow-dappled pines. An open field, white with untracked snow, glistened in the afternoon sun. Listening to the dancing bells that covered the almost silent hoofbeats of the horses, Laura thought that the land looked like a painting—so clean and still.

Despite the cold, she felt warm and safe holding on to Anatol, who had slept all day Friday while she had worked at the plant. Last evening they had dined on leftovers from their Thanksgiving dinner and then made love slowly and tenderly, both realizing that soon they would have to part—forever.

As the horse-drawn sleigh turned a curve in the snow-covered road, Anatol told the driver to stop. "I want you to see something," he said to Laura, then jumped down from the sleigh.

When she stood, he took hold of her waist and lowered her gently to the snow. Then, taking her hand, he led her off the road toward the edge of the hill. Spread out before them in the snow-covered valley lay Pavlovsk.

"It looks like a Christmas card," Laura said, smiling.

"To the left there," he said, pointing to a frozen lake, "that's where the dacha is." His hand moved to the right. "And there's the plant."

The plant, she repeated silently, tightening her grasp on his arm. "Anatol," she said, forcing the words out, "George arrives Monday."

"I know," he said, not able to keep from grinning. "I hope that means you won't be so tied down at the plant."

"No, I shouldn't be," she said, her throat feeling thick. "But as soon as he gets adjusted, I'm . . . going to return home."

"What?"

Not looking at him, she explained, "He won't have any problems during the transition period. There's no reason for me to stay on for more than a few days, a week, maybe."

"No reason?" He swallowed the lump in his throat, realizing that his remaining time with Laura had dwindled suddenly from a month to a week. "I love you, Laura. And you love me. Why leave before you have to?"

"Because the longer I remain here, the harder it will be to leave. I'll always remember you," she said, her eyes stinging.

Anatol felt as if his body had suddenly caught fire. He stomped back to the sleigh without a word.

"Anatol!" she called, rushing after him, "what are you doing!" Catching up with him, she grasped his arm.

He jerked free. "You're right, Laura. This is too painful. The sooner, the better for both of us. I'll move back to Leningrad today."

Stunned, Laura sagged against the sleigh, her tears crystallizing on her cheeks. In a choking voice she said, "Please, let's return to Pavlovsk. I . . . I want to move my things back to the apartment."

GEORGE HARDCASTLE and the American managers arrived at the plant Monday morning. Thankfully, during the day, Laura was almost busy enough not to think about Anatol and the harsh way they'd parted. Evenings and nighttimes were a different matter. Depressed, she would wander from room to room in her lonely apartment, trying to think of something other than him. But it was useless. Through the long nights she would count the hours, anxious to get to the plant again in the morning to bury herself in work.

As Laura entered the plant Wednesday morning, George was close on her heels.

"And I thought *New York* was a bitch in the winter. But this Russian weather is really something else!" he complained, shoving back the hood of his fur-lined Eskimo parka.

Laura stomped her boots on the water-soaked throw carpet and smiled at George's tearing eyes and scarlet-hued face. "You'll get used to it."

"When do I get used to it getting dark in the middle of the afternoon?" he asked as he pulled off his gloves. "I feel like half my workday is spent on overtime. Also," George confessed, "Chernov's driving me crazy."

"What now?" Laura asked as they stepped into her office.

"He won't stop nagging me about this business of a percentage of Biomed's profits going for better housing for personnel and a bigger day-care center. The guy can spend all of the state's share of the profits on whatever he wants, but he's got to keep his hands off ours. Doesn't he understand what a contract is?"

"He understands," she said, checking the papers in her in box. "He's just trying to wear you down."

"And that Krivtsov guy. As I was leaving last night, he comes up with the idea of eliminating the production of patient-monitoring equipment and increasing the plant's production of pharmaceuticals."

"What kind of drugs?" Laura asked.

"The kind we try to keep off the streets in New York. I haven't seen the necessary controls around here if we're going into business on the scale he's proposing."

Frowning, Laura turned pensive, then said, "Until the first of January we don't officially have a big say in what the plant produces."

"True. Well, catch you later," George said with a wave, and headed for his office.

Alone, Laura struggled with her conscience. She knew she could just walk away from the problems at the plant, return home and leave George, Yuri and Anatol to deal with them. Deep down, though, she didn't want to.

Most worrisome was Pavel's motive for wanting to increase the production of pharmaceuticals. Perhaps he was only trying to increase profits at the plant. On the other hand, she thought darkly, knowing from TV reports that drugs had a ready market on the streets, perhaps he was in the process of establishing his own criminal territory.

Coffee cup in hand, she went to Pavel's office for their daily meeting.

"Good morning," he greeted her pleasantly. "Are you still determined to leave us next week?"

"There's no need for me to stay. These past two days have proved that George can handle the adjustment period for our managers and yours. Everything has gone smoother than any of us had a right to expect."

"Thanks to the exemplary groundwork you did, I'm told by everyone."

"That's my job."

"I hope Biomed is paying you what you're worth."

"I've no complaints." Handing him a printout, she said, "George's projected production figures should please you. Of course they're based on the timely installation of the new automated assembly lines. That alone should increase profit by twelve percent, considering the back orders we're holding."

Pavel scanned the paper, then looked up at Laura. "Do you have faith in these figures?"

"I have faith in George."

"Blind faith?"

"It's not blind. I've worked with him for almost five years now."

Slipping the printout in his top drawer, Pavel said, "It's a shame you won't be here for the official beginning of the venture. We're planning quite a celebration, the press and all that."

"I'm not much for official parties. Being here has been an interesting experience—" *to say the least,* she thought "—but I'll be glad to get home."

"I take it you're not much for roughing it, either."

"Pavel," she said curtly, having had it with people assuming she desperately missed the creature comforts of home, "there's more to life than being able to pick up a phone and order whatever you want, using a credit card. What I wasn't prepared for were the problems that almost brought this venture to a halt. To be frank, your Ministry of Health wasn't a great help."

"You mean my father-in-law wasn't."

Not wanting to say more than she thought she should, Laura merely lifted her eyebrows.

"I imagine he's sorry he didn't help more. If you haven't already heard, he's being investigated by the Ministry of Internal Affairs for graft and corruption."

Laura fought to keep her lips from spreading into a wide smile. "Is that right?" she asked as casually as she could.

"He was always a greedy man, and apparently his greed caught up with him."

"You don't appear broken up about his problems with the law."

"I told you, I'm my own man."

And an ambitious one, Laura thought. She recalled Anatol's having told her that several crime organizations were engaged in a power struggle. If Dmitri Karnakov was one of the losers in that struggle, she wondered if Pavel, who she felt had the instincts of a piranha, might be one of the winners. She wondered if he was actually ruthless enough to have had a part in his own father-in-law's downfall. If so, why?

"Perhaps with you here," she suggested, "the Ministry of Health will be more supportive of this venture."

"I have every intention of keeping it operating smoothly."

"That's good to hear." She paused, then said, "George told me you were thinking of increasing the production of pharmaceuticals."

"That's nothing for you to be concerned about. You're leaving."

"Yes," Laura acknowledged, then mentally added, *but not for a few days.*

Back in her office, she stared at the phone on her desk, trying to decide whether or not to alert Anatol to what Pavel had in mind at the plant. She wasn't at all certain that he'd care to hear from her, not after the way they'd parted. In her heart, though, she wanted to grab at the chance to talk to him again, to try to soothe his deeply hurt feelings.

Throwing caution to the wind, she dialed the private line in his Leningrad office. When he answered the phone, she felt the usual ache in her heart. But she managed to calmly explain what Pavel was up to. He told her to sit tight and that he'd be there in half an hour.

PAVEL CLOSED the file folder he had on his desk, leaned back in his swivel chair and greeted Laura and Anatol when they entered his office.

Taking a seat, Anatol got straight to the point. "I understand you're planning to increase the production of pharmaceuticals."

Pavel glanced at Laura, then looked back at Anatol. "Word travels quickly."

"Why discontinue the manufacturing of patient-monitoring equipment? It's as necessary as pharmaceuticals, if not more so."

"I imagined that the reason for that would be obvious—profits. After all, we have an obligation to the workers who invested their savings in the profit-sharing scheme Laura recommended. If they don't receive interest soon, they could be tempted to withdraw their money. That would put the plant on the brink of bankruptcy again."

"Bankruptcy shouldn't be a consideration any longer," Laura said. "I've told George why we initiated the profit-sharing plan. After he calmed down, he decided the long-term benefits for Biomed were worth the risk I took. Yuri has tightened security, and the computerized system of inventory control that Sergei set up will instantly alert George to any missing supplies, which was the real problem."

"The real problem," Pavel said with a smile, "was in management here at the plant, a situation which you resolved quite nicely."

"Pavel," Anatol cut in, "if the approval for increased drug production goes through, have you thought of enlarging the plant so that it can continue to produce other needed supplies and equipment?''

"I've not only thought of it, I've sketched out a plan for that purpose. This plant could be a showcase, a model for others."

"I'd like to see the plans before you submit them to the Ministry of Health."

"Of course. Without your concern and guidance, this plant would have folded a long time ago. Unfortunately the plans are in my apartment just now."

"The one here in Pavlovsk?"

"Yes."

Standing, Anatol said, "Good. I have time for a ten-minute drive."

Pavel offered Anatol a twisted smile. "You are a suspicious one, Comrade."

"The State Planning Committee would say 'thorough.'"

Pavel rose and took his coat from a rack, then gestured toward the door of his office.

"I shouldn't be too long, Laura," Anatol said. He glanced at his watch and saw that it was almost closing time. "I'll stop by your apartment later."

Lowering her voice, she said, "Wait for me if I'm not there. Sergei and I have some work to do before we leave."

Anatol nodded, and she followed the two men from Pavel's office, her eyes lingering on Anatol as they went down the corridor. She had feared she would never see him again, and she found herself almost happy that yet another problem at the plant had brought them together again. But seeing Anatol once more also renewed her heartache.

Bidding good-night to employees as they filed toward the front doors of the building, Laura went to Sergei's office. He wasn't there. She waited several minutes, then decided he might be with Olga. As she neared her office, she heard Sergei shouting.

At the open door Laura saw Olga boxing personal items from her desk. Sergei was pacing like a caged animal, his face flushed, one hand raking through his disheveled hair.

His eyes, wider and darker than usual, darted toward Laura when she entered. "She's leaving!" he spit out. "Just like that she packs up and runs off." With a wild swoop of his hand he sent a stack of folders on the desk swishing through the air.

"Olga?" Laura asked as calmly as she could. "What's going on?"

"I'm moving up in the world," she stated firmly, disregarding Sergei's burning eyes.

"She's moving to Moscow," he said, a tortured twist to his grin. "Dmitri's gotten her a job with the Ministry of Internal Affairs."

"A promotion," Olga insisted.

"Wake up, Olga. He's using you again! He just wants inside information on how the investigation against him is going. Can't you see that?"

"I don't care why he's doing it. I'm just thrilled to be getting away from this place."

Grabbing her arm, Sergei growled, "It used to be good enough for you."

"Leave me alone!" Olga ordered, jerking her arm free.

Seeing his hands ball into fists, Laura went to Sergei and touched his shoulder. "Please," she said, trying to end their bitter words, "maybe it would be better if you did go. The two of you are upset right now. You won't accomplish anything this way. I'll just be a few minutes. Then we'll talk."

Sergei gave Laura a desperate look, then rushed from the room.

"Olga," Laura asked, once they were alone, "are you sure you're doing the right thing in leaving Sergei? He loves you so much."

She shook her head. "I can't live with his insane jealousy any longer. Even the mention of Dmitri's name sends him into a fury...just as it did the night he stormed out of our apartment after you and Anatol left."

"The night Misha died?" Laura asked.

"Yes, Sergei was so crazy I thought he was going to hit me."

"I can't believe he'd do that."

Olga chuckled caustically. "He did once, just before he and Misha went to Odessa."

"Odessa? When was Sergei in Odessa?"

"During the plant shutdown. Sergei wanted me to go with them, but I had business meetings at the Ministry of Health in Leningrad. Oh, it's not just Dmitri. Sergei accuses me of having an affair with any man I talk to for more than two minutes. No, it's better this way." Closing the top of the cardboard box, she said, "I will miss you, Laura. I'll call you here at the plant and give you my new address." She looked at her with moistened eyes. "I'm sorry I won't see you again before you return home."

Laura stepped closer and kissed Olga on the cheek. "I hope you'll be happy."

"I hope so, too," she said softly, then slipped on her coat, picked up the box from her desk and hurried from the room.

Laura started down the hallway toward Sergei's office, her thoughts whirling. He had been with Misha in Odessa when Taras Luryn was murdered. And where did Sergei go after he'd stormed out of his apartment the night Misha died? Had he followed Misha into the park? Was it Sergei who Misha had been arguing with? Could Sergei have been working with Misha and the black marketeers?

Reaching his office, Laura expected that Sergei would be waiting for her, but he wasn't there, nor was his coat. He'd left the plant, she decided. Quickly she sat down at his computer, intent on finding out if he was manipulating funds the way Olga had been.

Laura was concentrating so deeply on recent bank statements she was calling up on his computer that she jumped when Sergei spoke.

"I almost forgot we were supposed to meet, Laura," he apologized, then peered at the computer screen. "What are you doing?"

Steadying her voice, she said, "I was just checking to make sure that . . . uh, Pavel wasn't doing any creative accounting. Anatol doesn't trust him."

"I would know," he said, switching off the computer. "I handle plant finances now."

"Yes," Laura said uneasily, "that's right. There have been so many changes around here recently that I forgot."

Sergei smiled strangely. "It's not like you to forget a thing. I've never come across anyone as sharp as you are." After a deadly silence, he asked, "Where's Anatol?"

Laura realized that she was probably alone in the plant with Sergei. But so what? Her suspicions about him were no more than speculations. And now was certainly not the time to check them out!

To answer his question, she said, "He went with Pavel to his apartment." She rose, planning to go to her office to phone Anatol, but Sergei blocked the way to the door. "We can go over the figures in the morning," she said matter-of-factly. "I'm going to leave."

"You seem upset," he said, lifting a hand and cupping her arm. "And you're trembling." He glanced down at the computer, then looked back at her. "What were you really checking for?"

"I...I told you," she insisted, averting her eyes from his steady gaze. "I was afraid that Pavel was—"

"Why can't you look at me?" Sergei asked, his tone darkening.

"I have to go. Anatol's expecting me."

"You said he was at Pavel's apartment."

"He is, but he's going to pick me up any minute now."

"Your car's parked in the lot," he said, narrowing his eyes. He released his hold on Laura and draped his fur-lined coat over the back of a chair. "What did Olga tell you?" he asked, shutting the office door.

Laura's heart sank. "Only that she was very upset," she answered, a taut smile on her lips.

"She didn't mention Misha?" Sergei saw Laura's face tense.

"No. Why would she?"

"Or that I was in Odessa with him the same time you and Anatol were there?"

Her insides quivering, Laura asked, "Why should that be important?"

Moving nearer, Sergei examined the fear in her eyes. "You seemed to think that Taras Luryn's murder was important."

"How did you know his name?" she blurted out.

Cocking his head, Sergei shrugged. "You or Anatol told Olga and me the night you were at our apartment."

Her memory was as good as Sergei had suggested, and Laura knew she had only said "a man" had died in Odessa. Neither she nor Anatol had mentioned Taras Luryn by name. Now she was certain Sergei had killed Luryn!

Her pulses pounding, she grabbed for the phone, but Sergei's movement was as swift. Her heart lurched when she felt his rough hand come down hard on hers.

"YOU HAVE a suspicious nature," Pavel said, watching Anatol as he pored over the rough sketches he had made for enlarging the plant.

"It's all part of my job," Anatol said curtly, seated at the desk in Pavel's apartment. Closing the folder, he placed it on top of the other files Pavel had shown him. "You've really done your homework. These figures do show that the increased pharmaceutical production should add to the plant's profits, and quickly, too."

"Not to mention that the quality of the drugs will be superior to those manufactured at other plants."

"I hadn't guessed you'd be a man to concern yourself with quality medical care."

"I worked at the Ministry of Health, remember?"

"Only too well."

"Is that an across-the-board condemnation of any-one connected with the ministry?"

"Not at all. The vast majority of the employees working there want the best health care possible for our people."

"Then you don't like me because I'm Dmitri's son-in-law."

Anatol draped his arm over the back of the chair and scrutinized the man's smug expression. "There's talk that he was taking bribes from organized crime."

"If he was, he wasn't the only one at the ministry."

"Feel like naming names?"

"I feel like living to a ripe old age."

"Doing what—siphoning off drugs from the Pav-lovsk plant for a little extra spending money?"

"You are cynical, Anatol. Haven't you heard that new ways of making legitimate money are opening up? I plan to be a model assistant director at the plant. Chernov won't be there forever. I'm young. I can wait until he retires. By then the Ministry of Health should have had a good housecleaning. They'll need experi-enced people to fill top positions."

"People like you."

"Exactly."

Anatol stood, towering over Pavel. He glared down at him. "You sound too righteous to be believed. My instincts tell me you're as much involved with orga-nized crime as your father-in-law."

Pavel backed away. "I'm not."

Anatol followed and grabbed the man's tie. "Con-vince me."

Struggling to get the words out, Pavel asked, "Haven't you heard that parliament's added presumption of innocence to Soviet law?"

"This isn't a matter of the law right now. I want some answers." He tugged hard at the man's tie. "Talk to me, Pavel, or I'll dream up stories and tell Dmitri they came from you. Would you rather deal with him or with me?"

"Do I have your word this is off the record?" Pavel asked, his frightened eyes meeting Anatol's hard ones.

"You have it," Anatol said, releasing his hold on the tie.

Pavel tugged at the collar of his shirt as he widened the distance between him and Anatol. "When Dmitri got me the job at the ministry, I honestly didn't know what he was involved in. I soon found out and learned that the work I was doing implicated me, as well. I wanted out, but he said no one who was in got out, and I was in for life."

Picking up a pack of cigarettes from the desk, Pavel flicked one out and lit it.

As he nervously blew out a stream of smoke, Anatol asked, "Was it your idea or Dmitri's that you take the job at the plant?"

"This conversation is still just between us, isn't it?"

"I said you had my word."

"It was Dmitri's idea."

"Increasing the manufacturing of drugs was his idea, too, wasn't it?"

"His order."

"So you're still working for him."

"Not for long," Pavel said, taking a quick drag on his cigarette. "Who do you think informed the Ministry of Internal Affairs about his dealings with the syndicate?''

Anatol mulled that over, then said, "You were the one who passed on Dmitri's orders to Misha...and the one who killed him."

"I passed on the orders, but not to Misha, and I never killed anyone."

"Are you saying someone else was working with him at the plant? Who?"

"You still haven't figured that out, have you?"

"Save us both a lot of time and tell me," Anatol suggested, taking a step toward him.

"The one who killed Misha...was your friend Sergei."

Anatol grabbed a fistful of Pavel's jacket. "You're lying!"

"I'm not. Where do you think Sergei got the money for those trips he and Olga used to take?"

"Are you saying that Olga knew Sergei was working for Dmitri?"

"No, and she still doesn't. Neither does Chernov. They both got their instructions from Misha."

"Who got them from Sergei," Anatol muttered to himself, releasing his hold on Pavel's jacket. "Good God, I left Laura alone with him!"

CHAPTER SEVENTEEN

SERGEI SHOVED THE PHONE out of Laura's reach and shook his head. "You and Anatol wouldn't let well enough alone, would you?"

"Why are you doing this?" she asked, her head throbbing.

"It's your fault. The day you arrived at the airport I told Dmitri you would be a problem here at the plant. You're too inquisitive, Laura, and just as troubling to me as Taras was."

"You did kill him!"

"It was Luryn's greed that killed him. I just supplied the bullet. It was stupid of him to offer black market goods to just anyone who walked into his shop—particularly to you and Anatol."

"How did you know we were there?"

"The syndicate has been following your every move ever since you arrived."

Laura backed away from Sergei and grasped the edge of the desk. "And Misha?" She already knew. "It was you I heard arguing with him in the park."

"He wanted out of the organization. But no one gets out, not even me. After you and Anatol left my apartment, I went to Misha's. I had to stop him from talking to you. I arrived in time to see him entering the park, and I caught up with him. He wouldn't listen to reason."

"Reason? You call what you did reason?" Laura could hardly believe what he was telling her.

"Misha was weak and terrified of being caught. There's no place in this world for weakness."

"Even in someone like Misha? He was so gentle, so defenseless."

"That made it easy for me to use him, just as Olga used me."

"What kind of a man are you!"

"I'm a survivor. The strong always are. Take a good look at my face." He turned the scarred side toward her. "Does it disturb you as much as it does Olga?"

Laura's eyes darted toward the door.

"Don't bother calling for the guard." Sergei told her. "I sent him home early. His replacement won't arrive for another hour. By then it won't make any difference to you."

Sergei inched closer, a wild look in his watery eyes. Her back to the desk, Laura fumbled behind her for something to defend herself with.

"It's a pity," he said. "I really like you. But then, I liked Misha, too."

Laura's fingers gripped the stainless-steel letter opener's handle, shaped like the Empire State Building. Sergei came closer and closer, raising his hands. He lunged at her. Desperate, she thrust the steel opener through his sweater.

Sergei gasped and staggered backward. Laura sped across the office into the hallway and through the first door she came to, entering the large room where X-ray machines were assembled. Her heart pounding, she ran to the far side of the room to the door that led to the reception area. If she could just make it to her car!

She pushed at the door again and again, but it was locked from the other side. Her head jerked around when she heard Sergei curse her from across the dimly lit room.

Frantic, she grabbed the wooden railing of the staircase near the door and bounded up as fast as she could, hearing Sergei's footsteps pounding across the concrete floor.

Reaching the top of the stairs, she twisted the handle of the office door, knowing there was a phone inside. Desperately she tugged on the knob, but this door was also locked. Terrified, she turned back toward the stairway. Sergei was standing at the bottom, glaring up at her, one hand pressed tightly against his blood-stained sweater.

"Don't make this any more difficult than it has to be," he warned as he took one step slowly up, then another.

Laura stood frozen, her eyes burning, her throat dry. Holding on to the railing for support, she turned quickly, searching for another way out, but the landing went no farther than a few feet.

Trapped! Only one way out—back down the stairs. Sergei was almost at the top now. He was weaving.

Her last chance. It was now or never. When he reached out to grab her, she clutched the railing and thrust a foot at his chest with all the strength she could muster.

His arms flew out and he fell backward, his body curling as he plummeted down the wooden stairs.

Laura covered her mouth with a hand when he hit the concrete floor with a thud that echoed throughout the cavernous room.

Then he lay still, crumpled, his eyes staring blankly at the high ceiling.

Fighting the sickness roiling in her stomach, Laura gripped the railing, stark terror immobilizing her as she stared down at Sergei's prone body. With an effort she dragged herself down the stairs, using every bit of her courage and energy.

A step from the bottom she stopped and swallowed hard. Sergei was lying just in front of the stairway. Her breaths sounding like moans, she began to step over his body.

Sergei grabbed her foot.

Laura screamed. He tugged. She pulled desperately, dancing wildly like a crazed woman, kicking at him. Then suddenly she was free.

She stumbled backward, turned and ran from the plant.

Outside, the winter wind struck her like a wall of ice. The falling snow blurred her vision. Wearing only a cardigan, she hugged her arms and squinted, seeing her snow-covered car across the parking lot.

She staggered through the deep snow and jerked at the door handle, her heart sinking when she realized the key was in her purse in Sergei's office. She whirled around. No, she couldn't go back in there. She just couldn't!

But she knew she had to. Otherwise she'd freeze to death.

Brushing the snowflakes from her eyes, she dragged herself toward the door of the plant, forcing one freezing foot before the other.

Almost at the door, she told herself, drawing upon every ounce of strength she had. Peering into the darkened plant through the window set in the door, she could see no sign of Sergei. Her hands like ice, her fingers numb, she touched the knob.

She shrieked and jumped back when Sergei stepped into view and fell against the door, his battered face contorted with rage.

Not knowing where she was going, Laura turned and fled through the snow toward the woods next to the plant. She lost a shoe, stumbled and fell. She tried to lift herself up, but couldn't. Fear and exhaustion paralyzed her. She glanced back toward the plant and saw a dark figure plodding toward her.

"Oh, God!" she moaned.

She flattened her hands on the slippery snow and pushed herself up to her knees, then to a hunched position. As though through a murky veil, she saw trees ahead and staggered to them, losing her other shoe.

Falling against one tree, then another, she dragged herself up the steep incline, driving herself on, using trunk after trunk for support.

Finally she had to stop, bracing her shoulder against a pine. Her lungs felt numb from the freezing air she sucked in with every gasp. Through slitted eyelids, nearly frozen shut, she saw Sergei's dark figure weaving closer.

A long, pitiful groan rose from her throat, and she propelled herself to the clearing at the top of the hill. Collapsing on her knees, she found herself only inches from the edge of a precipice. Below, the frozen river; behind her, the crazed, wounded Sergei.

"Anatol," Laura sobbed, wishing she had one last chance to tell him how much she truly loved him.

From her kneeling position she forced her aching head to turn. She gasped when Sergei lunged toward her! Her eyes closed. Inky blackness winged over her as she crumpled into the snow, the night silence broken only by a diminishing, terrible scream.

ANATOL PUT ANOTHER LOG into the fireplace in Laura's apartment and returned to the sofa, where she sat huddled at one end, the afghan around her shoulders, her glazed eyes staring at the glass of brandy in her hand.

"When I heard Sergei's cry and found you," he said grimly, "I thought you were—" He couldn't finish. "I never should have left you with him."

Laura tilted her face toward his, her eyes still red from the tears she had shed after Anatol had brought her to the apartment. "You had no way of knowing Sergei was behind the problems at the plant. I still can't believe what he did." After a sip of brandy, she asked, "Do you think Pavel will cooperate with the authorities?"

"He'll tell them everything he knows. Now that Sergei's been arrested, he's too frightened not to. When I phoned the Leningrad militia from the plant, they said they'd pick up Dmitri." Anatol chuckled nervously. "It would be poetic justice if he and Pavel ended up in the same labor camp. But it's you I'm worried about. You were in shock when I carried you into the plant. The story that you told the militiamen about Sergei's chasing you—"

"I don't want to ever think about that again."

A lengthy silence hovered over the room, then Anatol said quietly, "I want to apologize for the way I behaved last Saturday. I was so upset I didn't know what I was saying."

Putting the brandy glass down, Laura took hold of his hand and pressed his palm against her cheek. "I know," she said softly.

"Do you forgive me?"

"There's nothing to forgive. We both knew my leaving would be difficult for us."

"We're all going to miss you. You know that, don't you?"

She lowered his hand to her lap and began stroking it slowly. "I'm going to miss everyone here."

"I don't know what's going to happen at the plant without you."

His innocent statement triggered Laura's jagged nerves. She threw back the afghan and leaped up from the sofa. "The plant!" she shouted. "I'm sick and tired of worrying about the plant! I don't care what happens there! For more than two months now my entire existence has been given over to worrying about that place."

"Laura, I only—"

"I don't want to hear another word about it. I just want to pack my things and go home. I want to forget I ever came here. Forget everything!"

"Everything?" he asked quietly, feeling as though she had torn his soul from him, leaving him empty.

"Yes, everything!"

Anatol had hoped for a kinder response, some word that would have indicated that what they had shared together had been as beautiful to her as it had been to him.

She had every right to be angry, he told himself, every reason to want to escape to a saner, safer life. But he desperately needed one sympathetic look from her, one word of understanding of just how miserable he was going to be without her.

Rising from the sofa, he stood immobile. He wanted to go to her. He wanted to take her in his arms and hold her close until she felt secure again. If he could drain himself of peace and offer it to her, he would do so gladly.

"Laura," he said softly, her name sounding to him as though it were echoing from a great distance, "I...I can't just walk away from you, not with this gulf between us. We can't end what we had together like this."

She turned slowly, trembling, her thoughts disjointed, her eyelids stinging. "Anatol—" his name came with pained difficulty "—we had something lovely together. But now it's over."

"Without regrets?" he asked hopefully.

Lifting a hand, she caught a tear before it slipped over her cheek. "How can you ask that? Little by little I'm dying inside. How long will it take before I can stop thinking about you and remembering about us? A week, a month, a year? Longer? Will I ever be able to forget the feel of your arms around me, the sound of your voice, your laughter? Will I ever want to?"

When he moved toward her, she raised a hand, palm toward him. "It's got to end here and now. And, yes, I do have regrets. I was wrong to think I could fall in love with you, then return home as if nothing had happened. But, regrets aside, I am going to try to forget you. I have to.''

"I'll never forget you," he said. Moving close, he grazed her face with his fingertips. "I'll cherish every moment we had together, replay every memory of you in my thoughts. I'll never stop loving you, Larashka.''

He leaned down and touched his lips to hers softly, then left the apartment, closing the door behind him quietly.

Numbed, Laura sank down on a chair. "Goodbye, Anatol.''

AT NOON THE NEXT DAY Anatol and Valentin strode under the vaulted arcade of Leningrad University after having filled out the necessary entrance forms for the next school year. As they walked, Anatol told his son that Laura was leaving.

"That's it?" Valentin asked.

Stopping, Anatol leaned back against one of the square stone columns. "What am I supposed to do—kidnap her? She can't wait to get away from here, and I can't stop her from leaving. It would be wrong of me even to try.''

Valentin braced a hand on the side of the column and shook his head. "Boy, you have mellowed since you met her. Time was when you were prepared to fight the entire government to get done what you thought was right. Now you sound like a wounded animal.''

Anatol turned his head and stared at him. "You don't like the new mellow me, huh?''

"Some of it, but I'm a little disappointed, too.''

"Thanks for trying to cheer me up.''

"I'm trying to wind you up. If you really love Laura and she loves you, why don't you go to New York with her?"

"Just like that?"

"Listen, Dad, for years you've nagged me about growing up and planning for my future. Well, I have. I'm going to get an education and Katya's going to marry me when I finish school. So pat yourself on the back for helping me get my life organized. Now take some of your own advice and get your own life in order. If this country falls apart, it's not going to be because you move to New York."

Anatol eyed him sideways. "Are you and Katya so desperate for an apartment you want to get rid of me?"

"Hell, no. I'd miss you, but New York's not at the end of the earth, and don't forget there are things like telephones and planes. Besides, if you and Laura get married, you'll probably start your own family. If you don't—" his blue eyes sparkled "—you'd probably want to spend your old age living with me and Katya."

"Fruit of my loins," Anatol mumbled, starting down the long arcade again. As they reached the front of the building, he said, "Even if I applied for an exit visa, Laura would probably forget me before it came through."

"That's negative thinking."

"That's practical thinking."

"You see what I mean about your having changed? It used to be you decided on a goal, and then you'd work like crazy to achieve it. You're giving up too easily on this challenge."

"Even if I could maneuver it, I can't just walk away from my work here or the problems in this country."

"Oh, but you expected Laura to do that. Sounds like a double standard to me."

"Maybe she doesn't want me running after her."

"Or maybe she does. From what you said happened to her, can you blame her for being as upset as she was?"

"I don't blame her."

"You will wind up blaming yourself if you let her get away. Face it, Dad, you're not going to make it in the singles bar scene here."

"How do I know I could make it in New York, or that the United States will even let me in?"

"There you go again with that defeatist attitude."

"Where did you learn to be such a nag?"

"From you. You're a master at it. Do you want to be with Laura or not?"

"Yes."

"Where's she going?"

"New York."

"Then it's your problem to figure out a way of getting there—and quick. Unless American males are stupid, one of them is going to latch onto her while you're twiddling your thumbs, deciding what to do."

"I don't have the background to work at the United Nations," Anatol said, thinking out loud.

"Keep going," he son prodded.

"Most of the people in the Soviet consulate are KGB."

"Forget that."

"There is one way maybe. No government red tape, no delays ... if I can talk the State Planning Committee into it ..."

Anatol squeezed his son's arm. "I've got to run, Valentin. I've got to get back to my office and make some quick phone calls."

AFTER CHECKING HER LUGGAGE at the airline office on Nevsky Prospekt, Laura took a seat, waiting for the bus to take her to the airport. She glanced at the clock on the wall and realized it would still be more than three hours before her plane would leave for New York. She tried telling herself she would be thrilled to be back home again. She had good reason to be.

Yesterday at the plant had been a nightmare. The day had been filled with constant explanations to George Hardcastle and his staff about why the investigators and government auditors had descended on the plant. The disruption had brought out the best in George, and he and Yuri had joined forces, determined to protect the plant and to make it a shining example of what a joint venture could be.

Should she phone Anatol and say goodbye? she wondered. She hadn't had a moment's peace since she'd just about ordered him out of her apartment in Pavlovsk. She'd berated herself again and again for the things she'd said to him, but then she would tell herself that the clean break was for the best. But still she'd vacillated and had reached for the phone time and again, only to pull her hand back once more. For two nights she'd tossed and turned, whispering his name in her half sleep.

She recalled their first evening together when he'd taken her to dinner and they'd walked along the Neva River afterward. Her thoughts raced on, presenting her with fleeting images of Anatol: his face aglow from the light in the fireplace at the dacha, his laughter ringing in the air as they ice-skated together, his holding her close in the horse-drawn troika. But the mental picture that lingered was that of him standing tall on the hillside by his parents' home, the sun brightening his face and the breeze ruffling his hair as he gazed over the Russian countryside.

"Oh, Anatol," she whispered, wondering if she were doing the right thing in running away from him. Was there any way they could reconcile their different backgrounds, their hopes and dreams? No, she decided sadly for the hundredth time. But, she determined suddenly, at least she could say goodbye to him.

ANATOL SAT NERVOUSLY at his desk, waiting for a return phone call. He'd made many since the talking-to his son had given him yesterday. All the pieces of his plan were in place, all except one. "Ring, damn you," he complained, holding the little crystal swan Laura had given him.

The buzz of his intercom tore him from his anxious thoughts. "Yes," he said halfheartedly.

"Miss Walters is here to see you," his secretary announced.

"Laura! Send her right in."

He rushed to his office door and swung it open, his eyes hungrily taking in the sight of her.

"Am I interrupting you?" she asked, trying to burn his image into her mind for all time.

"No, no, come in. I was just thinking about you," he said, his heart in his throat.

She looked back at him and noticed he was holding the crystal swan.

"I keep it on my desk," he said, unable to take his eyes off her.

"Anatol, I want to apologize for the way I acted the last time we were together."

"There's no need to," he said, inching closer.

"Yes, there is. I won't be able to leave unless I do."

"When are you leaving?"

"In just a few hours."

"No," he objected. "Yuri told me you weren't leaving until next week."

"I changed my reservation last night."

"There's something I—" he began.

"Please, Anatol. Let me speak first. I didn't mean what I said about not caring what happens at the plant. Of course I do, and I'm thrilled that the joint venture is going to succeed, most likely beyond our expectations."

"Don't you think I know you care? After what you'd been through, I'm surprised you're still here." He managed a crooked smile. "I'm certainly happy you are."

"And I want you to know I'm not sorry I came here. I never will be. And I'll never, never be sorry we met. I used to think that my work was the most important thing in my life, but I believe differently now. Loving someone deeply and being loved in return is far more important." Fighting the thickness that tightened her throat, she turned away slowly. "I'd like you to remember what I'm saying now, not what I said in my apartment."

Setting the swan on his desk, he moved in front of her and took hold of her shoulders. "You remember this, Larashka. I love you and I need you desperately."

She lifted her eyes and placed her hand on the side of his face. "I love you, too," she said softly, her voice breaking. "And there's nothing we can do about it. Crazy world, isn't it?"

"There is something we can do about it, if we both want to."

"Anatol, we—"

"Don't say a word. Just give me a minute."

He rushed behind his desk and quickly dialed a number on his phone, tapping the receiver with a thumb as he waited, his eyes holding Laura's steadfastly. "Alexei," he said, "have you heard anything yet? They're on the other line? Good, I'll hold." He raised a hand and crossed his fingers.

Wondering what had Anatol so excited, Laura moved closer to him.

"They did! Tell them we have a deal." He listened for a moment, then answered, "The sooner, the better. Let's say two weeks. Right. Alexei, I owe you."

His breathing deepening, Anatol cradled the receiver and took hold of Laura's hands. "Are you due for any kind of a vacation—two weeks, maybe?"

"Well, yes, but—"

"Would you mind spending your honeymoon here in Leningrad? I've got tons of work to finish before—" he smiled at her shocked expression "—before I start my new job in New York."

"Honeymoon? New York?"

"You're familiar with the city, I believe."

"Anatol...when...how?"

Crushing her to him, he said, "You didn't think I'd be crazy enough to let you walk out of my life, did you? I'd follow you to the ends of the earth if I had to."

Laura drew her head back, confusion clearly written on her face. "What are you talking about? What job?"

"With Amtorg Trading Corporation. The State Planning Committee has arranged for me to be a permanent adviser to American businessmen in New York. Will you marry me?"

"Oh, yes, Anatol!" she cried, her eyes shining joyously.

"There is one hitch. The Committee wants me to spend three months a year here in Leningrad. New York would be our home, but do you think Biomed would let you go for three months of the year?"

"If the Pavlovsk venture is the success I think it will be, and if you can open the doors for Biomed at other plants, I know they would. Besides, I have a feeling I'll be needing maternity leave by the time you're due back here."

"You do plan ahead, don't you, Miss Walters?"

"Mrs. Vronsky," she said, testing the sound of it. "I'm just thinking the nights are very long here in Russia at this time of year...."

Anatol smiled. "Are you suggesting we could start producing little Vronskys right away?"

"We could try, Comrade."

This April, don't miss #449, CHANCE OF A LIFETIME, Barbara Kaye's third and last book in the Harlequin Superromance miniseries

Hamilton
H·O·U·S·E

A powerful restaurant conglomerate draws the best and brightest to its executive ranks. Now almost eighty years old, Vanessa Hamilton, the founder of Hamilton House, must choose a successor. Who will it be?

Matt Logan: He's always been the company man, the quintessential team player. But tragedy in his daughter's life and a passionate love affair made him make some hard choices....

Paula Steele: Thoroughly accomplished, with a sharp mind, perfect breeding and looks to die for, Paula thrives on challenges and wants to have it all...but is this right for her?

Grady O'Connor: Working for Hamilton House was his salvation after Vietnam. The war had messed him up but good and had killed his storybook marriage. He's been given a second chance—only he doesn't know what the hell he's supposed to do with it....

Harlequin Superromance invites you to enjoy Barbara Kaye's dramatic and emotionally resonant miniseries about mature men and women making life-changing decisions.

You'll flip . . . your pages won't!
Read paperbacks *hands-free* with

Book Mate · I

The perfect "mate" for all your romance paperbacks

Traveling • Vacationing • At Work • In Bed • Studying • Cooking • Eating

Perfect size for all standard paperbacks, this wonderful invention makes reading a pure pleasure! Ingenious design holds paperback books OPEN and FLAT so even wind can't ruffle pages — leaves your hands free to do other things. Reinforced, wipe-clean vinyl-covered holder flexes to let you turn pages without undoing the strap...supports paperbacks so well, they have the strength of hardcovers!

Pages turn WITHOUT opening the strap

SEE-THROUGH STRAP

Reinforced back stays flat

Built in bookmark

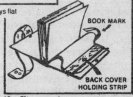

BOOK MARK

BACK COVER HOLDING STRIP

10 x 7¼ opened.
Snaps closed for easy carrying, too

COMING IN 1991 FROM
HARLEQUIN SUPERROMANCE:

Three abandoned orphans,
one missing heiress!

Dying millionaire Owen Byrnside receives an
anonymous letter informing him that twenty-six years
ago, his son, Christopher, fathered a daughter. The
infant was abandoned at a foundling home that
subsequently burned to the ground, destroying all
records. Three young women could be Owen's long-
lost granddaughter, and Owen is determined to track
down each of them! Read their stories in

#434 HIGH STAKES (available January 1991)
#438 DARK WATERS (available February 1991)
#442 BRIGHT SECRETS (available March 1991)

Three exciting stories of intrigue and romance by
veteran Superromance author Jane Silverwood